Out of My Mind

Sam Jenkins

For Mom and Dad- ta-da!

CONTENTS

ACKNOWLEDGMENTS

Every author will tell you that it took an entire village to write their book and then go on to thank everyone and their grandmother. You always wonder if it's true. Trust me- it is. If they say different then they're lying.

From a young age I was encouraged by my parents and teachers to put my imagination to paper. Before I could write I made picture books of the wild stories that I was constantly dreaming up.

It would take every page in this book to thank all the people who have supplied me with a lifetime of encouragement- my parents who allowed me to think my weird was the new normal, teachers (Mrs. Ayers, Mrs. Boardwine, Mrs. Brewer, Mrs. Arritt, Mrs. Suleski) who allowed me to read my stories in class, no matter how painful it was to my classmates. All of those who instilled in me an insatiable appetite for reading and telling stories. My grandparents, aunts, uncles, cousins who refined my talent for storytelling. My college professors (Deborah, Rodney, Shan, Mary Ann) and peers (Brandie, Nina, Heather, Eamon, Christian, Thomas, Tony, Victor, CeDarian) who helped hone my ability to express myself. I also very much appreciate all of the friends who kept me accountable to following through with my book and offered those every day encouragements (Adrian, Steph, Jeni, Mylissa, TK, Tanner, Alex, Sharon, Rick, Ashley, Josh, Shelly, Stan, Jeff and all the ladies of Memoirs and Martinis). And, of course, to all of the people who ever told me I couldn't do something. I can't forget my editors and friends (Crystal, Libby, Karen, Linda) who helped me put this together, set me straight and pushed me through. If it weren't for you all reading my terribly typo-heavy first draft (and second and third and...) we wouldn't be here.

I wish I could thank everyone individually but I hope that even if your name isn't on these pages you know who you are and that I love you- if you don't know this then I haven't done my job as a friend. Believe me- it took all of you to produce this book- it just happens to have my name on it.

CHAPTER ONE

I was perched on a chair at the local hangout- a coffee and tea place that was marginally affordable on my meager babysitting pay. Sunlight was streaming in the front windows and everything was bathed in a glowing gold light. It felt so warm and cozy and perfect. For maybe the first time in my life I was completely relaxed. I wasn't worried about homework or chores or classes or anything.

I was surrounded by my friends, cocooned in their mirth of the moment. My best friend, Lexa, was laughing at something Sawyer, our geeked out, sometimes self-deprecating, always- good- for- dry- humor- in- awkward-situations friend had said. I had no clue what it was.

In the midst of Lexa's laughter, Sawyer turned to me. "Email. That way you won't have to digitize." The random comment barely registered as I swept the table once more with my eyes.

There were other faces at the table. Allison, a girl that Lexa and I had hung out with on and off since elementary school. Allison was one of those girls that kept everyone at arms' length so you could never really be good friends. She was grinning despite her efforts to the contrary at what Sawyer had said. I heard a booming laugh from Ethan, who hovered at a corner of the table. Ethan was the "good guy" all the girls were after. At least, that's

1

what I'm told. Like Lexa, Ethan and I had been friends since elementary school and I had always found it difficult to think of him like that.

Hana was there, too. Smiling, not laughing with the others, but her face lit up with a glow I attributed to the sunlight cascading through the window. Hana was the youngest person in our class and almost a full year my junior. We usually had several classes together every year and had become close acquaintances, if not friends, during our time together. As I continued to watch her I began to feel a tugging at my memory. I felt as if I should recall something about her, something I needed to remember right now. I could feel the corners of my mouth start to turn down in a frown as I concentrated. Hana looked at me and I smiled reflexively, derailing my train of thought.

The melodic tinkling of the door's bell caught my attention and I looked up. Not at the patron coming in the door, but toward the bar. A man sat there, briefly illuminated by the spotlight of rich golden sunshine that poured in when the door had been opened. He had longish, wavy dark brown hair that glowed like a halo and a warm smile that he seemed to be wearing for no one in particular. I kept looking at him. I knew him, I was sure of it. His name was on the tip of my tongue. I searched for it. I desperately wanted to say his name and have him turn to me.

As if by the force of my will alone, he swiveled on his stool to face me. Suddenly, I was the only person in the room. My friends vanished as he slid from the bar stool and walked over. He said something, I laughed, we talked. I can't remember what about. I just remember that talking to him, just being near him, filled me with incredible warmth. I was insanely happy.

⁊ ⁊ ⁊

My happiness followed me into my waking hours. As I got up, stumbling around in the pre-dawn light before I remembered to turn on the lamp, I tried desperately to hang on to my dream, cursing it for being so detailed and so vague at the same time.

With my mind half stuck in the dream and half issuing warnings about the extensive list of to-dos for the day, I pulled on jeans and the first t-shirt I could find. I ran my fingers through my long mousy hair, forgoing the search it would take to locate my brush. Acting like I didn't care gave me permission to ignore the mirror, though I knew exactly what I would see there- limp hair, light brown eyes, a tiny nose that made me look twelve instead of eighteen. I was the vision of plainness that everyone measured themselves against to determine their most outstanding qualities. Thinking about this didn't have its usual sting today, however, as my dream continued its dance through my head.

It was so vivid that I actually had to force it to the back of my mind before I could go through my mental checklist for the day. This was the last week of my senior year. The week to end all weeks that would culminate with a tedious graduation ceremony where I would be presented with a piece of paper that I had diligently pursued for the past thirteen years of my life.

This week had brought on a whole new set of stress for me, which was saying something considering "stressed" was my middle name. The last week of school always had its own schedule- everything that you had done on every other day of the year suddenly went topsy-turvy. There were tons of meetings, especially for the seniors, end of the year exams, final projects- suddenly there were so many things to wrap up and no time in which to do so.

To make it worse, I had somehow believed that taking on extra projects like the senior slideshow couldn't possibly take that much more time out of my cramped schedule. It had temporarily slipped my mind that I'm awful with creative projects. The only thing I'm worse at is anything done on computers. You would think someone born in the technological age would be better with electronics but no, not me.

I had hoped to sweet talk Sawyer into stepping up as my partner in crime but so far no luck. I think he's enjoying watching me squirm under the pressure. I made a mental note for the dozenth time to stop being a spineless pushover who could be talked into these things but I shuddered to think of what kind of miracle it would take to make me change my ways.

Distracted with thoughts of everything I had to do this week and the ever-present fear that I would forget something, I headed out of the house without thinking of stopping for breakfast. I grabbed my book bag and my keys on the way out the door, calling good-bye to Mom, who was in the living room with a book and a cup of coffee.

She laughed at my breathlessness while calling out, "Have a good day, Aren!"

I headed for my humble gold Camry, throwing my book bag in the passenger seat. My parents had been amazing enough to offer me the hand-me-down after Mom bought a new (well, new to us) car when Dad happened across a great deal. The Camry had a lot of miles on her, but she was mine and I loved her.

We lived just outside the city limits, just far enough that driving to school was necessary. My destination was on the far side of town, through the two sleepy stoplights that made up the "downtown" section of Main Street. I slipped into autopilot as I took the too-familiar drive to school, my thoughts drifting toward that blasted slideshow.

At school I parked in the upper parking lot. I was one of the first cars there so I was able to snag a spot close to the stairs. Early as I was, there were already a few people gathered on the picnic tables outside, talking quietly and enjoying the crisp, clean late spring morning as I made my way to the front doors.

I shouldered my bag and walked in, smiling at Mr. Kessler who was on bus duty out front. I greeted the door with my shoulder then made my way down the foyer and into the gym/ cafeteria. I took a seat at the first table I found. I fished in my bag for my day planner, going over it again to make sure I wasn't missing anything.

Oh Mondays, the joy you bring never disappoints.

Since there was nothing I could do about the

slideshow but sulk, I flipped to the back of my planner where a little notepad was affixed to the cover. I started reading over my notes for the valedictorian speech I was expected to present this Saturday at graduation. If there was one thing I was good at, it was bookwork. Memorizing and reciting facts and formulas that I would probably never use in real life was a talent I extorted to its fullest during my time in Jefferson High School. I had known since freshman year that an outstanding academic record was going to be the only way I could pay for college. My parents worked hard and would have loved to pay for me to go if they had the money but it was a conversation we never needed to have because I knew they couldn't help me.

I looked over my speech notes for the second time without really reading a word. I had been writing things down as they came to me and I expected to actually put my thoughts into complete sentences in the next day or so. I had to turn in a copy of my speech to the vice principal for review prior to what I hoped would be a rousing delivery on Saturday. My speech was about dreams. I wasn't really a speechwriter so I figured I'd stick with a tried and true topic. I had no delusions about anyone actually remembering what I said. As long as I kept it short, it would be a hit.

As I pretended to read through my notes while pondering how speech delivery became a reward for academic achievement, Lexa and Sawyer entered the cafeteria. I smiled in their direction while returning my planner to my bag.

"Happy Monday," Lexa said dryly. She sat down beside me on the bench. Sawyer walked to the other side of the table to sit, dumping his book bag unceremoniously in front of him.

"Hey," I smiled. "So, about this slideshow-" I glanced over my shoulder casually at Sawyer, who rolled his eyes. His problem was he couldn't fathom how this could be a difficult task for anyone.

Geek.

I decided quickly that what little charm I possessed

wasn't going to work. So I let loose with the complaints. "I just don't understand. We do this every year, people know it's coming. They look forward to it. So why do we wait until the week before graduation to saddle someone with it? This thing has to be together before Friday." I slouched back against the table.

"Email." Sawyer suggested cryptically. "That way you won't have to digitize."

I turned sharply to look at him. Something about his suggestion was startlingly familiar. My brow creased as I tried to figure out when he had told me that before. He took my look to mean I wasn't grasping what he was saying, which wasn't far from the mark. He sighed. "Send out an email to everyone requesting photos be submitted via email. That way you won't have to scan all those photos everyone brings in. You'll save a step, and then there's no way you could possibly lose someone's prints. Honestly, I don't know why someone didn't think of it before."

"Probably because it's not the computer club that gets stuck with the slideshow, it's some poor schmuck from student council," Lexa quipped, shooting me a toothy smile to soften the blow.

I sighed. I was fully aware that I was the schmuck in question. Ethan, the student council president, had volunteered me for a place on the council board. No one had run for the dubious honor of secretary so I had been recruited. I knew it would look good on my college application so I had only staged a meager protest before caving. It was times like this, however, that I kicked myself for being such a pushover. I wasn't sure this line on my list of accomplishments was worth the work this slideshow was going to cost me.

"Ok, fine, I'll help. Well, I'll walk you through it. After you learn how to put one photo on there you just have to repeat repeat repeat." Sawyer rolled his eyes as he said this.

"I don't know how I could do it without you," I told him. He shrugged.

"Just don't forget to send out the email this morning,"

he instructed.

"I won't," I promised, making a mental note to do it first thing.

The last week of school was usually pretty light on class work for me. I had finished what few end of term projects I had early so I could concentrate on the task of graduating. I always elected at the end of the year to forgo finals in exchange for my outstanding attendance record. At the beginning of each term we could sign a contract exempting us from finals if we maintained an A average and missed less than three days of school. I always saved my three days for the end of the semester so I could skip the test preparation days for the finals I never had to take.

The bell rang for first period and I waved to my friends as I headed to Mrs. Donovan's room. Mrs. Donovan was the upperclassman history teacher and adviser to the student council. I was a senior with an extra time block on my hands so she had picked me up as a "peer assistant." When she had nothing for me to do, which was frequently the case, she let me work on projects at her desk as long as I kept quiet while she taught. I walked swiftly to her room, wanting to make sure I sent out the email before I was sidetracked.

Mrs. Donovan was at the front of the classroom fiddling with the DVD player when I came in. I called out a "hello" and she half turned to acknowledge it with a smile while still bending over the machine. There were only a few kids in the class, Early American History, when I got there. I didn't expect a large crowd since it was the last week of school. The final project in this class had been a paper, which they had turned in last week. Mrs. Donovan had said she didn't want to add to all the tests they had to cram for so she set her due date before finals started. Now everyone got to watch movies for the rest of the week, if they showed up.

I headed straight for Mrs. Donovan's computer and opened a new browser window so I could log on to my school email remotely. I clicked "compose new message," check marking the contact list for all seniors and typed out a brief request for slideshow photos by Wednesday morning. That would give everyone two days to get me photos. If I started making slides as they came in I could keep this project from becoming the runaway train that wrecked on Friday morning when it was due to be played for the entire school assembly.

I hit "send," feeling like I had already accomplished big things on a Monday morning. Now all I had to do was wait for the photos to start pouring in. I logged out of my email, rebelliously refusing to look at my inbox, and sat back as the bell rang for first period to begin. A few more students had trickled in to class making a grand total of ten. Mrs. Donovan had finished with the DVD player and had turned to face the room, probably taking mental notes as to who was present. I ruffled some papers on her desk until I uncovered her attendance book. I flashed the book toward her to show I was marking attendance while I slid onto a plastic chair beside her desk, facing a counter that ran along the wall. I quickly marked attendance then flopped the book back onto her desk. Mrs. Donovan was telling everyone what they had the pleasure of watching and reminding them to keep noise to a minimum. She nodded to someone to turn off the lights in the front half of the room before she hit the "play" button and headed back to her desk.

My feeling of accomplishment was fast in fading. I realized I now had ninety minutes of nothing to do. I briefly considered working on my speech but I'm not good at doing anything if there's noise in the room. I turned toward the TV and propped my head up in my hand. Hopefully the movie would be good.

The half dark room and drone of the movie was starting to make my eyelids heavy. Mrs. Donovan was going through some papers on her desk, probably still grading the essays she'd had everyone write. I leaned farther into my hand, closing my eyes. I wasn't in danger of falling asleep but I figured a little daydreaming wouldn't hurt.

I wished for a dozen freak things that could get me out of what was becoming a tedious Monday. I should have tried a little harder to get myself out of coming today. There was so much stuff I needed to do and none of them could be done while I was mindlessly going from one class to another.

The day was still young so I felt justified in clinging to the hope that I could get out of here early. My mind touched on all the things that could happen, each one wilder than the next- a fire alarm, the power going out, the principal deciding to dismiss us after lunch, rabid dogs invading the school...

Maybe I should just leave after Mrs. Donovan's class. I could just walk out the front door. Not even go to Mr. Wiley's class. Just the thought of enduring another day in that room made me want to flee. Mr. Wiley was our mercurial Advanced English teacher. His mood swings were enough to give us whiplash and had a way of infecting everyone around him. When he was irritable, the whole class was. It was as if he had some kind of super power that allowed him to project his mood onto us. The student body as a whole attributed this to the fact that Mr. Wiley lacked any ability to interact with another human being with a modicum of competency. Mr. Wiley could talk at you but not to you. He was like this with students as well as other teachers. No one was surprised he wasn't married. I definitely wouldn't miss his class when I was gone. This brought me back to wondering if I could get out of it.

I let my mind drift, relinquishing any control I had over the direction it wandered. I felt myself slipping into that warm fuzzy place somewhere between waking and sleeping.

ॐ ॐॐ ॐ

I was at the door outside Mrs. Donovan's room but everything seemed fuzzy. I walked down the hall, turning toward the lobby. I could feel my car keys in my hand. Other students walked by, taking no notice.

Suddenly, I found myself in Mr. Wiley's classroom, which lay in the complete opposite direction from the parking lot. He was standing by his desk at the front of the room, rifling through papers. He glanced toward the door when I walked in then, without smiling, he looked back down. He had seen me so I couldn't turn around and leave now. I took my seat, halfway down the last aisle.

As the last students filtered in, Mr. Wiley began to talk. The harder I concentrated on what he was saying, the less I heard. I began to panic, convinced that whatever it was had to be important.

When he finished, Mr. Wiley sat down at his desk. Students began taking out books and notes, intent on whatever Mr. Wiley had told us to do. I seemed to be everywhere at once, noticing the oddest details while not being able to make out the more obvious. I could not read what was written on the board, for example, but I did notice a shiny ring on the hand of a girl who sat at the front of the class. I looked back toward Mr. Wiley. I was sure he was going to call me out for my lack of studious behavior any moment.

All of a sudden I saw him pitch sideways after a strange groan and crack issued from his chair. The heavy wooden center leg split apart as the rollers on the legs sent the bottom half of his chair one way and the seat carried Mr. Wiley another. He tried to both keep himself from hitting the floor and from getting hit by the chair but the fall was so short he could achieve neither. He went down, narrowly avoiding a collision between the back of his head and the wall. He was trying awkwardly to get up but his knees were against the leg of his desk, his head near the wall and his chair still half cradling his back.

❧ ❧❧ ❧

My eyes popped open and I glanced guiltily around the room, trying to see if anyone had noticed that I had actually dozed off. I had never fallen asleep during class in my life. I looked over at Mrs. Donovan but she seemed oblivious. I shook my head, wondering where such a random scenario had come from. Sure, I wanted to get out of class but I would never sabotage a teacher to do it.

I looked at the TV hoping it would distract me. I wasn't even sure what movie we were watching. It looked like some old civil war movie. Probably something straight to DVD like most historically accurate movies.

I leaned forward, squirming in my seat and rubbing my neck. I pulled out my planner and pen. Lacking anything to actually write, I began doodling in the margins. The first battle of the movie was underway and I could hear shouting and cannon fire coming from the TV.

I don't know where the time went, but suddenly the bell was ringing to signify the end of first block. I got up mechanically, the conditioned response every student has to hearing the bell. I waved to Mrs. Donovan then headed out of the classroom. Zigzagging between other students who were trying to get to their next class, I turned the corner to the English wing at the same time as Lexa, who had come from the opposite side of the building. She grinned as she hipped into me by way of greeting.

"Hey," she sang.

"One more day, huh?" I asked, needing reassurance that I wasn't going to have to show up for class tomorrow for some awful reason.

"Yup. Our last class with Wiley. Kinda makes you feel all gooey inside, doesn't it?" Lexa raised an eyebrow and I snorted. Whatever I was feeling, it was definitely not gooey.

We walked in and took our seats against the wall opposite the door. Mr. Wiley was at his desk, which faced the class at the front of our row, ignoring us as we came in. One good thing about Mr. Wiley, he never started talking before the bell sounded. I figure this was more because he really didn't want to talk to us longer than he had to as opposed to him respecting that the time before the bell wasn't actually class time.

"You have plans after school?" Lexa asked. I was dutifully hauling my English book and notepad out of my bag, in case we were actually going to do work today.

"No plans. All I have this week is a slideshow and a speech to write. No biggie." I shrugged sarcastically.

"Oh, good- I was afraid you'd actually have something important," Lexa responded to my sarcasm in kind. "Do you want to go down to the C&T? I'll help you with your speech thingy."

The C&T- Maddie's Coffee and Tea- was a little café on Main Street where everyone hung out. Of course, it was one of the only places in town to hang out. I was suddenly reminded of my dream from last night. It wasn't so much whatever we were doing, but the warm feeling of being with friends. I was about to say I would go when the bell rang. Mr. Wiley looked up like he was noticing for the first time that we had invaded his space. I glanced around, about two thirds of the class had shown up. This seemed pretty impressive since it was, for one, the last day of regular class and, two, the class was Wiley's.

"Since this is the last day for most of you," Mr. Wiley began without preamble, "I thought you could do something fun to conclude your class. I have crosswords here-" he raised a daunting stack of stapled papers "-that cover the texts and terms we have studied through the course of the semester- this will be especially helpful for those of you who will be taking the final. You may work in pairs and I have a prize for the winning team. Books and notes are allowed- if you took good notes you will possibly survive. But-" he paused to glare over his thick glasses- " keep it down. If you get loud then it must mean you would rather work on your own. And yes, this is a graded assignment so do not think you can get away without finishing it."

He gave us a moment to shuffle around, moving desks together so we were beside our partner. Lexa and I shoved our desks together while Mr. Wiley began handing out the crosswords, three sheets stapled together printed front and back. The first page was dedicated to the gigantic crossword itself. I hate crosswords.

Lexa and I began reading through the clues, trying to see if we could recall any of the answers by memory before we opened our books. The classroom was relatively quiet with everyone at least going through the motions of doing the assignment. Mr. Wiley sat down at his desk so he could begin to ignore us in earnest.

It was almost like I felt it instead of heard it- the sudden tension in the air. The classroom was quiet as we feigned taking the assignment seriously. A loud crack sounded at the front of the classroom. Before I could turn my head I heard something heavy thud against the wall to the left of Mr. Wiley's desk.

Mr. Wiley had abruptly vacated the area directly behind his desk and now lay on the floor, stunned. He looked like he was trying to defy gravity by sitting horizontal to the ground. Everyone turned at once when they heard the noise. A few had even leapt out of their chairs. After a beat, one of the students went over to try to assess how to extract Mr. Wiley. He tried offering his hand but Mr. Wiley was still trying to comprehend what happened and refused the proffered hand.

I couldn't process the scene before me. The strongest feeling of déjà vu had washed over me, burying me. I couldn't move. Hysterical laughter bubbled up and I had to bite my lip to keep it inside. Chairs break all the time, don't they? Totally normal. Everyone has experienced déjà vu. This was just a weird coincidence.

As I was trying to keep myself calm I noticed one of my classmates, Jimmy, enter with Mr. Jones, the assistant principal, in tow. Mr. Jones quickly assessed the situation, taking in our stunned faces, and went to help Mr. Wiley, who was still struggling to get out from between the desk and the top half of the chair.

"What happened?' Mr. Jones asked.

No one answered and Mr. Wiley started hissing furiously, his words indecipherable but his tone all too clear. He was glaring at us as if he suspected one of us.

"That really scared me for some reason," I said to Lexa, feeling like I had to explain myself. Explain what? Jumping at an unexpected occurrence was completely within the realm of normalcy.

"Yeah," Lexa agreed vaguely.

I looked up as Jimmy reappeared at the door (I didn't even see him leave again) with Mrs. Jones, the underclassmen English teacher and wife to the vice principal. Apparently she was going to baby-sit us during her free period while Mr. Jones led Mr. Wiley out of the classroom, probably to the nurse.

Mrs. Jones smiled at us while we waited expectantly to see what she was going to have us do. She glanced at the crossword on our desks. "Let's just keep working on those. I'm sure it won't hurt anyone." She smiled as if she were remembering what it was like to be given such ridiculous assignments, though I doubted she had ever found an English assignment to be ridiculous.

I sat back in my seat, breathing slowly in an effort to stop the room from spinning. My face began to burn as a wave of shame and guilt swept over me.

How could I have possibly seen that coming? Could I have prevented it? Sure, I could have looked like a lunatic and told Mr. Wiley he could never sit down in his chair.

My stomach had begun to churn along with my thoughts. With shaky legs I walked to the front, intending to ask Mrs. Jones if I could be excused for a moment, but when she saw my face she gestured toward the door before I had the words out.

CHAPTER TWO

I practically ran to the bathroom, bursting through the heavy metal door to the girls' room and into the first stall I came to. Fortunately, or unfortunately, I didn't have anything in my stomach to rid myself of. I struggled to get my heaving body under control I was hit with a massive headache. I flipped the lid down on the toilet and sat. This was not the Monday I had in mind. I leaned my head against the cool metal wall and shut my eyes.

A few seconds or minutes or days later – I wasn't sure-Lexa came in the bathroom calling my name.

"In here," I breathed, so tired I thought the words wouldn't come out.

"Are you okay?" she asked. I unlocked the stall door and she peered in at me. "You look like hell. What happened?"

I let her comment slide. She was probably right after all. "One of my headaches. I've been fighting it all morning and then all the noise-" I stopped. The best lies were vague ones. Besides, I really did have a headache. Now.

"Let me get your stuff. You should go home," Lexa, ever the empirical decision maker, declared. "Can you drive?"

I opened my eyes, taking stock of my ability to see. The pressure behind them was steady but I didn't seem to be having any problems with my vision.

"I think I'm fine. I can make it home." I didn't know if I wanted to go home. Of course, I didn't want to stay here. "I just need a nap. I'll be fine, honest." Lexa pursed her lips but didn't say anything before turning toward the exit.

"I'll tell Mrs. Jones," she said as she left. I sat for another moment or two then dragged myself to my feet. I had to hold on to the wall to steady myself but otherwise found the walk to the door lacking in difficulty. Outside the bathroom I met Lexa who had come back with my book bag. I shouldered the bag and gave her a hug.

"Call me?" I asked. "I just need a nap. I should be good to go to the C&T."

She rolled her eyes dramatically, grinning. "I'll talk to you later. And then I'll decide if you're fit to be seen in public."

I headed toward the office, my legs still a little shaky. My addled brain, trying to focus on anything but Mr. Wiley's fall, pondered how badly my grade would suffer by not completing the crossword. I went through the motions of letting the secretary know I was taking myself home. She took one glance at me and I knew by her sympathetic look she wasn't going to argue. This wasn't the first time a headache had put me out of commission. It took me two seconds to sign the ledger where they kept track of all student comings and goings during the school day before I was free.

If I could have run out of the building without attracting attention, or falling on my face, I would have. I had an overwhelming need to be as far away from the school as possible. I was working overtime to fight the swell of unreasonable panic building inside of me. I got to the car and threw my book bag into the passenger seat before taking off, feeling slightly rebellious as I sped through the school parking lot doing about eighteen in the posted ten mile an hour zone.

I drove home on autopilot, parked and dragged myself out of the car. I groaned inwardly when I saw Mom's car. She worked part time at a gallery downtown but was apparently off today. I really didn't want to have to explain to her why I was home.

Mom was in the kitchen when I entered. I gave her the most pathetic look I could muster and she nodded in acknowledgement of my pain, her brows drawn together in sympathy for my plight. I headed to my bedroom and flung myself onto the bed, kicking my shoes off. I was practically out before they hit the floor as I succumbed to the intense exhaustion that had followed me home.

I was heading toward the door to the C&T, anxiously grasping for the door handle a step or two before I was in arm's reach. I was so caught up in my excitement that I bowled over my tall, handsome, wavy haired friend. I looked up and couldn't look away. His brown eyes, which had little green flecks floating in them, were warm and happy. He was so incredible and so perfect and he didn't even seem to realize it, which made him even more so.

One of the ways I knew he was amazing was due to the fact that I wasn't. I wasn't the girl that guys thought was pretty. For a moment, despair gripped me to the point that the sunlight outside the café seemed to dim. But then I looked back up.

Up into his eyes. There was something about him. He literally radiated warmth and kindness. His good looks didn't seem to alienate me as some people's did. Instead, I felt by just being near him I was important, beautiful- that I mattered.

It was like a switch had been flipped again. The despair came back- a choking weight that sat on my chest. The sunlight dimmed again as I looked away from him. I had never mattered to a guy- ever. Somehow everyone came to me for their relationship advice without stopping to think that I'd never been in one. It could be so lonely, having to live through everyone else's ups and downs- being left out when things were good and sitting with them watching sappy badly-written movies while they cried when things were bad.

He touched my arm, just the faintest brush of his fingertips, and my eyes came up, boldly searching for his.

I tried to soak in his radiance as if I could store it for a rainy day. He smiled at me and I immediately smiled back. He brushed my cheek with one finger, barely making contact, before sliding past me out the door.

I walked through the doorway, the residual happiness from our brief encounter infusing me with warmth. The C&T was packed- or maybe it wasn't. I felt like I was being pressed into a room that could barely hold another person but the only face I could make out belonged to Lexa, who was sitting at a table in the back, gesturing to me.

As I made my way toward Lexa I looked toward the right and could make out people-shaped silhouettes. No, it wasn't like I looked- it's more like I felt them there. I felt vaguely familiar presences. One of them suddenly became clearer than the others. It was Hana, sitting at the bar with her back to me. I couldn't see her face, or any distinguishing features, I just knew it was her. I felt like I hadn't seen her in a lifetime and suddenly I was sure there was no way I could approach her- there were too many years between us now.

I continued through the café but the back table where Lexa sat seemed to get further and further away instead of closer. I began to move faster, trying to push myself toward her as if I could outrun the table.

A shadow overtook me so suddenly that I saw it in the same moment I hit it. I heard ringing in my ears as I backed away to get a better view. I had expected to see a brick wall but instead a young man stood in front of me seeming larger than life thanks to the blur of my unfocused eyes. His dirty blonde hair was spiky and had the faintest hint of red highlights throughout which I wouldn't have seen if the sun shining through the door hadn't stopped to rest on his head. He took hold of my arms to steady me, his face radiating concern, and I lost my grasp of the dream's tenuous laws of physics. I was floating, moving so rapidly I was standing still. Flashes of faintly familiar scenes raced before my eyes, moving so fast I could only tell they were numerous but not able to really hold on to any of them. I knew I had witnessed them before and I would remember them if only I could focus.

I tried to narrow my eyes on the flashes of color and light that were speeding past me. They began to slow. I saw a woman, older than myself, with black hair pinned up on top of her head. My first instinct was that she was me even though we didn't look all that similar. She had extremely dark glossy hair and her nose was slimmer than mine. She was taller- but her eyes and the curve of her mouth- they were so intimately familiar I felt I was looking into a mirror. The dark haired woman was wearing a long dress with a modest collar and standing in an expansive yard flanked by orchards. The sun glinted golden off of everything it touched, exposing the silhouette of a large house in the background.

The woman was laughing. She spun around once in the yard, stopping to glance around for any witnesses to her unladylike behavior and discovering she wasn't as alone as she'd thought. However, her audience didn't seem to affect her mood as the smile on her face widened instead of shied itself away at being caught out in the sunlight.

A man stood several feet away from her, attempting to maintain a look of wry amusement but unable to hold in the smile that illuminated his entire face, making the blue sky bluer.

The woman approached the man, his long blonde hair looking yellow in the sun. I could see them from a distance and see him through her eyes simultaneously. They closed the gap between them as if they were being pulled into one another. Their world, in that moment, seemed so perfect and full of happiness I felt like I was going to burst simply by being near them.

He went still as she held her hand up and lightly brushed his hair with her fingertips. He blinked slowly at her touch. Emboldened, the woman reached up again, drawing her fingers though his hair. She left her hand on the side of his face, not wanting to break their connection. It seemed such an intimate moment I felt the need to look away.

The scene began to blur. My eyes were locked on the two people who were still standing together closer than would be considered seemly, her hand still resting on his face. Things began to focus again and I noticed only his face was still blurred. It changed, became slightly more youthful. His eyes shifted, becoming darker. His hair was darker, too, as if someone had taken away the sun and his locks no longer shone in the light. His hair rippled and became wavy. I knew this person in a different way than I knew the man who had previously stood there. But something about it felt wrong.

His face morphed back to the one framed by blonde hair that I had seen previously, the man who belonged to the woman in front of him. The sun shining on his blonde hair exposed glints of red in it. I watched them stand there, feeling ashamed at my intrusion on their private moment.

I felt a tug as the hands that had caught me in the café moved to my waist, grounding me somehow. This feeling was all that kept me from fainting as the images sped up once again. The happy couple in the sunlight was gone and I felt a loss deeper than anything I had ever known. I pleaded for the spinning images to stop again, to show me more so I could share their happiness for a little while longer. Instead, the images spun even faster, showing me nothing but blurs of color.

Then everything went dark. I struggled to catch any familiar glimmer that would let me know where I was now. Light began to return, slowly. I was in the C&T being steadied by the blonde man who had run into me. His eyes met mine. They glowed a malicious red that seemed to bore right through me. He leaned toward me quickly and I felt a horrible pressure as if I were being suffocated.

CHAPTER THREE

I was awakened violently by the stomach dropping feeling that happens when you fall off a cliff in a dream. My eyes flew open but I was afraid to move. I had brought my fear and distress with me from my dream. Irrationally, I moved my eyes all around, looking to make sure the man from my dream had not followed me. When I didn't see him in my immediate area I sat up.

I had been asleep several hours according to my bedside clock. Lexa should be calling soon. I reached for my laptop to check my email for slideshow pictures to pass the time.

Sure enough, I had forty-seven emails in my inbox, some with multiple photos attached. I began saving them, trying to label them as descriptively as I could.

It wasn't long after I'd saved the last photo that my cell beeped with an incoming text. I stretched across the bed and snatched the phone off the nightstand. It was Lexa letting me know she was headed to the C&T. I said I'd meet her there and put my laptop in my book bag in case I could corner Sawyer into getting me started on the slideshow.

Bag over one shoulder, I headed toward the front door. Mom was right where I had left her when I'd come home so I stopped in the kitchen to let her know I was leaving. When she caught sight of me she abandoned the cookbook she had been looking at and came over to stand beside me, placing her hands on my temples.

"Are you feeling any better?" she asked as she searched my face with a level of concern only a mother could muster. I gave her a half smile and shook her hands off. My headaches were becoming so commonplace I rarely brought them up any more, although Mom still wanted to rush me to the doctor every time I mentioned having the slightest pain.

"I'm going to meet Lexa," I told her. She had taken a step back from me but her searching gaze never left my face.

"Are you sure? Are you going to be long? I was going to make dinner tonight when your dad gets home," she informed me.

"Shouldn't be," I reassured her. I fished my keys out of my book bag. "I'm just going down to the C&T. I'm hoping I can get Sawyer to help me with that slideshow for Friday."

"Good luck with that," she chuckled as she turned back to her cookbook. She glanced up again. "Are you sure you're feeling better?"

"Fine," I called over my shoulder dismissively as I headed for the door.

The C&T didn't seem very busy from the outside. It was a little after three and all I saw were a few students like myself headed toward the café. The sun was warm and welcome after the long rainy spring and it still made me feel giddy. I parked across the street and jaywalked to the front door.

The little bell tied to the door rang its familiar welcoming jingle as I pushed it open. I could smell fresh baked pastries and coffee. Lexa was already at a table toward the back with Ethan who, in addition to being the reason I was saddled with this slideshow, was also Lexa's cousin. Ethan was the guy other guys wanted to be and every girl wanted to date. With one exception. Somehow I was immune to whatever pheromone he secreted that made him so popular. I can remember when Ethan was all baby fat and pudgy hands and somehow that image had remained with me into our teenage years. Whenever I almost got caught up in someone else's Ethan-worship I would recall those memories.

I smiled to Ethan and Lexa in turn when I reached the table. I deposited my burden in the chair next to me not only to get it off my back but to make sure no one tried to spirit the unoccupied chair off to another table.

"Hey," Ethan called.

"Hey, I didn't see you today," I returned.

"I didn't come in 'til after lunch. I don't have any tests my first two periods so I slept in," he grinned. "I didn't see you either."

"Aren developed a headache from watching Wiley go down during second block," Lexa smirked. "I'm not sure how he hits his head and she gets the headache."

Ethan looked from Lexa to me. "Yeah, I heard about that. Did someone do it to him? A bad end of year prank?"

Lexa shrugged. "I don't think so. They were looking at the chair- it didn't look like someone messed with it. Who knows?"

I kept silent while Lexa and Ethan discussed Wiley's mishap. My head was still a little fuzzy and my stomach had that strange slightly nauseated feeling I sometimes get after too short a nap. It's like I interrupted my stomach's digestive ritual and it's pissed.

"I'm going to grab something to drink- anyone?" I raised an eyebrow to Ethan and Lexa. Ethan shook his head while Lexa held up her mug of some unknown concoction to signal she was good. I scrounged around in the side pocket of my book bag until I came up with sufficient small bills and coins to cover the cost of most of my usual beverage choices.

Stuffing the money in my pocket, I walked over to the bar and hopped onto a stool, waiting my turn. Amber, one of the few full time baristas Maddie had hired, looked over at me from the espresso machine and smiled, indicating she would get to me as soon as she could.

As I sat at the bar I read through the chalkboards hung high behind the counter listing the various items the C&T offered. I was horribly indecisive about anything in life so it was just as well Amber couldn't get to me for a second. As I was reading through the list a second time, fully aware I wasn't absorbing anything I read, I felt my bubble get a little smaller as someone took the stool next to me. I look over, hoping it was someone with which I could start a conversation and thereby avoid making a decision about what to drink. Decisions always made me queasy and I liked to postpone them as long as possible.

It was him.

CHAPTER FOUR

My mouth dropped open and I gaped at him in a stunning impression of a large mouth bass. I thought I had invented him. Maybe I had met him before and that's why I dreamed about him. But I still didn't know who he was and I certainly hadn't expected to see him here. My heart was playing double-Dutch as I watched him. I wondered if he could hear it.

Luckily my dark haired and painfully handsome stranger was engrossed with the chalkboards as if his life depended on his choice. I watched the intensity in his face as he studied the menu, my eyes drinking in his dark lashes and the curve of his jaw. I couldn't take my eyes off him.

I had to have seen him before- hadn't I talked to him at- no, that wasn't it-

I felt like it was on the tip of my tongue but I couldn't spit it out. My eyes continued to brush over him, trying to fix every detail firmly in my mind. As was inevitable, he finally noticed my stalker-like stare.

"Hi," he said, turning toward me as if my stare had been a physical tap on his shoulder. "Ah, Aren, right?"

I gripped the counter to avoid falling off the stool.

Holy crap, he knew my name.

So we have met before. But how did I forget his name? How could I forget someone who looks like that? I frantically searched my memory but my subconscious had buried his name and was now laughing hysterically at my awkward situation. I cursed her.

"Yes, um-"

Should I guess? Maybe I could try Matt. Lots of guys are named Matt. He didn't seem like a Matt though.

"Noah," he said, watching to see if it rang any bells. It didn't but I was determined not to forget his name again even if I had to tattoo it on my forehead. He leaned back and gave me a crooked smile. "It's okay, I didn't think you'd remember me. From the Christmas parade?"

I was about to fall off the stool in fits. The Christmas parade? What about the Christmas parade?

I had been guilted, no surprise there, into marching in the Christmas parade last year in the freezing weather because the living nativity had been short a few shepherds. It felt like we walked for years in the freezing cold wearing bed sheets over our sweaters and insulated boots. It was the polar opposite of a warm and fuzzy memory, pun intended. That almost explained why I hadn't remembered him.

"Oh, yeah," I said, trying to sound like I knew what I was talking about. My face began to redden, belying my feigned understanding.

"What can I get you?" Amber asked as she leaned over the bar in my direction. I looked up at her, unable to hide my surprise at the reminder that he and I weren't the only two people in the world.

"I'll have-" I was searching desperately for something to jump out at me from the chalkboards. The harder I looked the more everything began to resemble Greek- just familiar enough to make me think I should know it but I still had to admit I had no idea what it was saying. "-a- um-"

"Can I have a large mocha with whipped cream, please?" he asked Amber, shooting me a conspiratorial grin as he saved me from the spotlight.

Not he- I reminded myself- *Noah.* What an amazing name, Noah. I hadn't known anyone named Noah before and it sounded like such a strong name. I had to move fast to hide my sneer at the way Amber was looking at him. Apparently my indecision also made me forgettable. Amber was still nodding at him when he turned to me, one eyebrow raised. Distracted by my musings about his name I had completely forgotten I was supposed to be making a decision about coffee.

"Um, what he said sounds good." It was after Amber walked away that I processed what I had agreed to. Thankfully, I liked mochas. At least I didn't agree to a caramel latte or something. I wasn't a caramel fan. I had always been more of a chocolate girl.

"So, what have you been up to?" he asked me as if we were old friends. I stared at him. He wanted to know what I was up to? Surely I had heard him wrong. No one who looked like him wanted to know what I was up to. I began to twirl a strand of my dull brown hair around my fingertip nervously. I wished I had done more than run my fingers through it. I was trying hard to think of something cool to say just in case this was a joke. I had to struggle not to look around to see if someone was laughing at my inability to speak to a guy. Or maybe there were hidden cameras somewhere like the TV show that sets people up in weird situations then makes fun of them.

"Nothing really. Finishing up with school for the year, you know," I said vaguely.

"Yeah, me too," he said. "So, do you have any plans for the summer?"

"Um, not really- I don't think."

Clearly, you don't think, Aren. I mentally facepalmed. What a genius I turned out to be. Noah, being the perfect gentleman he was, continued on as if my mental train hadn't just jumped the track while crossing a bridge.

"Yeah, I always say I'm going to do all these things, I have all these plans but the next thing I know summer's over and it's back to the books." He shrugged then smiled. I assumed he attended the college here. Jefferson boasted a small private college whose campus began at the opposite end of Main Street from the high school.

"Yeah," I finally breathed in response. I rationalized

that the less I said the better. Hopefully it would give me fewer opportunities to say something dumb and thus give the hidden cameras nothing entertaining to share with the rest of the world.

It was at that moment Amber arrived with our drinks, placing two identical mugs on the counter. "Anything else, guys?" Her question seemed to address both of us yet she never took her eyes away from Noah.

I shook my head as I fumbled for my money. I tried to twist my hand into my pocket without standing up but I couldn't get it far enough to reach anything. I felt like Amber and Noah were just staring at me, which made me even more flustered. I refused to look up. Instead, I tried to force my fingers painfully into my pocket but I could only feel the edges of the bills. My fingers were starting to go numb from lack of circulation so I tried to work them back out of my pocket, defeated. My face, which had only just begun to return to a normal hue, burst into flames again. How in the world do I manage to make getting money out of my pocket difficult?

I was contemplating how I could stand up with any kind of grace to get to my money when I chanced looking up. Noah was handing Amber a few bills. "For both. Keep the change," he said.

My pride bristled and as I started to protest I realized he was probably just trying to spare them both the torture of watching me lose a fight over money with my jeans.

Stupid jeans. Stupid, back-stabbing jeans.

"Thank you," I said, "that really wasn't necessary." There- I made the cursory protest that was required to keep me from looking like an ungrateful mooch. The truth was my red fingers were starting to tingle as feeling returned to them and I was hoping I didn't have to try to use that hand soon. Take two of getting into my pocket would probably prove just as fruitless. And I had never had a guy buy me something before. I kind of liked it.

"Sure," he dismissed his act of kindness- or mercy, depending on how you chose to look at it. He made no move to go nor did he endeavor to continue our conversation. I found myself staring, mesmerized, as he bent down to take a sip of his mocha since it was filled to the brim. When he raised his head, a faint trace of whipped cream remained on his upper lip. I realized I had been holding my breath. I relaxed my shoulders and turned to slide off the stool. I had to leave before my cheeks could burst into flames yet again. I turned to pick up my drink after both of my feet were safely on the floor.

"Thanks again but I have to get back to my friends," I said more to my cup than to him. I glanced up wondering if he had even noticed I had vacated my stool.

"It was good to see you," he said warmly with a preposterously cute crooked smile that made me feel like he actually meant it. "See you around," he called as he headed in the opposite direction.

I had to concentrate ridiculously hard to get back to my table without spilling my drink. I felt as if I was moving through a dream. The good kind where I was invincible. The euphoria that was spreading through me, and consequently causing me to lose feeling in my extremities, was amazing. I attempted to breathe steadily and deeply, hoping my face could regain some sort of normal shade of pink before I got back to the table.

No luck. The minute I caught Lexa's eye all my hard work was tossed out the window as my face blazed again.

I sat my drink down on the table, determined to see my task through to the end. Now that my drink was on the table I proceeded to seat myself. I leaned over to sip some of the steamy mocha from my mug. Realizing I had just mirrored what Noah had done a second ago, I allowed myself one goofy grin before looking up at Lexa, who had slid into the seat next to me.

"So, who was that?" Lexa tried to sound casual to put me at ease therefore causing me to potentially spill more details than I intended. I was up on her tricks by now. And besides, I had nothing to tell. Still, I couldn't keep the smugness from my voice as I told her his name.

"Noah," I answered taciturnly. As I had concluded with him, I figured short answers were best with Lexa, too.

"I don't think I know him," Lexa said nonchalantly. Again, a tactic designed to ferret out information by getting me to try to remind her where she may have met him. She was good at this game, but for the first time in a long while I was feeling up to her challenge.

"I don't exactly know him either. We were in the Christmas parade together." As I said this, it didn't sound right. I shrugged, a million things had happened since Christmas. Besides, I didn't spend long pining over guys who were out of my league. I was nothing if not a realist.

"Really? Maybe I should start doing the parade thing. He's cute," Lexa said with a conspiratorial smile. Again, my face began to heat up. I wondered if were possible to cause my cheeks to peel from all the blushing.

"Yeah," I agreed. "I don't really remember him. I don't know why he remembers me."

Lexa frowned. "It's not unusual that a guy would remember you, you know." I smiled gratefully at her. Lexa was the pretty one who wasn't without a date when she wanted one. It was so natural for her that she couldn't understand it wasn't so effortless for other people. And she was my best friend so it was required she say things like that to me.

"Hey," Sawyer called out from behind me, making me jump. I grabbed my mug to steady it. He sat his bag down in the seat currently holding my own bag then placed himself in the chair next to it.

"Hey," I greeted him, taking another sip and feeling inexpressibly grateful at the excuse to avoid any more probing from Lexa. "So, I just have a teensy question about that slideshow..."

Lexa accepted that our conversation was over for now and had slid back over to Ethan whom she was attempting to help with his science final. Sawyer cocked his head to the side to look at me. I wasn't as good at the nonchalance as Lexa.

"Where's your laptop?" he asked bluntly. I chalked his answer up to a victory in my favor and fished it out to show him I had taken the initiative to download the photos I had already been sent.

After another hour or two the C&T started to get crowded with the after work mob. By then Sawyer had done a good job of thoroughly confusing me then bringing me back to a state of near comprehension. Lexa was making to leave after taking all the Ethan she could handle so I said my goodbyes as well and we walked out together.

We made our way through the café to the door and into the sunlight. It was something bordering on a miracle for me that it was still full daylight after five. Out on the sidewalk we stepped away from the door and paused, our cars being in different directions.

"I didn't get to ask earlier- are you feeling any better?" Lexa inquired. Her brow was drawn up in concern and I felt a wave of warmth for my friend.

"I'm fine. It was just one of those headaches, you know? They come on so fast," I reassured her. I was actually starting to believe it myself. I had worked all afternoon to forget what had happened in Mr. Wiley's class but the reminder of my headache instantly brought back thoughts of the trigger.

"Are you going in tomorrow?" Lexa moved on to her next question, apparently satisfied with my answer to her previous one.

"I don't know. I don't have any tests but I do have a few projects I need to get from art class. I may just swing by in the afternoon and pick those up. Ms. White's free block is after lunch, right?" I asked.

"Sounds right. I don't think I'm going at all. Call me before or after or something. If you're not busy- or if you need help." I wasn't sure if she meant with getting my stuff out of the art classroom or my speech or the slideshow. Of course, I know if I asked her to help with any of the above she would.

"I will," I promised. I gave her a quick hug then ran across the street to my car. I headed home, determined to get a few hours in on the slideshow before I had forgotten everything Sawyer had taught me. Even then, I figured he'd be expecting a phone call or two so he can answer my questions about something he had already explained three times.

My dad's truck was in the driveway when I pulled in. After parking my car I dragged my book bag out, which was heavier than normal due to my laptop. I went to deposit it on my bed before doubling back to the kitchen where Mom was finishing dinner- spaghetti and garlic bread from the smell of it.

Mom turned toward me from her place at the stove, still stirring her homemade spaghetti sauce. "Would you get the plates and glasses down, honey?"

I nodded as I started to pull glasses, plates and silverware from their various cubbies and put them on the island. Mom was pulling the garlic bread out of the oven when Dad sauntered into the kitchen.

My dad is a nurse at the local doctor's office. He works five, sometimes six days a week and he has put to rest any rumors I may have believed that nurses get paid handsomely. But he seems to like his job so I'm guessing that makes up for it. My mom just recently began working part time in an art gallery/ gift shop downtown after being out of the work force for years. She had decided to start working again once I was able to shuttle myself around. Of course, that was about the time most job opportunities dried up. She had been grateful when this job came along since it was something she enjoyed and it did help pay a few bills.

"Hi, Dad," I said as he came in. He was running his hand through his floppy brown hair, the same uninteresting shade as mine. He grinned at me then wrapped me in a huge hug. I squeaked as he squeezed the air out of my lungs. He chuckled and released me.

"So how's your last week of high school turning out?" he asked.

My mind flashed briefly to the incident in Mr. Wiley's class then firmly filed it away as a bad dream. "Ok, I guess. I don't think I'll get to enjoy it though, I have way too much to do."

"Oh yeah. Working on the slideshow?" he asked me as he poured himself a glass of milk. He waved the jug in my direction to ask if I wanted some. I nodded and he reached for another glass.

"Sawyer showed me what to do this afternoon so I'm going to work on it this evening. People are already sending photos and I'm afraid to get behind on it."

"How's your speech?" Mom asked as she began piling spaghetti on a plate.

"Not exactly a speech yet. I wrote down what I want to say- it's just not in complete sentences." I moved over beside Mom to dole out my own food.

We sat down at the table to eat and continued talking about my upcoming week. Sometimes being an only child was great, but the more we talked about my extensive to do list the more I panicked. This was one of reasons I didn't like being an only child. There's no one else to distract your parents from every little thing you're doing.

After dinner I rushed off to my room, shutting the door firmly in hopes of keeping out my anxiety as well as my parents. I put my phone face down on the nightstand and took my laptop to my desk. I plugged it in, turned it on and sat back to wait impatiently for it to boot up. As I sat there I glanced around the room, noting I needed to clean. Books and clothes had congregated on the floor in somewhat untidy little piles. I was amazed at how they did that all by themselves since I don't remember putting any of them there. My shelves needed dusting as well. I hated dusting. Both my books and my figurine collection were coated with a thin layer of the stuff. I looked over my figurine collection, wondering what I would do with it when I went to college. I knew my room probably wouldn't change much when I left seeing as how my parents didn't have a need for another room but I knew eventually I would have to do something with them.

My parents had begun collecting figurines for me when I was very small. I had gotten a new one each birthday of a little girl with brown hair like me holding a number corresponding to my age. There were also ones that marked firsts for me- a porcelain whale from my first trip to Sea World, a Mickey figurine from Disney, etc. Over time other members of my family began adding to my collection. I could look at the shelf and recall the first time I smelled the ocean and the first time I rode a horse. My entire life had been captured in those tiny porcelain figures.

I turned back to my laptop, which had completed its start up routine. I debated on whether I should finish the few pictures Sawyer and I didn't get to or if I should go ahead and check my email so I could do all of them at once. The idea of checking my email made me want to hyperventilate so I opted for wrapping up what Sawyer and I had started. That way I could make sure I remembered everything he had told me.

Sawyer had been right about repetition. I was soon flying through the slides. I quickly added all the photos I had downloaded that afternoon and now I felt brave enough to check my email. I shouldn't have done that. I about fell out of my chair when my inbox informed me I had sixty-two new emails.

Crap.

I began dutifully downloading the pictures, noticing some of them were duplicates of ones I already had. I gleefully deleted them. After a little while my mind started to wander while my fingers continued to label and save picture after picture. I tried to stop it, but it went right back to the café and Noah, previously the mystery guy from my dreams.

I wondered why I waited five months to start dreaming about him only to run into him the same day. It was more like I had conjured him up from nothing rather than simply remembered him. For a moment, the idea of being able to conjure cute guys out of nowhere made me giggle. Then I remembered what my "conjuring" did to Mr. Wiley. That wasn't as funny.

I continued to download and save, all the while letting my mind run amok with fantasies about running into Noah again, him asking me out and professing his love for me. Even I had to roll my eyes at myself. I hadn't ever been giddy over a guy before so these feelings were completely new. I couldn't decide if I liked it or if it scared me. I left the jury deliberating on that one.

I hadn't realized how long it would take to save all the

photos and a few hours had passed before I knew it. I yawned and stretched, trying to work out the kinks that had set in from being hunched over my computer. I told the laptop to shut down and went to find something to sleep in.

I was happy to crawl into bed though surprised by how tired I was given I had napped half the day away. I tried to read for a little while, telling myself it was still early to go to bed when I didn't have to get up at any specific time in the morning. After a few pages, however, I had to put the book down and turn out the light.

CHAPTER FIVE

I was walking through a landscape comprised of every place I had visited in my life all stitched together along one path. Or maybe I was standing still and the places were rushing by me. I wasn't sure and it didn't seem to be important enough to dwell on. One thing I did know, I was alone. No matter where I looked I didn't see another soul.

Every new scene recalled a different memory, some I had no idea even existed. I barely grasped one before the next one took its place. It wasn't long before I felt exhausted. I tried to keep the memories and the accompanying emotions from overwhelming me but it was impossible. I thought the onslaught would end after exhausting all images from babyhood but my mind kept going- reaching back further to places I might have visited years, decades, or even centuries ago if I had been alive. I had just begun to believe that I was getting myself under control when I felt the pressure of eyes on me. I wasn't alone anymore.

I forgot about trying to stem the rapid flow of images as I panicked at the discovery of the intruder. The memories came at me with crushing force, bringing every feeling- good and bad- with them. I felt like I could choke on so much emotion.

I tried to regain my breath without much luck.

Twisting around, I attempted to catch a glimpse of whoever was invading my mind. I couldn't see anything but the dimming tableaus of places in the past.

I faced forward again- and caught the briefest flash of red streaked blonde hair in the sunlight in a memory of a family vacation at the beach. My eyes locked on the scene but I was unable to stop my forward momentum to get a better look. Then I saw dark, wavy hair and one brown eye in the bluish light given off by the tanks at an aquarium. Then again, the blonde hair in the dappled sunlight under the trees at the zoo- then dark hair again-

I felt someone, or possibly several someones, catching up to me. The memories of random places kept coming and I had no energy to spare to fight the newcomers off. I heard a voice but all I could make out was "must" and "self." Suddenly, my progress was halted when a hand came down on my shoulder. I was spun around, dizzy from the memories and the chase.

"It will all seem better come morning." I recognized the speaker as Noah. I had barely had time to put a name to his face before I was distracted by movement to my right. I turned to witness the blonde guy launch himself at us. I was immediately enveloped in blackness.

∾ ∾∾ ∾

I woke up with a start, clutching at the sheets to ground myself. It was pitch black in my room except for the little patch of moonlight on the floor with which to orientate myself. I tried to rein in my breathing. When the room stopped spinning I put my hand to my forehead to wipe the sweat from it. My eyes ached from exhaustion. I closed them, making my way to the bathroom by touch. After splashing water on my face and neck I slipped quietly back to my bedroom feeling marginally better.

I climbed into bed wondering how in the world I was going to get back to sleep. I felt as if I were still being pursued. I lay down, staring at the ceiling while attempting to think of anything that would take my mind off the chase. The only other thing I could find in my head was Noah. I ran over and over our conversation trying to analyze it for clues as to his motives but soon my eyes hurt too much to keep open and I drifted off.

ᕲ ᕲᕲ ᕲ

When I woke, it was past nine in the morning. After last night I was thankful I had been able to take advantage of not having to be in class early. Of course, that may explain why I woke up feeling exhausted since I had deviated from my normal weekday schedule. I wrote off my morning fog as getting too much sleep and wandered into the kitchen. It seemed Mom and Dad both had to work today so I had the house to myself. I grabbed a glass of orange juice and sat down with plans to take a long time in deciding what I would do with my day just because I could.

Obviously the slideshow and my speech loomed large on my list of things not yet complete. I wanted to have my speech finished by Wednesday and the slideshow done not too long after so I could try to glean some joy out of the remaining days of the week. I was gaining momentum on the slideshow front so I figured I could continue where I left off until I had gone through all the photos I had saved last night. Then I could switch gears and start on my speech, as long as I remembered not to check my email before three or so today.

I dragged my laptop out to the kitchen and sat in my flannel shorts and Jefferson softball t-shirt to work on the slideshow. It felt like it took no time at all to add the new pictures but it was after eleven by the time I was done. I leaned my head back to try to ease the kinks out of my neck. I didn't want to start on my speech but I couldn't put it off any longer. Logic stood to reason that if I wanted it done I had to work on it. I hated logic sometimes.

I saved and closed the slideshow so I could start typing my speech. For good measure, I turned my Wi-Fi off so I wouldn't be tempted to check my email. I took my notes out and struggled to make full sentences out of the scrawled snippets. I figured I would try to put the sentences into some kind of order after I translated them out of what read like caveman speech. I spent an hour staring at my notes and starting to write, stopping, deleting what I had typed then starting again. It was a few minutes after noon before I remembered I had meant to go to the art room and pick up my final projects.

I briefly considered letting them linger another day but knew if I put it off I'd forget. Besides, I'd probably need that time tomorrow to work on something else. I showered and dressed, tying my hair up in a knot. I grudgingly left the house and headed to the school, parking rebelliously in the visitor parking spot. In a few days I would be a visitor, I reasoned. Running inside, I didn't bother to stop at the office. This would take twice as long if I had to sign in only to turn around and sign right back out.

There was no one in the art room when I entered. The room looked sad without students sitting around with brushes or pens or pencils, entirely bent on whatever project they were doing. Making a tour of the room, I picked up the objects of the mission that had taken me out of my pajamas. I had a ceramic statue of my "artistic" interpretation of a woman that had been glazed last week as well as a watercolor and an oil painting that had finally dried. I screwed up my face at the watercolor. Watercolor was definitely not my thing but I figured I should keep it to prove how bad I was if anyone ever asked.

Ms. White was coming in the door as I was reviewing my mental checklist to make sure I hadn't forgotten anything.

"Hi, Aren," she said as she came through the door, a mug in her hand.

"Hey. I was just getting my things. I didn't want to forget them," I explained.

"No problem." she said. "I'll certainly miss you in my class next year." A wave of nostalgia threatened to wash over me but I just smiled and mumbled something that sounded like agreement. Considering my lack of true artistic skill I decided she must say this to pretty much everyone.

I attempted to wave goodbye though my arms were

full as I headed out the door. I wanted to get out of here before I was caught parking in the visitor's space. I was hurrying along, two paintings in one hand and the statue in the other, while trying to figure out how I was going to get my keys out of my pocket when someone rounded the corner right before the office and slammed into me. I staggered back, losing my grip on the paintings. I heard the wood crack as the oil canvas took a direct hit from the tiled floor. I went into the wall trying to maintain my grip on the statue. I looked up to discover my assailant was an underclassman whose name I didn't know. He had a lineman's broad shoulders and was kind of baby faced with dark blonde hair and vacant blue eyes-evidence that he had likely taken too many hits to the head. Being several inches taller he had to look down to glare at me, kicking at my unoffending watercolor at the same time.

"What do you think you're doing?" he growled at me like our collision had been entirely my fault. As if I could do any damage to someone with at least sixty pounds and twelve inches on me. My mouth dropped open as my eyebrow raised in astonishment. He must be joking.

He rolled his eyes and went out of his way to shoulder check me as he continued down the hall. I had no idea what could be so important that he thought the additional abuse was warranted. The more I thought about it, the angrier I became. If I didn't have plans to graduate on Saturday with an unblemished performance record I would have turned around and bashed the guy in the back of his head with my statue.

No, that would be a waste of a perfectly good lump of clay.

I gathered my paintings and headed to the car, trying to quell my impotent anger. I refused to look at the damage done to either painting until I got home and put that kid safely out of harm's way. Setting the paintings on the ground, I wrenched open the car door so I could place everything in the back seat.

I definitely should have put this off until tomorrow.

CHAPTER SIX

I inspected my artwork as soon as I got in the door. The frame of the canvas wasn't too bad, it had splintered but it hadn't broke. I figured if I slathered enough wood glue on it I could fix it. The watercolor had a few scuffmarks but was otherwise unharmed. I decided they added a certain artistic quality it had previously been lacking. A statement regarding what I thought about watercolors, maybe.

Accepting that I probably wouldn't get anything else done today I threw myself on the couch and called Lexa. She answered on the second ring.

"Hey, did you already go up to the school?"

"Yeah," I answered, flashing back to the idiot in the hallway. "I'm at the house now. What are you doing?"

"Nothing. Why?" she drawled.

"I thought maybe you could help me go through a few of these slideshow pictures. Just for a little while. I was thinking about heading out to the park later." I was hoping the promise of another activity that didn't constitute work would convince her that it couldn't possibly be too bad. Besides I felt bad about asking her. The park was the first place that came to mind- although it wasn't like we had a lot of places to go around here.

The park was a sprawling complex situated around a small lake on the edge of town near the high school. It had several baseball fields, a playground, a basketball court, soccer fields, a running track and mini golf in the summer. Summer ball was already starting up for everyone from kindergartners to adults. Most everyone, whether they played summer sports or not, spent part of their time at the park during the warm months.

"K, sure. I had thought about going out there anyway. I'll see you in a bit," she said as she hung up.

I let my head loll backwards across the arm of the couch. I was still mad at the idiot in the hallway. I wish I had punched him. It didn't take much to imagine how the incident should have played out.

ɠ ɠ∾ ∾

He comes around the corner and bumps into me but I remain on my feet. I drop the paintings to free my hand up so I can punch him. He's taller than me but not so tall I can't connect with his nose and the impact catches him off guard. His head is thrown back and his body follows. He goes down hard several feet from where he had been standing and hits his head on the lockers behind him. He grabs his nose, I'm sure it's bleeding. He rolls over, backing away from me with a look of sincerest regret tinged with newfound respect.

ɠ ɠ∾ ∾

My head whipped forward as I heard a loud knock on the door.

That was quick.

Lexa was on the porch, her laptop under her arm.

"Hey," I said as I stepped aside to allow her entrance. She rolled her eyes at me in mock exasperation. At least, I thought it had a mocking quality about it.

I grabbed my laptop off of the dining room table and we headed for my room. She threw herself across my bed and kicked off her shoes.

"You owe me, woman," she sniffed at me, though her smile belied her aggravation.

"I'll buy you a hot dog at the park," I told her. She made gagging noises; Lexa hates hot dogs.

"How do you want this done?" she asked.

I showed Lexa how Sawyer had basically set up the

slideshow. Lexa was much better than me at this kind of thing and she picked it up immediately. After my brief tour of the work done so far, she and I both started downloading photos from my web-based email. She started to put her half together on her computer while I worked on mine. We chatted as we worked but after a few hours I judged that Lexa was near the end of her rope. Luckily both of us were near the end of our list of photos.

I used a flash drive to transfer the portion of the slideshow Lexa had completed to my computer, tacking it on to what I had already done. I hadn't timed the slideshow yet but I was sure I had to be approaching the limit. I hit the save button, then hit it again just in case. After a second, I decided to back it up on the flash drive.

The emails with photos had started to slow down so I was hoping there wouldn't be many more between now and the morning. I was determined that I would automatically delete any photos that came into my inbox after the deadline. If you can't be on time don't expect to see your face in my slideshow.

Lexa had shut down her computer and rolled over onto her back, her arms flung over her face while her legs moved back and forth over the edge of the bed. Lexa was dressed about like me, jeans and a t-shirt, but somehow jeans and a t-shirt looked a lot better on her. I tugged at my hair tie self-consciously, letting my still-damp hair fall. For a second I tried brushing it out with my fingers but gave up almost as quickly. As I wound it back up on top of my head I decided I was going for that devil may care look.

"Are we done?" Lexa moaned, her arms still over her face. Clearly she had decided that my actions warranted her dramatics. I smiled and hopped up, taking my laptop over to my desk to charge.

"Waiting on you, *chica*," I said, slipping on some flip-flops that I found near the desk. I stood in the doorway with hands on hips.

Leaving her laptop on the bed, Lexa rocked to her feet and follow me out. I volunteered to drive as I sent a quick text to Mom so she wouldn't be trying to hunt me down later.

For the second time that day I found myself headed across town. This time I drove past the school and turned onto the wide paved road that was the park entrance. It was about four o'clock and the park was already packed with kids and parents. Three of the four baseball fields were taken with either practices or games. This would last until about nine or ten tonight and later than that on the weekends. I cruised around a little bit, looking for a parking spot that wasn't in foul ball territory. I ended up across from one of the picnic pavilions near the soccer fields.

Within minutes I had already spotted several people I knew and had waved greetings as Lexa and I headed toward the walking track that meandered through the park. Walking and talking was one of our favorite pastimes. With a poignant ache I realized this activity had its days numbered.

An unspoken agreement between us said we wouldn't talk about the changes autumn would bring. Lexa and I had wanted to go to college together but the program she wanted to get into wasn't at any of the schools where I had secured an offer for scholarship. Deciding to face this next step of life apart was one of the first adult decisions we had made. So far, being an adult sucked.

So Lexa and I talked about everything else. About what we were doing with our summer, what we were wearing to graduation, our plans for celebrating after, what other people were doing after graduation. We could practically run down the entire list of our graduating class by memory. If I thought about it hard enough, I could probably do it alphabetically considering there were only sixty-seven students graduating on Saturday.

When we made our way around to the playground we appropriated two swings near the edge of the mulched area. Technically we were too old to use the playground equipment but park security never said anything. Most of the parents there turned a blind eye as well. Probably because most of them grew up in this park and sat in these swings way beyond their elementary school days, too.

"So..." Lexa pursed her lips to draw the word out while swinging her head around to look at me at a weird angle. I braced myself for whatever was about to come. That "so" was always followed by an interrogation. "So what about that guy at the C&T yesterday?"

"Oh, Noah," I said, unable to stifle the little giggle that escaped my lips along with his name. A tingle started in my stomach and I felt my fingers go numb. I immediately rolled my eyes at myself. When did I become the chick that goes crazy at the mention of some guy?

"Yeah, Noah," she prompted. "I've never seen you like this."

I wasn't sure if that was a good thing or a bad thing. "What about him? I talked to him for less than two minutes yesterday. I don't really know him. He's just a guy." I wasn't sure if I was saying this more to Lexa or to myself. I was trying to describe the situation using logic but the tingly feeling in my stomach was telling me logic had little to do with it.

"Yeah, but he remembered you. Do you like him?" There it was- what she was really after. Lexa was a perpetual matchmaker who had made it her mission in life to find a guy I would go out with. I had long ago chalked my disinterest in dating up to having very few options in this town. Lexa just thought I was weird.

"I...I don't know how to answer that. I don't know him. So yeah, right now he's fantastic. I mean, how can I tell?" I was flustered and the words flew out of my mouth before I could think them through.

"Alright," she said as if she were backing off. She used her toe to push her swing back and forth a little, scanning the park. I realized I had only gained a temporary reprieve. Suddenly, Lexa sat bolt upright in her swing. "Aren, he's here."

Some part of me was praying she was talking about Noah, another part was hoping desperately it was anyone but him. I slapped at Lexa's arm, shaking my head at her, hoping she would be less obvious. She sat back in her swing again and pushed off, but she still kept staring. My face was turned toward the ground but I couldn't help peeking up through my lashes to see if it was Noah. I could feel the strain in the back of my eyeballs as I tried to look up far enough to see who was there without lifting my head.

Sure enough, it was him coming around the bleachers of the nearest baseball diamond. I had thought I had committed his face to memory when we were in the C&T but I became breathless all over again when I saw him. He was dressed in t-shirt, jeans, tennis shoes- nothing special. But then, he probably could have worn a trash bag for all I cared. Part of my brain pointed out that he may have been wearing a trash bag yesterday but I never looked any further than his jaw line.

"Would you look at him?" Lexa hissed between clenched teeth.

I warred with myself for a moment before my head shot up. I had meant to raise it slowly, casually, but instead I looked like a rabbit sensing danger. It was no good hoping Noah hadn't seen my desperate move since he caught my eye and smiled immediately.

I melted. I tried to remind myself that I was not the kind of girl who melts but it wasn't working. I had never experienced anything like this before and I was completely unprepared. My rational side tried to rein me in since this couldn't end any way but badly. The emotional side of me was doing cartwheels.

Noah sauntered over to us, a slow rocking gait that was mesmerizing to watch. He grinned and leaned against the metal upright of the swings. "Hi," he said to me.

"Uh, hi, Noah," I breathed. I realized talking in his vicinity was so difficult for me because my head was all fluffy when he was around.

"This is Lexa," I said as I motioned to Lexa. She smiled and raised a hand to him then stood, stretching.

"I'm going to go look for Sawyer, I'll find you later- okay?" She didn't wait for a response before she started walking quickly across the lawn. As her words set in I became confused. I was sure that of all our friends Sawyer would be the last one to come to the park willingly. He hates anything remotely associated with physical activity or the outdoors. Then it dawned on me what she had done. She had left me here so I would be alone with Noah.

Embarrassed, I kept my seat on my swing and looked down at my toes. I could feel Noah's eyes on me. I felt like I was twelve again, all thumbs and awkward conversation no matter how hard I tried to appear grown up.

"It's a little strange running into you two days in a row. I would almost think you were following me," Noah said.

I jerked my head up, an incredulous look on my face. "I'm not following you, why would I follow you?" As soon as the words were out of my mouth my face colored. Noah's eyebrows raised a fraction as he smiled.

"Good question. You don't even know me yet. Walk with me?" He pushed himself away from the metal pole and I got up automatically as if his motion prompted me to match it. His words had been half question, half statement as if he knew I would go with him before he asked.

We picked up on the walking track about where Lexa and I had left off. We walked slowly, not speaking at first, which was good. I wanted to make sure I remembered how to walk before I added talking to the mix. Emboldened by the knowledge that my feet knew what to do, I plunged forward.

"So, did you say you were in school?" I asked him.

"Yeah, my first year at the college," he answered. When he didn't elaborate I figured it meant I had to ask more questions.

"What are you studying?"

"I haven't really picked a major yet. I'm weighing my options. I thought it would be English but now I'm thinking about Psychology. There's just something fascinating about what the mind does. I took the 'Intro to Psych' class this semester and I think I might be hooked," he glanced sideways at me, his crooked smile sliding up one side of his mouth.

"Psychology seems tough to me," I finally said after a beat. I looked down at my feet again, watching one foot move in front of the other. We were coming around to the lake now and a faint breeze was blowing. I could see a small boat out on the water and a few geese were picking at the shoreline. The grass was a bright spring green from all the rain.

"There's a lot to it but I think if you really want something the work is easier." For no reason I felt my cheeks get hot. Was he still talking about his major? I mentally kicked myself for trying to read into his words. He continued, "I'm very interested in dreams, actually."

I stumbled a little, a weak cough escaping my throat as my breath caught. Noah stretched out a hand toward my elbow as if ready to catch me.

"I'm fine," I said, embarrassed. "So, dreams, huh? I just thought they were kind of the sorting phase before your subconscious filed thoughts away. Like a little secretary," I said, trying to continue on as if nothing had happened. Noah laughed a little.

"That's one way to put it. And that's probably one purpose dreams serve. But I don't think that's everything. I think dreams can have real power to them."

I bit my lip as a ball of ice formed in my stomach, pushing aside the tingly feeling Noah triggered. If I kept reading in to what he was saying I would talk my way into being a case study for his class. But if he professed to knowing more about dreams than your average person then maybe he was exactly the guy to answer a few questions. I bit my lip.

"What?" he asked when he saw my expression.

"I...don't think I really have any opinion about dreams. They're kind of, well, they are what they are, right?" My tongue seemed to stumble on the word "dream."

"I think there's a lot to dreams that people haven't even imagined. I think dreams are a tool that inspires, you know, sets things in motion." His odd choice of words made the ice ball in my stomach grow. A knot in my throat was making it hard to breathe.

"Really?" was all I said. My mind was going so fast my head was starting to spin and I felt unsteady on my feet. I hadn't given much thought to my déjà vu. I had tried to persuade myself to write it off as a coincidence. But faced with even the most remote opportunity to talk about it I felt afraid. I had to admit my dreams frightened me.

"Aren?" My chest gave a flutter as the sound of my name passing Noah's lips caused me to turn toward him. I guess he had noticed I'd stopped listening to what he was saying. He was looking at me with his eyebrows slightly raised in what I wanted to believe was concern-friendly concern, not clinical concern.

"Sorry, I don't know where I went," I said to my feet.

"Has something got you distracted? Or are you just not that interested in dreams?" he asked with a smile in his voice.

"Oh, no, I want to hear what you have to say. It's very interesting. My mind just took a detour for a second. Go on." I admonished myself for not paying attention. It had to be the first sign of my mental instability if I could drift off when someone like Noah was talking to me.

"I was asking you about your dreams. You know, do you remember them? What are they about?" My breath caught again. I couldn't tell him about my dreams. I couldn't tell anyone, not even Lexa. They were so private and, recently, almost terrifying in their clarity. I had always been someone who recalled more of my dreams than the average person but now I carried them with me into my waking hours. The line between what was dream and what was real had become very blurred recently.

"I remember some of them I guess. Pieces, really. But not for long." This answer seemed better than the truth. I was almost ashamed by how much I wanted Noah to like me. I didn't want to scare him away with my creepy dream stories.

"Hmm. I would have pegged you as someone who can remember all her dreams," he said. I wasn't sure what to say. I couldn't help wondering again if he might know something. How could he? Was I wearing a sign on my forehead? My mind oscillated between telling him and not telling him. He continued, "Dreams aren't something I think you should share lightly with someone. I think they tell a lot about a person."

I mentally patted myself on the back for not blathering everything that happened the last few days, waking or dreaming. I didn't know a lot about talking to guys but I'm pretty sure that conversation would send him running for the hills. I had no desire to test my hypothesis however.

We walked a few beats in silence. It felt natural, comfortable, to simply walk with him. As natural as it could be for someone who feels like they're walking on a cloud. I'd never felt this way before and I was learning that familiarity with the feeling was not causing it to diminish. Instead, the numbing effect made me feel like I had fallen asleep again somewhere. My body felt lighter and I began to feel bolder. I was constantly trying to remind myself this was real, that what I did would have consequences and when it was over I would not wake up. But I was finding it hard to believe.

My emotional high was causing me to rethink the decision to not tell Noah about my dreams. Something about him made me want to tell him everything, lay everything out and let things happen as they would. There was an appeal to laying out your whole hand then sitting back as events unfolded. I could set in motion everything- or nothing- but I couldn't say I'd held any moves in reserve.

I shook my head, needing the physical action to clear my mind. Noah seemed to understand exactly what that meant.

"What are you thinking?" he asked.

"Nothing really. Just thinking about what you said," I responded. A sharp, shrill shriek from a child on a ball field made me jump. Until then I had forgotten there was anyone in the world but us. I was enjoying our little bubble, even if it had only existed in my mind.

"A little jumpy, are we?" he prodded when he saw my reaction.

"I, uh, a little- I guess. I haven't been sleeping well lately," I mumbled. While I recognized the rote response most people give to almost any situation of this nature, I had to admit it was more than true in my case. It seemed like I was sleeping all the time- but good sleep had been in short supply.

We were coming down the straight stretch that cut between the last baseball field and the back parking lot heading toward the playground, having almost made a full circuit of the park. I didn't feel like I had been alone with him for thirty seconds but we must have been walking for at least fifteen minutes. Clusters of people were beginning to come into view. My reaction when I picked out Lexa's head in the crowd was a sudden stab of dismay before the panic set in. I didn't want to come off this cloud. I wanted to stay here in this hazy, dreamy place. I thought about asking Noah why he was here with me in the first place. If I could make him seem less perfect by getting him to admit his dark ulterior motives for talking to me I could go ahead and crush my own spirit- allowing me to skip to the healing process. I was praying Lexa didn't see us coming around the track so I had a few more seconds to make Noah admit he only started talking to me because he heard I was good at math or something.

I must have left my luck with my other flip-flops because no sooner had I asked that Lexa not see us than she looked up and caught my eye. She smiled and waved. She was lounging on a picnic table with a few familiar faces.

"I'm sorry I kept you from whatever you were doing," I said as our feet carried us closer to my friends. I noticed there was a profound lack of sorry in my voice but I hoped he wouldn't notice. At any rate I figured he would want to go before being trapped in an awkward situation with my friends from which he would have to try to extricate himself.

Instead, he knocked me off balance when he blurted out, "I came here hoping to see you."

"What? Why?" I scoffed. The whole idea seemed

ludicrous. Not for the first time, I wondered if this was some elaborate joke and I couldn't help but feel hurt.

"No, I didn't mean I knew you'd be here," he seemed to be the one fumbling for words now. "I know a lot of people come here and- well- I was just hoping you would be here." His explanation seemed to pour out of his mouth of its own volition, his words tripping over each other like puppies racing after a ball.

If I had been walking on clouds before, now I was flying at a speed that would launch me into deep space in seconds. I felt so numb from the tingly feeling in my stomach that I didn't know which way was up. I shoved my feelings of hurt from the imagined slight aside and gave myself over to this feeling of absolute, utter and complete infatuation. I let it engulf every part of me as if I had been submerged in a deep pool. I almost choked from the weight of the giddiness. My breath hitched for a moment. Then, in the space it takes to pick one foot up and put it down again, all of those feelings were back under control. I had been completely saturated before drawing everything back into that private part of myself where I could keep the most intimate pieces of me safe.

His awkwardness had made him fly a little closer to earth since it let me see a little crack in the perfect and daunting man I had met at the C&T.

Lacking anywhere else to go, our feet soon brought us to the edge of the picnic table's shadow. Lexa was there along with Hana and her younger brother whose name escaped me at the moment. I said hello and after an awkward pause I introduced Noah. I wasn't sure what etiquette required as far as introducing him or even how to introduce him so I just threw out his name to everyone, who waved in unison.

"Hey, did you hear about what happened at school today?" Lexa asked, turning to me.

"No, I didn't go- remember?" I reminded her. Hana piped up then.

"After third Josh Melman was coming out of Science, rounded the corner right there at the office, and tripped or something. He ends up sprawled out against the lockers and somehow bloodied his own nose. He made a huge scene- saying he had been sucker punched or something, but there was no one around. He was a mess. I figure it was karma," Hana said as if that explained everything.

"His name sounds familiar," I said, trying to place his face.

"He's on the football team- tall, not too bright. Blonde-"Hana continued on with her description but I didn't hear the rest of it. I realized who he was. I sank down onto the bench. He was the guy who had run me down in the hall.

The same guy I had punched in the face in a daydream.

"Wow. I mean, how many people can bust their own nose?" Lexa was saying as she shook her head. I was pained to admit she made a good point. How did someone send themselves flying and bloody their own nose? It was almost as if my daydreaming had caught up with him.

"Aren?" someone asked. I looked around from face to face as I came out of my reverie. It was as if I were trying to look at everyone from underwater. I hadn't been sure who said my name. I felt an unnatural sense of dread- I was afraid my face would give me away as the person responsible for what had happened to Josh. One part of my brain was screaming that this was completely irrational while another part told me that there was no other explanation.

"What?" I finally asked, my voice sounding unusually high. I pinched the bridge of my nose, hoping that faking a headache would explain my crazy behavior. "Sorry, I've picked up a headache from somewhere." I thought I sounded ridiculous but faking a headache seemed like a better explanation than the truth. At this point my version of the truth went something like 'I didn't like Josh so I dreamed I punched him in the face which sent him flying across the hallway at school.' Yeah, definitely sticking with headache. Of course, by the time the night was over, I was almost sure to actually have one.

"Sweetie, you've been having those a lot lately. Are you

okay?" Lexa asked, genuine concern in her voice.

Before I could answer I felt a hand on my shoulder. I had assumed it was Lexa and colored when I looked up to see Noah. I had forgotten all about him, which made me blush harder. I could feel Lexa's eyes on us, desperately wanting to know what was going on.

"You okay?" he asked. I tried opening my mouth to talk but nothing came out so I simply nodded.

But I was definitely not okay. I tried to listen as the conversation moved to a different topic but I couldn't focus. I kept coming back to Josh and his nose. I had no logical explanation for my panic but I was panicking nonetheless. I felt responsible. I was suddenly aware that my distress came from a fear of myself. If these are the things I dream of, students breaking their noses and teachers falling out of broken chairs, anything could happen next. I had been ready to write the whole Mr. Wiley thing off as a premonition of some kind but if Josh had bloodied his nose by fault of his own clumsiness wouldn't that have been what I saw in my dream? What would've happened if I had dreamed something worse? Like running him over with my car?

Scary scenarios started bouncing around in my head. Before it could get out of hand, I grasped at the one point I couldn't accept. My dreams couldn't have any affect on the real world. That's the one thing that made dreams *dreams*.

I kept going through what I could remember about my dreams and the events that followed. I couldn't recall much except the strong sense of déjà vu. At some point I got confused about what was a dream or a reality. Or maybe they were becoming the same. I wondered briefly if I were asleep now.

I tried to go back further to find some ground to stand on. If this could actually happen it would be some kind of ESP, right? Did I believe in that? I tried to remember if I had ever come to a concrete personal conclusion about extrasensory perception. I guess I was on the fence about it, which didn't help me find a place to start dealing with this. I vaguely bought into the idea that anything was possible but I think I was referring to me becoming president not killing people with my dreams. What if I did dream that someone died? I had no control over my dreams. I knew some people say they can control what they did in their dreams but I had always been content to let mine lead me where they wanted. Trying to control your dreams seemed like wasted effort. I thought dreams were supposed to flow freely so your mind could sort through all the stuff you had crammed in there.

I had no answers and no one I could think of to go to for help. I had blamed my plethora of dreams on my overactive imagination and had welcomed them. Somehow something as simple as dreaming had become a nightmare for me. I wanted to say I was overreacting but one thing I didn't believe in was coincidences. Which brought me back to the ESP.

All of this probably took me less than ten seconds to process but during that time I think I stopped breathing. I heard Lexa say my name and I jerked my head up.

"What?" I asked, my eyes wide as I took in my surroundings. I blinked, trying to regain the composure everyone had just watched me lose.

"You okay? Your face is bright red," Lexa observed. All eyes turned toward me and Hana nodded in confirmation.

"Yeah, I think I worked up more of a sweat than I expected. Walking. I'm going to go get a drink." I couldn't believe how much my voice was shaking. I paused before I stood up. I was having a hard time telling the ground from the sky and I really didn't want everyone to watch me fall on my face. It was bad enough the way they were staring at me. I tried to tell myself it was out of concern, but I felt like a freak.

"I'll walk with you," Lexa said, hopping up.

"Let me walk with her, Lexa," Noah said quietly. Out of the corner of my eye I saw her give him a hard look as if sizing him up. If Lexa was anything, she was protective of her friends. "We'll be right back," Noah called to the others and took my elbow before Lexa could say anything.

"Aren?" he asked as we were walking away. I was

shaking now. I hoped it wasn't too noticeable since I was walking but I had to get away from everyone. I didn't stop or look up when Noah said my name. I was so embarrassed to be half dragged across the park by this guy I hardly knew and who I definitely liked. He was not the person that should be witnessing my mental breakdown.

"I'm okay," I said mechanically. I had no room for thought at this point. My body was numb and now that I was moving I wasn't sure if I remembered how to stop. I certainly didn't know where I was going. Noah gripped my elbow tighter as he steered me toward the concession stand.

"Aren, I'm not sure what's upset you. Was it something with your friend? The one who got hurt?" Noah was speaking in low, soothing tones to me. For a minute I only heard the sound of his voice, not what he was actually saying. Then it started to sink in.

"My friend? Josh? He's not my friend," I snorted. He most certainly was not my friend. Sure, I had seen him at school but he really wasn't someone I had give much thought about. I hadn't even remembered his name. He was just someone who I bumped into in the hall, literally. If this was what I did to someone I didn't even know what might happen when I got mad at someone I did know? The panic became a lead ball in my stomach that began to grow, forcing itself up my throat so I couldn't speak. I felt like I was choking. I had to concentrate to remember how to breathe.

"I don't know what's going on, Aren, but if you need to talk-" he stopped. Hopefully it was because he realized how trite he sounded. I was about to hyperventilate and even I could hear it. "Just- it seems like something is really bothering you. I know you don't know me so I'm sure you think I'm not the person to talk to but, well, be careful. Careful of who you talk to. Not everyone understands."

His words temporarily cut through my panic. I waited, expecting him to say more. What was he talking about? His puzzling comment led to a spark of anger. Had he jumped to some crazy conclusion about me?

We had reached the cement concession stand by now. I watched Noah as he edged up to the window then reappeared with a paper cup of water that he handed to me. I leaned my back against the cool cement and drank slowly. My hand was still shaking a little but somehow I didn't slosh the water all over me.

"Feeling better?" Noah asked. I didn't trust myself to answer so I nodded. I wasn't sure if he believed me but I didn't really care. I only wanted him to go away. If I was going to collapse I wanted to do it in the relative privacy of strangers, not in front of the hot guy I had just met.

I finished my water and tossed the cup into the fifty-five gallon drum that served as a garbage can. By some miracle, I actually made it. Buoyed by this small achievement I straightened my shoulders.

"I think I'm going to find Lexa and go. It's been a long day and-" Noah was already nodding, which was good because I had run out of things to say. He gave me that lopsided smile of his.

"Maybe I'll see you some other time?" he asked. He glanced down at his feet then back up at me. It was so cute. Feeling bolder than I ever had in my life- I'm going to blame it on shock- I held my hand out and smiled. Noah looked confused.

"Phone," I demanded imperiously, channeling Lexa. He pulled his cell out of his pocket and handed it to me mechanically, a surprised look on his face. I typed my number in and saved it to his contacts. I handed his phone back smoothly. At least, I think it went smoothly. For all I know I was standing there for thirty minutes staring at his screen and drooling.

Noah realized what I had done and smiled again. "Later then," he said as he walked off. I was so relieved when I had a few soccer moms between him and me that I sagged against the building again. I took stock of my situation. My head was starting to clear. I wasn't sure if my shock was making its exit or if I was getting used to being in shock. I really wanted to find Lexa and get out of here. I was pretty sure I had myself under control but I felt like a time bomb. I needed to get home where I could fall apart in a place that offered both privacy and ice cream.

I started back toward the picnic tables with carefully measured strides, my need to get home quickly far outweighed by the need to not trip and kill myself. My whole body felt limp now, as if I had simultaneously tensed every muscle in my body and now they were all letting go. All of my muscles tightened again when I saw the picnic table we had previously occupied.

Lexa and our friends were gone, though that wasn't the part that surprised me. In their place, standing by the exact same table, was the blonde boy with the red highlights that were blazing in the late afternoon light.

He was tall, lean and intently scanning the crowd. An unexpected trickle of fear ran down my spine. I whipped my head around trying to find Lexa. Maybe she went to the car. I should go look for her. Anything to keep from getting a step closer to him. I wasn't sure who he was but considering what else had come from my dreams I didn't want to take any chances. I tried to move, to go anywhere, but my feet felt glued to the ground. The harder I tried to look for Lexa- for anyone- the less I actually saw. I couldn't make out any of the faces near me. The park seemed incredibly loud. My breath quickened and now the pounding heartbeat in my ears was starting to drown out any other sound.

It was then he looked up. His eyes widened and I knew he saw me. I was held by his gaze for a split second as something electric, almost violent, passed between us. I didn't wait to see what he would do if I stayed. The shock freed my body so I took off running for the car, praying Lexa was already there. In my mind I could see him following me, gaining on me, but I didn't look back to see if it were true.

I almost cried when the parking lot came in view. Lexa was near the car conversing with Noah. I tried to amend my frantic run into an eager jog but my heavy breathing gave me away. Lexa turned to me as I came crashing toward her.

"Are you going to make it?" she asked. She held up her hands as if she expected to be required catch me. Noah moved a few steps closer.

"Fine. Good. Let's go?" I almost pleaded as I fished the keys out of my pocket. Lexa was standing between Noah and I, trying to prevent him from witnessing my psychotic meltdown like any good friend would do. I turned toward the car and Lexa went to the passenger side. She climbed in and I opened my door to do the same. Noah stopped me.

"Hey," he said, still coming closer, "be careful. Trust me, it will all seem better come morning."

"You like that line, don't you?" I asked him. Noah raised an eyebrow. "Come on, you've told me that one before. And I'm not sure I'm buying it."

"I have?" he asked me dubiously.

"Yes, you-" I stopped talking when I caught the look in his eyes that said he had never uttered those words before. At least not in my waking hours.

"See you later," I said quickly as I climbed in the car. I realized another feeling had replaced my shock. It was the now-familiar feeling of déjà vu that swept over me like a rip tide, wanting nothing more than to drag me to the bottom of the ocean.

CHAPTER SEVEN

We were halfway through town before Lexa said something. "Aren, what happened?"

"I-" I started to tell her how I was beginning to believe my daydream had caused Josh to bloody his own nose but it seemed silly once I put it like that. Noah's warning about being careful of whom I talked to chose this moment to resurface. "I don't know. I'm just stressed and tired. I think I had a panic attack or something."

"You need to calm down," she advised sagely. "Everything's going to be fine. This time next week you won't even remember what you were stressing over."

I thought about her words. I knew she meant things like the slideshow, graduation, my speech. In truth, I had completely forgotten about those. Tension began building at the base of my skull as I added them to the list of things I was supposed to be worrying about.

After that Lexa started drilling me about Noah and I was busy answering all her questions and trying to pretend nothing out of the ordinary had happened. When we got back to my house the daylight was almost gone. Lexa came in to grab her stuff saying she needed to head home. We said goodbye and she reminded me that Noah or not, I still owed her anything but a hot dog.

After Lexa left I allowed myself to completely crumple with exhaustion. The emotional roller coaster I had showcased in a public park had taken every bit of energy out of me. I dragged myself to the living room to say good night to my parents before disappearing. While I was brushing my teeth it occurred to me that I hadn't eaten anything for dinner. At the thought of food, though, my stomach roiled.

I ambled into my bedroom and threw myself onto the bed. I glanced dutifully toward my computer but quickly dismissed the idea of working. Tomorrow was Wednesday. I had plenty of time to finish everything.

I couldn't believe tomorrow was only Wednesday. The last few days seem like they had taken years. Tomorrow was more finals at school so I had another free day. I resolved to finish everything in the morning. I was pretty sure I needed to turn in at least a rough draft of my speech for review by then. And I'd like to get the slideshow off my hands as soon as possible.

I crawled under the comforter and lay there for a moment, not even bothering to turn off my lamp. My mind seemed determined to keep spinning at a hundred miles an hour no matter how stern I was when I said it was time for bed. On the contrary, saying it was time for bed seemed to ramp me up. As tired as I was, I was scared to go to sleep.

After a few minutes of thinking about why I couldn't stop thinking, I reached for the book on my nightstand. It was a battered, yellowed paperback copy of a Michael Crichton novel. I had read it three or four times since middle school but I have a tendency to return to things I like. I always said I should branch out and read something new but I always come back to the same dozen or so books on my shelf.

I attempted to read a few pages but was too tired to concentrate. Now I was perturbed. If I couldn't sleep and I couldn't stay up, what was there? I put the book down and turned off the light. I lay back, determined to try to get some sleep. My body ached from all the tension that had been poured into it. I began chanting that it would be fine, I had dreamed for years and years and nothing like this had ever happened before.

CHAPTER EIGHT

I only knew I had fallen asleep by the fact that I woke with a start. It was pitch black in my room. I couldn't hear the television anymore so it must have been several hours later, after my parents had gone to bed. I turned my head to look at the clock. Two in the morning. I tried to remember if I had been dreaming. I couldn't recall anything. Do the dreams come true even if I don't remember them? I decided that probably wasn't how it worked. How would I know it was true if I didn't remember it?

I lay back in bed, consciously trying to relax my muscles. Two in the morning- not bad. I had made it almost halfway through the night. Just a little more to go. The slight adrenaline rush that had awakened me- or had happened because I'd woke so suddenly- was beginning to ebb. As I felt it slip away, I closed my eyes and tried to put myself back in that warm fuzzy place on the brink of sleep. I was hoping if I could get there the rest would be like falling down the rabbit hole.

I was warm and relaxed but still conscious some time later. It felt like I had already been there for hours but it was probably only fifteen or twenty minutes. I started wondering if maybe it was the position in which I was lying. I had been perfectly comfortable but once I got to thinking about it hard enough, I was convinced I couldn't actually be comfortable or I would be asleep. I started tossing about, first lying on one side then the other, then fluffing my pillow. I tried blankets off, blankets on, blankets placed strategically to cover various parts of me while leaving others uncovered for ventilation.

I drifted off for a little while but then realized around four thirty or so that my eyes had opened again of their own volition. After checking the clock to see how much progress I had made, I rolled into a little ball. My body felt so heavy from exhaustion it was like it was filled with lead. However, every time I closed my eyes they would pop open again a moment later.

The rational part of my mind was trying to tell my body to relax and go to sleep was working very hard to ignore the small part of my brain that said I could never go to sleep again because I might dream. I couldn't wholly dismiss this thought as irrational. I wasn't sure what dreaming meant yet but after seeing what had already happened I didn't want to chance it.

I kept hoping I would somehow fall asleep even after the gray pre-dawn light began to filter through my curtains. I wrestled with myself for a moment before I decided that going back to sleep now couldn't do any good. I sat up and switched on my lamp since the day was still too new to give me adequate light for reading. I opened up my book and passed my eyes over a few pages. It didn't take me long to put the book down again.

Since I was up this early I decided I wanted to be productive. I grabbed my laptop and checked my email. I only had a few more pictures. It took me no time to save those and add them to the show. The slideshow was looking pretty full so I figured it was a good time to call it quits. Besides, hadn't I told everyone this morning was the cut off for getting photos to me? If they didn't have their pictures to me by now it was their fault. I saved the show then transferred the newest version onto my flash drive. One project down.

Feeling motivated by crossing something off of the list I grabbed my notes and went back to my speech. I worked on it for a while but soon realized it wasn't going to get done this sitting. My mind was starting to wander and my stomach was growling. I noticed that while I had been working the sun had come up. The room was bright enough for me to switch off my lamp. I shut my laptop off and moved it to one side of the bed. I lay back, deciding I wouldn't move until I knew what I was doing for the day.

I really wanted to get my speech out of the way. Then I could take it and the slideshow to the school and be done. I wondered what Lexa was doing today or if I would run into Noah again. Butterflies erupted in my stomach when I thought about him. Then I remembered I'd given him my number. I reached for my phone on the nightstand. No missed calls, no texts. Well, that was okay. I didn't expect him to call me right away. How long would he wait though?

Excited by the prospect of possibly seeing him for the third time in as many days I got up and got dressed. I decided to be casual, jeans and a t-shirt, but I picked my jeans and t-shirt with uncharacteristic care. I found my favorite dark blue jeans and my teal v-neck t-shirt that fit me just right. I ventured into the bathroom and took a long, unhurried shower before dressing. I combed out my hair carefully and sprayed it with leave in conditioner, praying it would behave itself today.

With my stomach growling, I went into the kitchen. Dad was already there, reading the paper over a cup of coffee. I fished out a box of cereal and a bowl hoping to appease my stomach as soon as possible.

"Hey," I called to my dad as I was rummaging around in the kitchen.

"Hey," he called back. "Why are you up so early? I thought you didn't have school today?"

"I don't," I answered. "I couldn't sleep so I figured I'd try to get a few things done."

He nodded and went back to his reading. I carried my bowl over to the table and sat at the opposite end from Dad. I concentrated on scooping cereal into my mouth, chewing, swallowing then repeating. I hated soggy cereal so I tried to eat as fast as I could before it turned to mush.

"Well, I've gotta go- I'll see you later, sweetheart," Dad said as he stood. He came around to where I was sitting and planted a light kiss on top of my head.

"Bye," I told him. "Love you."

"Love you, too," he called back. He headed for the living room where I could hear the faint sounds of the news. Mom must be in there. A little while later I heard the front door open and close. Not too long after Dad left, Mom came in to tell me she had a half day today at the gallery and would be back this afternoon.

Finished with my breakfast, I put my bowl in the sink and went back to my room. My determination to finish my speech had returned now that my stomach was full. Unless something more important came up, I amended mentally. I went to my phone first when I got back in my room. Nothing. I had at least been hoping for a text. It was still early, I told myself, and I'm sure he wouldn't want to bother me if he thought I might be asleep. I was both disappointed and relived that I hadn't gotten his number. I wanted to text to see why I hadn't heard from him but I also didn't want to be that creepy stalker girl who constantly asked why she didn't hear from him.

Since I had no one trying to make plans with me, I went back to my laptop. I had chosen dreams as the topic of my speech a week or two ago when I was told I would be valedictorian. Now, my speech made me think of the new developments with my dreams and the sudden appearance of Noah. I recognized that somehow I had intertwined the two. This made it exponentially harder to concentrate. When I finally declared I was done it was partly because my mind was so filled with other things that I had no part of me left to concentrate. At least I had met one of my goals- my speech was short, a page and a half, double-spaced. I emailed it to the vice-principal so he could approve it. I wondered briefly what someone had said during their speech that made this approval process necessary.

By now it was mid-morning. I checked my phone again, still nothing. I was starting to wonder if it was broken. Just to have something to do I started picking up the clothes that had strewn themselves around the room and separated the clean from the dirty. I straightened up my bookshelves; I even took a stab at dusting around my books and figurines. My room hadn't been as messy as it had looked at first glance so I was done in no time. But now I had to find something else to do.

I grabbed my flash drive and decided I could get the slideshow off of my hands. Unfortunately the file was too big to email so I had to deliver it to the school myself. I was sure they wanted to look through that as well to make sure I didn't include anything inappropriate.

I put the flash drive in my bag along with my phone, double-checking that the ringer was on. It took all of ten minutes of my day to take the slideshow to the school. I had handed the flash drive to the secretary who dutifully put a sticky note on it and promised to get it to whomever needed to review it. Now I wondered what else I could do given it wasn't even lunchtime yet. I yawned as I headed back to my car. I checked my phone again before starting the engine.

If no one was going to call me, maybe I should just go home and take a nap. I was exhausted. I vaguely remembered why I hadn't wanted to sleep but now, in full daylight, it seemed silly. I drove back to the house, a palpable weight lifted from my shoulders now that I was done with the slideshow and my speech. I could now look forward to the various activities leading up to graduation. Of course, now my day seemed like it would be very long without any projects to complete.

One more reason to take a nap.

My phone had remained silent the whole way back to the house. Feeling surly, I turned the ringer off and put it on my nightstand. I kicked off my shoes and wrapped myself around a pillow, trying to get comfortable. The house was quiet with no one here. Outside, birds were chattering away. It didn't take me long to drift off.

CHAPTER NINE

I was running and I was scared. Terror blossomed in my chest, making it hard to breathe. There was only room for my fear or my lungs and my lungs were losing the battle. I continued to run, not knowing where I was or where I was going, only that I couldn't stop. I swung my head from side to side trying to make out familiar landmarks but everything was cast in shadow. I started to slow as I strained my eyes to see anything recognizable. The fear exploded in my chest again, reminding me I needed to run faster. I turned my eyes back to the ground in front of my feet and concentrated on moving.

I felt like my legs were on autopilot. I wasn't sure I could stop if I had to. Any time I began to slow down the fear in my chest ballooned, making it harder to breathe. A shadow behind me began to swallow mine as it overtook me. I couldn't bring myself to look. I could either look or run and I chose to run.

My path was becoming uneven, as if I had gone from pavement to a dirt road. I was dodging holes in the ground as well as maneuvering over lumps in my path, some small soft mounds and others resembling sharp rocks. My fear was telling me that I had somehow made a mistake. Without making any turns I had still ended up in the wrong place. I was somewhere isolated from which I would never be able to make my way back to civilization. I was fighting these thoughts as hard as I was fighting for solid footing.

I knew way before it happened that it was inevitable. I was sure ever since the terrain had become more uneven that it was only a matter of time before I lost my balance. Even with this new worry I still tried to keep my momentum up, trying to get as far away as I could. The fear in my chest had not subsided in the least and I could almost hear the breath of whomever –or whatever- was behind me. But there is a difference in knowing something might happen and knowing seconds before that without a doubt it was the only thing that could happen.

As my right foot came down after hurdling over a jagged mound in the road my heel hit the sloping wall of what I could only think of as a deep pothole. I had no purchase with which to push off so I could continue running. Instead of moving forward and putting my left leg down, my left leg swung forward and both feet went out from under me. I looked up at an empty sky as I fell onto my back. The impact I had been anticipating was even worse than what I had imagined. The ground was hard and unyielding and everything that had been in my chest, fear and air, was knocked out of me. I didn't have more than two seconds before whatever had been chasing me caught up. My throat seized. My arms and legs tried to go four different directions at once, as if they had suddenly declared it was every appendage for itself. My right hand found a sharp lump, a rock. My oxygen deprived body tried to muster enough strength to throw it, hoping to delay my attacker. I felt the last of my strength drain from me as I screamed and flung the rock. It felt like the entire rock-strewn ground heaved along the arch of the rock I had thrown. The flying rock and gravel made no differentiation between myself and my attacker. The rocks felt like sharp glass as they stung my face and arms while the ground fell away from under me.

෨ ෨෨ ෴

A violent spasm shook my whole body as I sat up, flinging my arms in front of my face. My nightmare had gone from the dark place of my dream to the daylight in my room. I could hear the ringing echo of my scream as it blended with the last of the shattering rocks. My face and arms stung in what felt like a million places. I heard pounding footsteps in the hall and my door was flung open. My mother stood there, her house keys still in her hand. A part of my mind registered that she must have just come home from the gallery.

"Aren!" she screamed, her eyes darting around the room. It was then I realized I hadn't left the shattering sound behind in the dream. My throat closed up as my eyes were drawn to my unusually bare bookshelves. I couldn't figure out what was wrong. I stared, puzzled. Mom had broken her temporary paralysis and was moving toward me, her footsteps crunching on the carpet. It was then I realized what was missing- my figurines. Instead, shards of glass and porcelain littered the floor, the shelves, my bed. My eyes dropped to my arm. Pieces of glass were glittering at the origin of the trickles of blood that were running down my arm. I felt the same wet, sticky sensation on my face. My stomach began churn at the sight.

"Aren, what the- come here-" Mom was on my right side, the side that had been further away from the explosion. She was trying to find a place on my arm where she could put her hands to help me up. My body felt as if it were made of gelatin. I couldn't figure out how to get off the bed. After a few rocking motions, I managed to pitch myself toward her. She put an arm around my waist, trying not to touch any of the tiny injuries. I froze at her touch, the fear of my pursuer catching me suddenly rearing up before I convinced myself that I was safe.

"Oh, Aren- how? Come on, we have to get the glass out. No, I've got to get you to the doctor- your head- can you talk? Answer me!" My mother lost the battle to keep the hysteria out of her voice. I wanted to say something but I couldn't remember how. The tightness in my throat had eased but now it felt so relaxed it couldn't form words. My mouth opened but I couldn't say anything. It felt dry and my head felt so heavy I thought it would fall off my shoulders. I was trying to keep my face turned away so I wouldn't see all the blood.

"Yeah," I finally mumbled as Mom helped my uncooperative body toward the front door. She placed me in the back seat of her car. Bemusedly, I wondered if I were getting blood all over her new upholstery. My left eye was starting to sting as blood from my forehead trickled down. I closed my eyes against the pain, telling myself it was shampoo so I wouldn't be sick. I was tired and numb and praying I'd gotten away in time. I had nothing else left in me to run and no matter how much I told myself that it was okay, I wasn't being pursued anymore, I couldn't shake the feeling. I finally gave up and let the daylight turn back into the darkness of my dream.

CHAPTER TEN

The nearest hospital was the next town over but the doctor's office where my dad worked was just a few miles from the house. My eyes half opened as I was jostled out of the car. There was no way to get my half comatose self out of the car smoothly while trying not to touch any of the dozens of cuts the glass had made.

I heard the buzzing of Mom and Dad's voices and figured it was Dad who had gotten me out of the car.

The world slowed its spinning a little after I was put down. For a second I thought about trying to open my eyes but I was afraid of what I would see. I wasn't entirely sure my pursuer had abandoned me. Instead I concentrated on my breathing. Maybe if I still looked unconscious I wouldn't be attacked again. It was then I felt a pinprick in my arm and I no longer had to fake my unconscious state.

When I woke it felt like someone had taken a baseball bat to my entire body. As my consciousness increased so did the pain. I tried to force myself back to sleep but it was if I were being propelled up and out of my blissful unawareness by an invisible force. I hadn't dreamed at all while I'd been out- be it an hour or a day. I heard people talking and I swung my head around to view my visitors. My whole world spun when I moved my head.

"Hey, honey," my mom said gently, her face full of concern as she looked down at me on the examination table. Mom started to say something else but the door burst open just then and Dad entered with a coffee mug full of water for me.

"Well, still have problems with a little blood I see- you passed out as soon as you got here," he chuckled as he tried to make light of the situation, probably more for Mom's benefit than mine. "It looked worse than it was though. You must have tripped into your bookshelves and knocked your collection down from what your mom said. You have a lot of little cuts but most of them you'd be wasting a bandage on. That one on your arm did need a couple of stitches," he pointed to the large gauze taped to my left arm. "Doc probably could have got away with some adhesive if you weren't allergic. I want you to go home and try not to break anything else, okay? I'll be there soon."

Dad kissed me on my forehead and gave Mom's hand a quick squeeze before leaving.

"Let's go, Twinkle Toes," Mom laughed weakly as she helped me down. I felt a little light headed but not too bad. I was glad I'd passed out so I hadn't had to see the stitches. My stomach got queasy just thinking about it.

This time I was able to put myself in the car. I climbed into the passenger seat and fastened my belt. I looked at my arms. I saw little tiny holes and a few scrapes. A couple looked kind of deep, but I was sure I'd probably given myself cuts just as bad in the kitchen. The square of gauze taped over the top of my left forearm made movement stiff. Both my arms were pretty stiff, actually. And sore. My face, too. I flipped the visor down to look at the mirror. I had the same pattern of holes and scrapes on the left side of my face.

"It really doesn't look bad at all now that you're cleaned up," Mom assured me. "There was just so much glass- but I'm sure they got it all out." She didn't sound like she was doing a good job of convincing herself of this. I immediately became paranoid about left over glass in my face.

When we got home, Mom took pity on my handicapped state and helped me clean up my room. There was glass everywhere. We picked up the big pieces then Mom started going over the carpet with the vacuum. I began sweeping all the hard surfaces for glass bits. We had to strip my bed down, too. We took the sheets outside and tried to shake them out before putting them in the washing machine. I rooted around in the linen closet for clean sheets to remake my bed. The soreness in my arms had become a dull throbbing by the time I finished. I sat on the edge of the bed, paranoid that I may have missed some glass. I tried to comfort myself with the thought that if I missed any of it I was sure walking around in bare feet would find it at a later date.

I glanced at my clock. It was only a little after two. I couldn't believe it. This day was never going to end. Out of habit, I reached for my phone. I was actually surprised to discover I had several texts from Lexa.

Goin to lunch w E n Allie where r u?

U wont guess whos here

Noah. He askd about u. I said we'll prolly b at C&T later

What r u doin?

While I was reading her messages and mourning my lost opportunity with Noah, another message popped in. Lexa was letting me know that she was getting ready to head down to the C&T. I weighed my tiredness against my desire to see Noah again- if he actually made an appearance. The emotional high I got when I was around him was quickly becoming addictive.

I looked in the mirror. I hadn't been hideously mauled so I was fairly certain the sight of me wouldn't chase him away.

I text Lexa to ask if she would swing by and pick me up. Then I went to the bathroom to find the aspirin.

CHAPTER ELEVEN

"Is it really a good idea for you to go out?" Mom asked me. She frowned meaningfully at my gauze.

Great, she was in full on Mothering Mode.

"It's just a few scratches, Mom. I'm only going to the C&T. Lexa's even going to pick me up," I said. She held on to her frown for a little while longer before allowing her face to relax.

"Fine, just be careful," she said.

I rolled my eyes, "I got three stitches not an arm transplant."

Just then the doorbell rang. I turned before Mom could say something else and opened the door for Lexa. "Be back soon!" I called, not even letting Lexa set foot in the house. She was still trying to take in my somewhat marred appearance while I was nudging her out with my good arm. She issued a short "bye" to my mom before I shut the door.

"What happened?" she asked me, taking in my puncture wounds. I was trying to carefully tug open the handle of her car without the use of my sore muscles.

"I had an accident. I fell into the bookshelves where my figurines were and a couple of them broke." I had to admit, it sounded plausible. The more time I put between me and my dream the less real the dream felt. It seemed much more believable that I had a bad dream and fell into the bookshelves. The bookshelves did not fling the figurines at me.

Some small voice inside me said my rationalization was all for nothing. Falling into the shelves would not account for why the entire collection looked like it had been wired with explosives rather than having rolled onto the carpet.

"Are you okay?" Lexa asked. I found the question to be somewhat ironic but I took it at face value.

"Yeah, I'm fine. My skin's a little sensitive around the cuts but it wasn't a big deal. They said they got all the glass and stuff out." Lexa glanced dubiously at me.

"So did you do anything else today?" she asked, trying to change the subject. I told her about my productive morning, leaving out the hour or so that was my ill-fated nap. She told me about lunch with Ethan and Allison to talk about their post-graduation trip to the beach. She kept it short, though, since I hadn't been able to talk my parents into letting me go.

Lexa parked in the bank parking lot across the street from Maddie's. The sun was shining brightly from an electric blue sky. The few cars rolling by seemed to be in no hurry to reach their destination. We crossed the street and made our way to our usual table at the back of the C&T. Lexa volunteered to get drinks so I didn't have to try to carry anything. I wasn't sure of my limitations yet so I was grateful.

While Lexa went to the counter I scanned the room. Then I scanned again. I tried to peer around the bar to the sitting area where a few couches and chairs were. I glanced back to see if anyone was coming out of the bathroom. I was having a hard time hiding my disappointment that Noah wasn't here already.

I pulled my cell out to check for any texts. Nothing.

Where could he be? If he had been asking about me and Lexa told him I would be here why wasn't he here? Maybe he wasn't coming at all? I wondered how long I could sit here before I started looking too desperate.

Lexa returned with her coffee and a peppermint tea which she placed in front of me. I pushed it away to let it cool. "Are you going tomorrow?" Lexa asked as she sat down. My brow furrowed for a moment as I tried to recall what was on the agenda.

Then I remembered- Thursday was Senior Skip Day. It was a long-standing tradition that one day during the last week of class all the seniors, well- most seniors- skipped classes. In an effort to stem the sudden drop in attendance the school had adopted the "if you can't beat them join them" attitude. Now they hosted a Senior Skip Day party, usually down at the park if the weather held. They had food and music, games and prizes. One year they even had a water balloon fight. From what I've heard, it usually wasn't too bad. And if it was, you could usually leave with little difficulty.

"I don't know. It's funny, before now we couldn't wait to be seniors but I'm not as excited as I thought I'd be. Are you going?" I asked.

"I'd hate for them to throw a party for me and I not put in an appearance. Maybe after you can help me shop for something to wear Saturday," Lexa added. I shot her a look. It wasn't like she hadn't already decided weeks ago on what she was going to wear to graduation. She even had a backup option. She probably had a backup to her backup. But if Lexa were given five minutes to herself, she would spend it shopping. I wasn't much of a shopper and I definitely couldn't compete in Lexa's league so our outings typically turned into quite the adventure.

My withering stare didn't seem to faze Lexa so I was about to tell her exactly how I felt about going shopping when Hana appeared.

"Hi," she said, coming to stand opposite us.

"Hey, Hana, what's up?" Lexa asked.

"Nothing much. How about you?" Hana looked expectantly at me when she asked this. I suddenly felt self-conscious about my wounds. I flashed back to my dream and felt my stomach knot up at the absolute terror I had felt. Terror that had somehow translated into physical damage.

Hana inspected me but I offered no accounting of my injuries. She turned back to Lexa who was dutifully answering her question about what was up with her take on Senior Skip Day. I looked toward the door, hoping Noah would walk in. Instead, Sawyer appeared.

"Hey, everybody," he said as he took the seat beside me, raising an eyebrow at my bandage. I shrugged and mumbled something about a little cut. He turned and put his backpack in the empty seat beside him, seemingly satisfied with my taciturn answer. Everyone said their hellos to Sawyer and Lexa asked his opinion about Senior Skip Day. I couldn't see the big deal. My mind was so full of other things it was hard to remember that I still had a few motions to go through before high school was completely behind me. I was amazed at how long ago school already seemed. I was definitely ready to move on to the next chapter of my life. I was wondering if Noah would be a part of that life before I could stop myself. This made my eyes start their sweep of the room again, just in case he had come in while I wasn't looking. He hadn't.

Hana had finally sat down and she and Lexa's conversation had moved on to Friday and graduation rehearsal. I tried to pay attention as I sipped my tea. It was still too warm and I burnt the end of my tongue. Sawyer had retrieved his laptop and was pecking away at the keyboard. I leaned over to see what he was doing, hoping it would distract me. He was playing some kind of online game. Useless. I turned back to the girls. Hana glanced at me every now and then while she twirled a strand of her strawberry blonde hair around her finger as if she were trying to puzzle something out. I wasn't as close to Hana as I was to Lexa but Hana seemed to be just a little too perceptive about people. I didn't hang out with her nearly as much as Lexa but sometimes Hana picked up on things that were bothering me before Lexa did. In the back of my mind I thought that could be a reason as to why we weren't better friends. It was hard to be friends with someone who seemed to be able to read your mind.

I tried my tea again. It was cool enough to drink without burning me but now it was in danger of turning too cold to drink at all. I took a large swallow in an attempt to drink it before it became undrinkable. I was feeling moody and thought it better I focus on my tea instead of taking it out on one of my tablemates.

It seemed the bell on the door of the C&T couldn't stop ringing. Every time it did I would look up but it was never the right person. A few of the people coming in the door noticed me eyeing them. Some would offer a wave, others would look at me like I was crazy. I focused on my now empty mug and tried not look up every time the door chimed. I didn't want Noah to come in and see me staring at the door like a lost lamb. I bit my lip and tried again to pay attention to Hana and Lexa's conversation.

Before I had figured out what they were talking about Lexa turned her face to the door and smiled a greeting to someone. "Hey," she said. I whipped my heard around to see Ethan. I couldn't keep the disappointment from showing on my face. Luckily, everyone noticed the bandage before they got to my face today.

"What did you do?" Ethan demanded as he took the seat beside Hana. He didn't seem to notice his choice of neighbor but I saw Hana glance at him from under her lashes and bite her lip.

"I got cut." I offered Ethan the same line I had given Sawyer but Ethan wasn't buying it.

"With what? A machete? That bandage is the size of Sawyer's laptop," Ethan cracked. Sawyer looked over at the bandage and back to his computer. I don't think he saw the resemblance. Hana giggled quietly. I felt my face turn red.

"No, I broke a figurine and it sliced my arm. No big deal." I tried again to dismiss it. Ethan's eyes had moved from my arm and were now studying my face.

"It looks like you went face first into the gravel. Were you playing ball out in the back lot? I've told you not to try to slide into home when you play out there." Ethan sat back in his chair and Lexa snorted at him. She and I had both played softball for as long as I could remember but if anyone was making the dramatic slide into home it was her. I hadn't slid into a base since freshman year when I tore a ligament sliding to third.

"You caught me," I sighed and threw up my hands. I immediately winced at the movement.

"Well, I guess maybe that's as good of an excuse as any," Ethan said.

"Excuse for what?" I asked.

"The slideshow," he stated matter-of-factly. "Mr. Jones emailed you the pics the faculty wanted to include from sports and stuff but Mrs. Donovan didn't see them in the show. They asked if you could get those in there before Friday morning."

My stomach sank. The satisfaction I had achieved this morning by finishing that stupid slideshow was replaced by despair. "When were they going to tell me this?" I squeaked.

"Mrs. Donovan emailed you. I told her I'd let you know when I saw you," he said dismissively, as if it wasn't a big deal. I sat back, thinking about all the time I had put into that slideshow. I had thought this morning I was finally free of it but here it was, my own personal bad penny. When was I going to find time to finish it? It was Wednesday night. I could stay up and work on it tonight, maybe. Otherwise I would have to work on it tomorrow, which meant skipping some or all of the Senior Skip Day party. I hadn't realized I even wanted to go until I was faced with it being replaced by more work. It was my last week of school before graduation- why did I have to spend it working? And why did no one think it was a big deal?

"Hey, don't worry about it. I'll give you a hand. We'll finish it in no time," Sawyer said to me as he glanced up from his game. Surprise then relief flooded through me. With Sawyer's help revising the slideshow seemed manageable. I shot him an appreciative smile but it still seemed unfair that we had to do it at all.

"This sucks!" I said a little more forcefully than I meant to. I folded my arms in front of me to pout, only to uncross them quickly when a thousand tiny pains shot up them.

"What sucks?"

My head whipped to the left as a new voice spoke up.

Noah stood on the other side of Sawyer, looking down at me. Caught completely off guard, I tried to recover while everyone watched. Lexa the eternal romantic was grinning at me. Out of the corner of my eye I saw that Hana had disappeared and Lexa was sliding over into her seat to open up a place beside me.

"Um, nothing. Just school stuff." I tripped over my tongue as I tried to talk. Hopefully I was getting all the tripping out now. I watched as Noah made his way smoothly around the table to take the seat Lexa had vacated.

"I'm sorry. Anything I can do?" he offered. I couldn't believe he could honestly be willing to help me with anything. I suddenly had a vision of the two of us sitting at a library table together, books open in front of us, while he tutored a twelve year old me. I shook my head, both at my vision and as an answer to his offer.

"No, thanks. I think I have it covered," I said, hoping to move on. Noah was smiling at me but his smile didn't quite reach his eyes. I noticed he was taking in all the tiny scrapes and cuts on the left half of my body. While he was occupied looking at my arm I took the opportunity to study him. His dark hair was hanging down in his eyes and he was wearing a green ribbed t-shirt that fit him snugly in all the right places. My heart fluttered just looking at him. I gave myself a moment to embrace my girlish side. Then I felt my face grow hot at my internal monologue.

"Do you need a refill?" he asked me as he turned his gaze from my gauze to my empty mug. I shook my head as he stood. I panicked momentarily, thinking he was leaving already. "I'm going to get something, I'll be right back." With another tight smile, he moved toward the bar.

"Don't forget to breathe," Ethan jabbed from across the table as soon as Noah was out of earshot. I felt the color in my face deepen. Lexa laughed.

"Shut up," was all I could think to say. I tried to think of a better retort to follow up with but was saved when attention shifted to Allison, who had just walked in, waving in our general direction.

"Hey, Allie," Lexa said.

"Hey, what's up?" I added mechanically. I didn't spend all that much time with Allison. I would say we're friends but she likes her space a little too much to have friends. That made it hard to get to know her. She was a much better listener than she was a talker, almost to the point of a fault.

"Hey, not a lot. Just trying to get through this week. I had to take the calculus final today, so I'm glad that's over." She came around the table to sit in the seat Lexa had previously vacated for Noah. I started to say something, but I was too late. Then I wasn't sure how to ask her to move. I chatted nervously for a few minutes, constantly checking to see if Noah was headed back toward the table. I was afraid if he saw his seat had been taken he might give up and go somewhere else. Finally I saw him turn this direction. I let out a deep sigh. I hadn't realized how slowly the time seemed to pass when he was gone until he came back and it resumed its normal pace. He glanced around at the lack of available seating.

"Let's go sit somewhere a little more private," he suggested quietly. My heart leaped as I followed him to the seating area at the front of the C&T. We settled down into the well-worn cushions of a small couch. I had never noticed that you couldn't really see anyone from here. I felt like we were the only two people in the world. The thought made me light-headed.

"So what did you do? I don't remember all the bandages last time I saw you," he said, blowing on his drink.

"Yeah, I had an accident. I broke a figurine."

I had given him the same story as everyone else but I could see it wasn't working.

"How did you cut your arm there? And what happened to your face? It looks like someone threw gravel or something at you," he said, taking a sip of his drink. My breath hitched. I suddenly remembered the feel of the rock in my hand that I had launched at my stalker before everything in my room exploded. His choice of words seemed an eerie coincidence. A shiver rolled down my spine and I stiffened. I relaxed immediately however, remembering that Ethan had said it looked like I had ran my face into the gravel as well.

"I don't know how it happened, it was all kind of fast," I said evasively. I mentally rolled my eyes at how dumb it sounded. I saw him raise an eyebrow and tried to elaborate before he could ask more pointed questions. "I had just woke up, I was still half asleep. I bumped into the shelf or something."

"It sounds like sleeping is becoming dangerous for you," he half joked. I couldn't keep flashes of Josh or Mr. Wiley out of my head when he said this.

"It does look that way. I'm not going to be able to sleep at all before long." I'd said the words before I'd thought them through and now I could see he was trying to figure out what I meant rather than take it as a random comment.

"Why not?" he inquired.

"I, well, I've been having some crazy dreams lately. I've been waking up more tired than when I went to sleep. It's been a stressful week though."

"That could be it," he mused. He looked away as he took another sip of his drink. "But it could be something more. Maybe your dreams are trying to tell you something."

I remembered Noah's fascination with dreams and hoped that was the only thing behind his comments. Momentary insanity overtook me as I mused that he may be the one person I could talk to who could shed some light on what was going on with my dreams. Obviously I couldn't tell him the complete truth but there was no way he would ever guess the truth on his own- I was still struggling to figure out the truth myself. I tried to dismiss the thought as soon as it occurred but the brilliant lightning strike that set me on this path didn't seem to have designs on recalling its suggestion.

"Well, if they are trying to tell me something I can't figure out what," I said, trying to sound nonchalant even though my breath had rapidly increased.

"What are they about?" he asked eagerly as he warmed to the subject. He angled his body toward me so he could watch my face as I answered his questions. I couldn't help but smile nervously in response to the way he looked at me as he prepared to hang on my every word.

"I see lots of people, mostly from school. Some of them I don't even talk to much. Sometimes I'm being chased," I shivered again, recalling the feeling of pursuit much more strongly than I thought I would in my waking hours.

"Who's chasing you?" he prompted.

"I'm not sure. I don't think it's someone I know but I never see them clearly. But the panic stays with me." I wasn't going to tell him about the blonde guy but the part about the panic was true. I was fighting it off now.

"What about the dreams with your friends? What happens in them?"

I pretended that I had to think back to remember the dreams but I was actually trying to buy time to get myself under control. I thought about my answer carefully, trying to phrase it in a way that didn't make me sound completely insane but make it close enough to the truth that I could keep up with the half-lies I was telling. "Well, just normal stuff. Like talking, hanging out."

"Do they say anything significant?" he pressed. I recalled the advice Sawyer gave me in a dream then again the next morning.

"Um, not that I remember," I said aloud, "but sometimes the situations in my dream are so normal everyday type stuff that I have feelings of déjà vu the next day. I guess everyone has those, though."

He paused before answering me. "That happens to just about everyone now and then. Is it just being in the same place or something someone says or does? Maybe something you don't remember them doing before but now it's like they pulled it out of your dream."

This was getting too close to the things I haven't been able to puzzle out for myself. I knew he had to be asking questions straight from his textbook but I was convinced no one in any of his books had experienced anything like I had.

"The places are all familiar. Sometimes someone says something that I remember hearing in my dream but it's never anything unusual. Maybe my subconscious is having a hard time sorting through my day. They have been pretty hectic lately and I have been stressed." I knew I was talking way too fast. I was hoping that offering my own hypothesis would redirect him from what I felt was a dangerous path but the unsteadiness of my voice screamed that it was a diversion tactic.

"Maybe. But it sounds like you dream about things that are going to happen instead of things that have already happened." His face looked intense as he considered this. My heart was beating faster and my face was burning as a result. If we kept talking about this I would blurt out everything just to get it off my chest. He looked up then and saw my face. His expression relaxed.

"Hey, maybe you're clairvoyant. There's a theory that time isn't linear, that everything actually exists at the same moment. Some people claim that when they're dreaming they can access other parts of time therefore seeming to predict the future."

I wasn't sure if he was joking or not. I decided to take it as a joke. I wasn't going to tell him I had seriously considered this possibility myself. I laughed, weakly.

"That has to be it," I said in what I hoped resembled mock seriousness.

"Before you fall asleep you should think about the fact that you are going to dream and that the dreams are yours. A lot of people who have problems sleeping due to runaway dreams have found that if they consciously remind themselves that the dreams are theirs, they can control them." Noah met my eyes, holding them for a beat longer than usual. For the first time I didn't feel like I was a freak because of my dreams. He made it all seem so normal.

"Thank you, I'll have to try that," I murmured. I told myself to relax, that it was over. I felt the tension in my muscles start to ease. I sat back into the couch and he mirrored my movement. He was still turned to face me, his knee only a small fraction of an inch away from mine. I could feel a build up of electricity between us that seemed like it would explode if we actually touched. Suddenly, I wanted to touch him. My heart beat a little faster at the thought of it. But then the pounding in my chest led to a pounding in my head. My headache was coming back with a vengeance, along with the soreness and stiffness in my arm and neck. I sat up straighter and tried to look over the bar toward our table to see if I could find Lexa.

"What is it?" he asked me.

I turned back to him. "I'm a little worn out after today. I need to go find Lexa, she's my ride." I said this last part reluctantly. I didn't want to leave him.

Noah looked like he had something he was trying to decide if he wanted to say. I hoped he was searching for a way to keep me here. "Aren," he started haltingly. I shivered at the sound of my name. "Sometimes people have dreams that are so powerful they affect their waking lives." He paused again, looking for the words to continue. "Occasionally they can even manipulate physical things around them."

My chest began to hurt and I realized I had stopped breathing. I took a slow, measured breath. His words were on rapid replay in my head but I still couldn't believe he was saying what I thought he was saying. As I heard his words again and again my mind skipped from one strange incident to the next. I began to panic, thinking he was too close to revealing something as truth that I was in no way ready to accept. If he said it out loud, that would make it too real. I would officially be some sort of freak. I would become what I had feared from our first conversation like this, a case study. He would study me then pass me along to others to study. I wouldn't be a person any more- I would be a science experiment.

"Aren," he said my name pleadingly this time, as if he were asking me not to think of him as the freak, "I know how this sounds. But I know this can be dangerous if it can't be controlled by the few who can do these things.

It's very hard when your mind can't tell the difference between waking and dreaming. I remember what it was like for me." He said this last part in a voice so low I had to lean close to hear him. It took a moment before the words had meaning. And then I just stared. I was afraid to speak in case what he said had a different meaning than what I heard. I pulled away from him, noticing the intensity of our conversation had drawn our heads within inches of one another. I glanced around the room. No one seemed to be paying a bit of attention to us. But my world felt like it had flipped on its axis and was now spinning backwards.

The tension that had been leaving my body only a few short moments ago had returned tenfold. I could feel everything knotting up as my body prepared to run. My eyes widened to take on what I imagined was a doe-like quality and my jaw dropped, though I managed to keep my lips pressed together. My clamped lips kept me from issuing any unintelligible noises but the stiffness was causing them to tremble. Like I had done the first time I met him, I glanced around for hidden cameras that were waiting for me to spill my insanely laughable story so the world would have undeniable proof that I was certifiable. I blinked furiously to keep myself from tearing up.

"Aren?" he said my name again. I tried to tune out my paranoia to focus on our conversation. I waited to see if he had anything else to add but he remained silent. I didn't trust myself to speak. I searched for something I could say that wouldn't be completely condemning.

"What was it like?" I asked him. A million questions had whirled around in my head but this is the one that came out. I couldn't make myself say anything that would confirm what was happening to me but maybe he would tell me what it was like for him. Then I would compare notes in the privacy of my mind so he nor anyone else could make fun of me.

"It was- difficult. I wasn't sure what was real and what wasn't. And I was alone," he gave me a pleading look. I knew he was trying to tell me I didn't have to be alone. But as much as part of me wanted that, another part rebelled against the idea of relying too heavily on someone I still didn't know as well as I would've liked. On cue, the paranoia reared its ugly head. His eyes moved down to my bandages and he ran his finger lightly across the medical tape. "How did this happen?"

"I got cut," I said automatically.

"How?" he was quieter, but somehow more insistent as his gaze wandered back to my eyes. His hand now rested lightly on my wrist.

"I had a collection of glass figurines- no-" my voice faltered a little. I could see the story I was trying to tell superimposed over the events that actually took place.

"Aren," he said softly, imploringly. Every time he said my name it shot a tingle down my back, each one stronger than the last. The tiny convulsions chipped away at my resolve not to implicate myself in any kind of abnormal behavior. As the last thin, fragile fragment fell away I felt as if a floodgate had opened inside me.

"I had a dream." My voice was low and quiet, its intensity startling even me. I licked my lip as if in preparation to say more but then I bit down on it. My eyes moved to stare at the floor. He didn't say anything this time as he gently gave my good wrist a comforting squeeze. "A dream," I said with more conviction than I felt. I wasn't sure which of us I was trying to persuade as to what happened. Suddenly, the fictitious story I was trying to tell disappeared and the only narrative I saw was the truth, strange but undeniable. I heard the glass exploding and felt the shower of stinging shards. A calm spread over me. I accepted this and that meant at least part of what he was saying and I was feeling had to be true.

"The glass shattered," I told him as I met his gaze. The green in his eyes flashed and I knew he heard exactly what I meant for him to hear. Somehow my cryptic words had not caused any miscommunication between us. I searched for anything in his eyes that said he was getting ready to drag me off to some lab but I saw nothing.

I had chosen to accept what Noah had told me about himself, at least for now. It was almost as if I could feel my perception of the world shift. I wasn't sure how big this new part of my world was but I knew it was sparsely populated by Noah and me. My reality was tied to him indefinitely. We didn't know each other well but we had been drawn to each other because we had something no one else did and that no one else would probably come close to understanding. Noah had given me the ability to trust in my sanity, my judgment. I wanted to leap across the small space to hug him but I didn't want to push my luck. I needed him now and I couldn't help but recognize how strong my dependence on him had become in so short a time.

CHAPTER TWELVE

We sat in surprisingly comfortable silence, studying each other. It was during the silence that my headache began to crash around again, reminding me it was still there despite my temporary distraction. It pushed aside any thoughts or questions I might have concerning the conversation I was still trying to process. I put my fingers to my temples. Noah leaned forward, concern displayed on his face. Knowing this look was for me made me melt a little.

"It's my headache. I need to go," I said. He only nodded.

"It was good to see you again," I murmured, suddenly feeling awkward.

"I'm glad I came," his grinned his lopsided grin. "I'm sure we'll run into each other again soon." The way he said it, however, sounded as if he didn't expect to leave our next meeting to chance. Of course, how could he given what he'd just told me?

I stood there for a moment longer then decided if I didn't go now I never would. Part of it was not wanting to leave Noah. I felt so giddy when I was around him, like being with him was a dream within itself. A very good dream at that. Part of it was if I didn't get going, this headache would render me immobile for a while.

Once I could see around the cases of pastries that had

been blocking my view of our usual table I noticed it was occupied by a group of people I didn't know. I frowned and started looking around. It would be like Lexa to strategically strand me here so Noah would have to take me home.

I checked my phone, no messages. I moved toward the back of the C&T, finally spotting Lexa in a corner seated at a table for two, my bag hanging from her chair. She was facing me, talking animatedly with some guy. I waved but she didn't see me so I began weaving my way carefully through tables to get to her, trying not to jostle my head as it continued its throbbing.

It wasn't until I only had one table between them and me that I noticed the boy's red-streaked blonde hair. The face of the guy from my dreams flashed briefly before my eyes. It was then Lexa caught sight of me and waved. Her companion turned to see who had caught her attention.

A physical shock went through me. I'd been telling myself the guy I saw at the park wasn't really the guy from my dreams. I hadn't been standing close enough to him to make out any facial features so I was sure my imagination had supplied the finer details, making him look like the guy in my dream. But there was only about ten feet at most between Lexa's table and me. I was too close to be seeing anything but what was actually there. I recovered from my shock with an awkward hop and skip that landed me behind Lexa's chair. Pain exploded in my head and I winced. Lexa was so caught up in her new friend she didn't seem to notice my strange behavior.

"Aren, this is Holden," she gestured to him, "he goes to the college." I smiled woodenly as every part of my body screamed to run away. My emotions were so wrung out that I wanted to lie down in the floor and sob. I couldn't do this, I couldn't navigate another minefield situation like the one I had barely survived with Noah.

"Hi, Aren," he said as his face split into a toothy grin. Suddenly he was on his feet in front of me, entirely too close. I took half a step back from him and nodded in greeting, not trusting myself to say anything. My eyes were still open wide and I forced myself to blink.

"Lexa," I said quietly, turning back to her and attempting to ignore his nearness, "I'm sorry but my head is really starting to pound and I need to go home. Could we go? Now?" I demanded. Lexa turned in her seat to look at me incredulously. "I'm sorry," I said again, though it was clear I didn't mean it.

"Um, Holden," she twisted to look up at him, clearly confused as to why he was still standing when she was sitting, "I'm sorry but we have to get going. Aren had a little mishap earlier today and it's catching up with her." She made it sound like I was a three year old who wet her pants.

"Really? Well, I understand. What happened?" He had glanced at Lexa when she was speaking but now his eyes were back on me, searching my face for the answer. His gaze moved slowly from the abrasions on my cheek to the bandage on my arm. I had to agree the thing stood out like a beacon but it had distracted most people from noticing the tiny cuts on my face- until now.

"I had an accident. No big deal," I quickly dismissed his inquiry. Lexa was in no hurry to get up so I stepped away to give her room while shouldering my bag, hoping she would take the hint. I could see she wasn't having any luck thinking of a reason good enough to make me stay as she studied me with growing concern. She glanced up at Holden, who was still on his feet, and reluctantly stood to join us. Lexa placed herself between Holden and me and turned on her most winning smile.

"It was nice meeting you," she said in her sweetest tone. "I guess I'll see you around?"

He smiled down at her but his eyes kept flicking over her shoulder to glance at me. They were standing so close she had to look up into his face. He was a little more than a head taller than Lexa and I was a few inches shorter than her. I felt like a little kid with an irrational fear of strangers. They continued to look at each other while I tried to find anywhere to look but at them.

"I'm sure you will," he told her. "I'll walk out with you."

Lexa started to walk with him, but I put my hand on

her arm. She gave me an odd look but paused while I stepped closer to link my arm with hers. The aisles weren't quite wide enough to walk two abreast so I was still partially behind her.

"Lexa, I know this guy-" it was kind of true- "he's bad news. Please don't talk to him." I whispered as loudly as I dared. Holden was walking in front of us, cutting a path through the crowded C&T. Lexa's eyebrow shot up. I didn't give her a chance to talk. "Please, Lexa." She heard the anxiety in my plea and bit back her retort. I didn't think she believed me but she wasn't going to push the issue until we were alone.

"I'll be around this summer," he said in what appeared to be an attempt at stalling since we were only halfway to the door. "Could I maybe get your number? I'd like to hang out again. Maybe we all could." He said this rapidly, shooting me a look as he did so. My trepidation evaporated as I was suddenly caught by his eyes. They were hazel with subtle yet constantly shifting shades of blue and green. Completely mesmerized, I couldn't look away. They had such depth to them, as if his eyes were trying to tell his entire story. I couldn't see any malice, which made me waver. The idea that was so firmly stuck in my mind saying he wasn't someone I wanted to associate with began to fray at the edges.

"Um, yeah, okay," Lexa said as she looked for something to write her number on. She was visibly less excited when he suggested including me in their future plans. Lexa reached for a napkin and a pen that was lying on the counter and began to scribble. She lay the pen down and handed over the napkin with a flourish. She smiled but it was a tight smile that didn't quite reach her eyes. Holden took the napkin and folded it carefully, still watching me as he did so. He tucked it into his pocket and turned again toward the door with a chivalrous wave of his hand, determined to see us out as promised.

When we got to the door, Holden opened it and motioned us through. Lexa exited first but stopped right outside the door. I had to turn sideways to slip past her, preparing to tow her away if necessary.

"We have to go, really," I said. I started to inch away, not wanting to turn my back to him. Unfortunately, it was Lexa who wasn't making a move to leave. "Lexa, come on. Please." My voice sounded plaintive and whiny and for the umpteenth time tonight I felt like a spoiled brat. The unsettled feeling was returning and I wanted to get away from Holden as soon as possible. My headache was starting to get worse, which didn't help. I was contemplating lying down on the sidewalk and crying when Noah came out of the C&T.

Noah's eyes went to me then slid across Lexa to rest on Holden. "Can I help you with something?" he asked Holden. His voice sounded completely cordial but his face told a different story.

"No, we're fine- I was just walking the girls out," Holden answered, seemingly unruffled by a stranger's interjection into his conversation. Noah raised an eyebrow in my direction, asking if Holden's response was true. I didn't exactly understand what was going on so I made no confirmation either way. I was still trying to decide if I was flattered by the white knight act or offended by the outdated chivalry.

"I'll see you ladies later," Holden said to us. He turned slightly toward Noah and Noah reacted in kind by putting his back toward us in a dismissive gesture. Wearing similar expressions of distaste at this ridiculous show, Lexa and I slowly turned to go, both of us straining to hear their conversation. The snatches we heard made us even more confused, however.

"You aren't supposed to be here," I heard Noah say to Holden.

"I could say the same for you. It's meddling." Holden's words came out clipped.

"Get out of here, I mean it," Noah responded. It sounded like he meant the conversation to end there but Holden continued.

"You can't make me go. You know what this means to me," Holden was speaking angrily in a voice a little louder than he probably meant to. Lexa and I were waiting to cross the street, pretending we couldn't catch a break in the almost non-existent traffic. Noah and Holden seemed to notice this at the same time and turned to us. Knowing we had been made, Lexa and I hurried across the street to her car. My head pounded in time with my feet as we jogged across the pavement. When I turned around from the safety of the opposite sidewalk, Noah was walking away from Holden.

By unspoken agreement we did not mention the strange interaction we had witnessed on our way home. I concentrated on keeping my head on my shoulders. Lexa seemed lost in thought. I tried to think of a way to bring up Holden and my bad feelings about him. I couldn't think of anything to say that didn't sound like I'd gone around the bend. The longer I said nothing, the harder it became to find a way to start the conversation.

"I really could use your help to find something to wear Saturday. Maybe after Skip Day?" Lexa asked me when we pulled into the driveway.

With a groan I said, "I've got to finish that slideshow before I do anything. Hopefully with Sawyer's help I can get it done early. I'll give you a call."

"Ok. Tomorrow then," Lexa confirmed. She gave me a gentle hug and I got out the car. I flinched at the sound of gravel crunching as she turned around in the driveway.

I was holding my head as I walked to the house. I could hear Mom and Dad's voices from outside the house but they stopped talking when they heard the door open. They stared as I came in the door. Mom gave me an overly sympathetic look from the dining room table. Dad rushed off to get me something for the headache that was evident from my use of both hands to steady my head. After an awkward silence I told them I was going to lie down, even though it was still full daylight outside. I dismissed their bizarre behavior as I changed into shorts and a t-shirt then plugged my phone in to charge. I lay down, not really tired but unfit to do anything else.

Luckily, I was unable to face the now-empty shelves that had most recently held my figurine collection. It seemed the stories those figurines told were slipping from my memory already to be replaced with tales from lives I wasn't sure were mine. A creeping sadness overtook me every time I thought of them, a sadness tinged with guilt that the blank spaces on the wall refused to let me forget.

I stared at the ceiling while replaying the events at the café in my mind. The highlight was the conversation I had had with Noah. However I couldn't dismiss my discovery that the blonde guy- Holden- existed outside of my dreams. Noah's reaction and subsequent conversation with Holden were also noteworthy.

I now understood why my conversations with Noah always seemed to come around to dreams. It seemed like they were taking control of most of my waking hours. I thought about his views on the subject. He seemed open to believing that dreams- our dreams- could do anything. He also didn't seem keen on petitioning to have me locked up for saying it. I certainly wanted to spend more time with Noah, but as his potential girlfriend and not a case study.

My breath caught a little as I allowed myself to consciously think about being Noah's girlfriend. That must be where this was headed, right? I thrilled a little at the thought. I hadn't ever considered dating anyone before but now the thought of dating appealed to me intensely. I felt a connection to Noah that had been hard to explain until now. But each time we were together I found it harder to part from him. Considering his knowledge about dreams and the sudden turn mine had taken, he seemed like a godsend. I felt like I could be completely honest about what was going on without fear of rejection, like Noah was my safe harbor. When I thought about it again it seemed that being his girlfriend was an inadequate term to describe the depth of the connection I felt to him. Dating seemed like such a superficial expression. It was more like we were made for each other, like soul mates.

I took a deep breath to try to alleviate the tightness building in my chest. In a moment of clarity I realized I must still be in shock from the accident. I was seriously thinking about things like soul mates and dreams that could change real life, could hurt people. I took another ragged breath and pushed the confusion away.

I tried to stifle a sudden yawn and the tension in my face caused my head to pound again. I climbed between the sheets as the headache sapped the rest of my strength. The medicine hadn't kicked in yet and I was exhausted. I closed my eyes, trying to take Noah's advice and prepare myself for the dreams I knew would come.

CHAPTER THIRTEEN

Everywhere I looked I saw indistinct shapes in greens and browns. Shadows seemed to move lazily, making the shapes undulate. The harder I looked at the shapes, the less defined they became. Their constant shifting made me feel like I was moving even though my feet were still. I could see my dream self shut my eyes, telling my surroundings to stop moving. Slowly, the forward motion stopped. Even in my dream I could feel the triumph of my newfound self-control.

While I was standing still, the scene changed around me. Some of the browns gave way to blues and I could see vaguely familiar but faceless people milling about. Suddenly, Lexa was standing in front of me. Her rich, deep mocha colored tresses shone in the light that played off the soft bronze highlights in her hair. Her skin was flawless and her warm brown eyes seemed to sparkle from within. Lexa had always been the pretty one but she had never made me feel ugly in comparison. Actually, I was proud of my best friend's acceptance of her looks and her restraint in flaunting it. I smiled as sisterly love overtook me.

"Why can't you see it? You haven't been yourself in a while and I don't know what to do. You aren't right anymore, you're not anything. You have to stop this. You took this on, you could have said no but you didn't – you didn't think of anyone but yourself." Lexa's verbal assault continued but her face showed only calm, as if she were speaking about the weather. I was so stunned I felt as if I'd grown roots. My chest began to cave in as each word hit me. I wanted to speak up and defend myself but I couldn't find a single point I could argue. She was right.

She continued, "I can't do this- if this is what we have to look forward to then maybe it's best that we aren't going to see much of each other soon. You decided to go away, so everyone would take notice and congratulate you on going to a great school. You're already changing- if this is who you are then I don't want any part of it. Don't you understand? This is not the person I thought I knew, I don't know you at all..."

My vision was starting to swim and I couldn't see Lexa clearly anymore. I couldn't hear her either. I was ashamed at the relief I felt that she was gone. I felt a change in the crowd around me. I felt attention turn to me that had previously not been there. The mood was slowly changing from indifference to dislike. I looked around, trying to find a break in the crowd where I could exit. I wasn't sure where the edge of the gathering was but I couldn't stand here, surrounded by all these people. I began moving through the crowd but it seemed like they swarmed wherever I was, pushing against me so I couldn't escape. The harder I tried to force my way through the more difficult it became. Even up close I couldn't make out any distinguishing features on the faces in the crowd, which added to my unease.

Suddenly the people parted and I fell forward, barely catching myself as I struggled to adapt to the lack of resistance. I could see the edge of the assembly now. Sawyer stood at the periphery of the crowd. I was so relieved at the sight of a familiar face I all but threw myself at him. Sawyer threw his arms up as if to catch me but I caught myself before I bowled him over. He kept his hands up once I came to a stop as if his intent had not been to catch me but to ward me off. His words confirmed my fears.

"I can't help you. You're on your own, don't you see

that? Which is fine with me because I'm sick of having to carry you on my shoulders everywhere I go. Poor you, so much to do- such a martyr. And I'm the one doing all the work- but no one will know, right? You'll be lapping the attention up until the end," Sawyer stopped talking and glared at me. His face contorted with anger and disgust.

I felt a lump in my throat. I couldn't answer, I couldn't breathe. And most of all, I couldn't believe Sawyer felt this way about me. I didn't recognize me in the person he was talking about- surely I wasn't so wrong about myself?

My vision blurred again but I couldn't tell if it was from lack of oxygen or tears. I looked up but the blue above me was blinding. I finally found the ability to move and turned away from him. Lexa came into my field of vision. She had the same menacing expression on her face as Sawyer. The crowd had gathered behind her and Sawyer. I couldn't see my way out no matter where I turned. Each person held a small figurine in their hands. I put one foot in front of the other hoping I could find a break in the crowd. The ground made a crunching sound and began to shift with each step. I was walking on gravel, thick gravel that threatened to put me on my face if I walked too fast. As if on cue, the tiny punctures on my body began to ache.

The scene around me changed once more, the greens giving way to grays. The gray seemed to reach up toward the blinding blue and I realized I was in town. Buildings rose up on either side of me as gravel transformed into sidewalk under my feet. Claustrophobia began to take hold as I was cast into the shadow of the buildings.

I saw Noah on the far side of the street, oblivious to my presence. I wanted to run to him but I was afraid he would reject me like my friends. They had found it necessary to point out the worst in me in such a way that I couldn't believe they were my friends any longer. That left no one in my life except Noah.

The prospect of his rejection became a physical burden. I was frozen in place with fear of it. I felt so strongly for him, as if I had known him all my life. It were

as if a part of me had been missing all this time and I
didn't know what it was like to be whole until he came
along. I needed him. I wouldn't be able to breathe again
until I was near him. At that moment he turned and
noticed me. He said nothing as he held out his hand to
me. Then he seemed to shrink as the street between us
grew wider from two lanes to the length of a football
field, probably more. I could barely make him out on the
sidewalk, still holding his hand out to me. The pain in my
chest became more severe with our physical separation.
The blue of the sky darkened to an ugly purple. The
weight of it seemed to sit on my shoulders. I took a few
steps toward him but came no closer to crossing the
street than when I first stepped off the sidewalk.

Everything I saw became red as the lighting changed
again. I couldn't distinguish any landmarks and I began
to shake violently at my blindness. The shifting vapors in
front of me solidified into a person. A head with red
streaked blonde hair towered above me. The sight of
Holden blocked out everything else. He was so close to
me I could have shut my eyes and the heat of his body
would have told me he was there. His hazel eyes glowed
hot. He didn't appear as if he were going to attack me as
the others did and I relaxed involuntarily. I knew I didn't
trust him but I was hurt and feeling reckless. I would take
any friend I could find now.

"Don't you want the truth?" he asked me in a quiet,
pleading tone. He spoke as if he were trying to soothe a
caged animal. I wasn't sure what truth he was talking
about but I was sure I didn't want to know his truth. My
mind bucked at the idea of any truth possibly coming
from him. He didn't seem to notice the conflict playing
across my face or if he did he didn't acknowledge it.

"Please." It was a statement not a question, as if asking
were only a formality and he was going to tell me anyway.

"Can't you see what this is? I know you feel it. You're
trying to put it together on your own, let me help you. I
know you don't trust me, I know what he's told you-
shown you- even before you saw him. But please, come
back to me." I wasn't sure if the last part was spoken out

loud or just with his eyes. They seemed to express such a longing that everything around me took on their hazel hue.

"But- she-" was all I could say before he looked away from me, shame on his face. I didn't realize until I saw his expression that I meant Lexa and what happened earlier in the café.

"I couldn't find any other way to get close to you. I'm sorry," his voice was thick with an emotion I couldn't quite place. His apology sounded formal, sincere, and my heart leaped in response. I couldn't feel my body anymore and I wasn't sure if I was standing or if I had fallen to the ground. The sense of my physical self had been replaced with the feeling that I was nothing but densely packed emotions. There was a war inside me between my wariness and distrust of him and the connection I was discovering. Or rediscovering. I shook my head, unsure how that was even possible.

"You know it's true. You know I've come for you. He just beat me to you and he's using you," he spoke quickly, urgently, with more passion than I expected. The intensity was like a physical blow. I reeled backwards, my distrust giving way to anger.

"Stop! Just stop!" I screeched. I rushed forward, shoving him. I could tell I had taken him by surprise because he offered no resistance. He flew backward off the sidewalk and into the street. I heard the high-pitched squeal of tires and had to cover my ears against the noise. I hadn't noticed before that heavy traffic had been zooming by us the whole time. Holden was a blonde blur as he was mown down by a car and disappeared from my sight. The crushing weight of the sky lifted suddenly. I felt like the only living being on earth. I couldn't even sense life behind the wheel of the car that had struck him. I couldn't feel his presence. The purple sky opened up then, dousing me in large raindrops so multitudinous that my vision was completely obscured. The drops fell heavy on me like I was being showered with golf balls.

When I woke I was curled up on my uninjured side,

my knees pulled to my chest, my head between them as if I were being pelted with glass shards again. Then I realized I was actually curled up to try to protect myself from the golf ball-like rain in the dream. I ran my hand through my dry hair several times to convince myself I hadn't actually been in a downpour.

The light in my room was hazy so I wasn't sure what time it was other than morning. I discovered my body ached worse than it had yesterday as I slowly unfolded myself. I lay on my back, waiting until my muscles finished their complaining before I tried to do anything. I didn't feel like I had gotten anything good out of my night's sleep. My face felt puffy and my mind seemed to have worked double time. I thought back over the last twenty-four hours, trying to separate my dreams from reality. I was having a harder time of it than I had imagined possible so I gave up.

Instead, I moved on to what I had to do today. If I were going to make the Skip Day party I would need to get the slideshow out of the way. I automatically reached for my phone to see if Sawyer could still help me. Then I hesitated. I was ashamed at the relief I felt a moment before at the thought of being able to ask for help when I remembered the last things he said to me. Was I taking advantage of him? Would he tell me so? But what Sawyer had said to me about using him had been said in a dream. He had offered to help me last night. All I can do is ask him if he still has time this morning to help and if he doesn't, well, I'm on my own. Still, I put the phone back on my nightstand, suddenly unprepared to face anyone this morning.

I went to the bathroom for something for my aches and pains then slipped back into bed. Until now I had avoided any contact with clocks so I decided I'd take a few more moments to enjoy this part of my day before my schedule became too pressing.

My mind had gone back to attempting to sort my dream from reality when my phone buzzed. It was a text from Sawyer asking me about the slideshow. I replied quickly before I had time to overanalyze why he was texting me. I let him know I planned to work on it first thing this morning so if he wanted to help he could come over whenever. I was already pulling clothes out of drawers when my phone buzzed again to let me know he was headed my way. I changed as fast as I could with one usable arm and took my laptop to the dining room table.

The house was quiet so I figured Mom and Dad must be at work already. I walked to the front door and peeked into the drive- nothing but my Camry. I unlocked the deadbolt in preparation for Sawyer's arrival before returning to the dining room.

I hit the button on my laptop to let it boot up while I grabbed a bowl of dry cereal. The slow pace at which my computer was moving gave me too much time to think. With a free moment, my mind started calling up images of Noah. I was afraid our conversation at the C&T had been part of my dream instead of reality. At the same time, I wished the entire thing were a fantasy. Finally, my computer finished its warm up ritual and I forced myself to turn back to the project at hand. I had the file up and had moved on to opening my email when there was a knock at the door.

"It's open!" I yelled, not looking up. I heard the door open and close and some shuffling as Sawyer sauntered into the room with his book bag in tow.

"Hey," he said as he pulled his laptop out of the bag and sat down next to me.

"Hey," I echoed, looking up at him after I finished typing my email password. "I don't know what the damage is yet, I'm just getting into my email." I spoke quickly with a note of apology. Sawyer noticed it and raised an eyebrow.

"That's fine. I just got here. Let me see what you've been doing and I can start duplicating slides."

I showed him what I had so far. I hadn't really changed it much from how he had shown me to do it so by the time my email dinged to let me know it had downloaded all my messages he was done looking at the setup. I scrolled through all the ridiculous emails about end of the year this and that to find the ones Ethan had been talking about. There were several emails so Sawyer and I divided them up after I gave him access to my inbox. As I watched the little progress bar fill up I couldn't help thinking that this was just like when I had made Lexa help me earlier this week. Even with all this help I couldn't seem to finish one task. I felt bad for ruining their week with my projects. I frantically began putting photos onto slides as soon as they downloaded in an attempt to not waste Sawyer's day.

"How many did they send?" he asked as he watched photos continue to download.

"I don't know," I said a little sharply. I quickly stuffed a handful of cereal in my mouth so I couldn't say anything else.

"Just asking," Sawyer mumbled. I heard him clicking away on his computer and wondered if his eager pace had to do with attempting to get away from me as quickly as possible.

I started going back through the slideshow trying to find places to fit in the faculty's pictures. I had so many slides that it was hard for me to remember what they all were. I was afraid I was putting duplicates in but I didn't want to take the time to go through the whole thing to check. Instead, I started inserting slides randomly. My laptop was running a little slow since it was still trying to download pictures and the delay annoyed me.

I was inserting photos in the slideshow faster than they were downloading so it didn't take long before I had to stop to wait for more photos. I leaned back from my laptop, hoping the physical space would discourage me from impatiently tapping away at the computer and slowing things down. I looked over at Sawyer who was still immersed in what he was doing. Or at least he looked that way.

"I really appreciate this," I said. He looked up, met my eyes, and flashed a smile.

"No problem. I know you've got a lot going on right now," he said. His gaze dropped back to his computer, which was a very good thing since my face went white at his words. His tone had said what his words had not.

That he thought I was playing the victim. Of course, for him this project would have been no big thing. He was a genius when it came to all things computers. If it hadn't been for him, I would've had no clue as to where to start for this stupid slideshow. And now he was going to hold that against me. I bit my lip, forcing back the retort that had leapt to my tongue.

"Yeah, thanks," I replied instead, hoping my voice didn't sound as hurt as I felt. Sawyer was one of my best friends and the sting of his tone was intense.

"Like I said, it's nothing. I didn't have any plans today. I'm not really big on all that pre-graduation stuff."

This time it was me who wasn't looking up from my computer. With every word he said I felt like Sawyer was confirming my fears. I felt like such an idiot. I started silently pleading with my laptop to hurry up so this could be over. I shoved the last handful of dry cereal in my mouth.

The silence had become awkward. I couldn't shake my self-consciousness no matter how many times I told myself that my interpretation must be all wrong. I chewed my cereal slowly then swallowed. I kept my eyes on the progress bar on my laptop. I desperately wanted to search Sawyer's face for clues as to what he was really thinking since asking him was completely out of the question.

A gray window suddenly flashed on my screen, bringing my focus back to the computer. Before I could read what it said it disappeared and I was left staring at my wallpaper. Every program that had been open had just quit. I rolled the mouse around, hoping everything would reappear. I began to panic as I realized I hadn't hit save once while adding the new slides. I would have to start downloading everything again. My panic turned to despair as I realized I would now have to go back and redo something I had already done on a project that I had thought was already finished.

Sawyer, sitting a few feet away from me, seemed to notice my alarm. He had looked up from his computer, a quizzical expression on his face. When I didn't respond to the question on his face he asked aloud, "What's wrong?"

"Everything closed on me. Everything. All my downloads, my slides- I hadn't saved anything," I squeaked, half dazed. I was still hoping everything would reappear before my eyes. Sawyer looked back to his computer, clicked a few buttons then got up.

"Here, let me see," he asked as he leaned over me. He angled the laptop toward him but I did him one better by sliding out of my chair so he could sit down. Without looking at me, he sank into my seat, all the while typing away at my computer. I backed out, taking my empty cereal bowl with me to the kitchen. I sat the bowl on the counter then leaned against the island. Sawyer was glaring at my computer.

"Hey," Sawyer called, not looking up, "you can start putting slides together on mine- I've got several of those emails downloaded. That way you don't lose too much time."

I bristled a little at that, but I did see his point. I sat down at his laptop, almost afraid to touch the keys in case it was me that had caused the computer to crap out. My need to have this project over with was stronger than my illogical fear of breaking Sawyer's laptop however, so I started making slides just as I had been doing before. Sawyer's laptop was unfamiliar to me but it was also faster than mine so I felt like I was gaining ground. I queued up several more attachments for download as I saved the work I had done so far.

Reflexively, I glanced at the clock. It was close to eleven. An entire morning wasted. My left arm was starting to hurt from all the movement. I dropped my hands in my lap so my arms could rest while more photos downloaded. Waiting on downloads would be the death of me.

"Done?" Sawyer looked up from my computer.

"No," I said, sounding more venomous than strictly necessary. I elaborated, hoping to soften my response, "I'm waiting for more to download." Another photo finished right then, and I added it to the other slides.

"I'm restarting your laptop then it should be good to go," he said as I heard the familiar beep the machine always made during start up.

"Thanks," I told him, though any note of gratefulness I should have had seemed to be absent in my voice. What was wrong with me?

"How many more do you have left? I can start downloading over here," he informed me. I looked back at my inbox. There were only a few more emails. It seemed like a miracle that there could possibly be an end.

"I haven't touched the last three," I said. Each email contained several photos, some of them being quite large. I don't know who had thought that was a good idea. I heard some more clicking then Sawyer stopped. I knew he was waiting on my slow computer to work. I felt embarrassed for my poor little laptop. This embarrassment only fed my defensive posture. I tried to tell myself that I was interpreting what he was saying the wrong way, that he hadn't actually come out and said anything damning. But I heard how closely his words this morning echoed what he had said last night. Clearly my dream had tried to warn me that this was coming.

I looked at the progress bar on the screen to see how much longer I had to sit here. Usually I didn't have a problem sitting in silence with Sawyer. He has always made it so easy. Sawyer was one of those rare people who would say what he needed to say and listen as long as he needed to listen. He was usually the referee in our little group since he was good at seeing both sides of an argument. Of course, that also made for a good devil's advocate.

But today I wasn't handling these admirable qualities very well. I felt like I was being judged, and if it was Sawyer who was judging me then he was probably right in whatever conclusions he came to. That made it doubly worse.

I watched as the progress bars filled up and the download windows closed themselves as they finished. I went in and began to put the pictures into slides as soon as I possibly could. After I finished adding the last round of photos I hit save.

"How many are left that need to download?" I asked Sawyer.

"I went ahead and queued what was left. They only had a picture or two each," he said. "Did those finish?"

"Uh, yeah. I'm done. I just need to get this part of the slideshow to my computer," I told him. He reached into his bag and pulled out a flash drive. I saved my portion of the show on it before handing it back to him so he could finish the transfer onto my computer.

"There you go," he said. He stood up from my laptop to move back toward his own. I stepped back to make room for him. He started the shut down sequence.

"Hey, thanks," I said to him. He half-turned to look at me over his left shoulder.

"No problem," he said offhand. He slipped his laptop into its neoprene case and put it in his bag. "So, do you think you can handle this by yourself from here on out?" he asked as he shouldered his bag.

I bristled. I was trying so hard to be nice but his attitude kept grating on my nerves. "I'm not that helpless. I think I can finish a few slides," I snapped. This time, Sawyer caught the tone in my voice and looked up at me. I had worked through being hurt and now I was angry.

"I didn't say you were," he answered slowly, putting the right amount of confusion into his voice.

"Look, if I hadn't have really needed your help I wouldn't have asked. If you didn't want to help, though, you could have said no. I didn't volunteer for this," I spat. Once I started talking I couldn't make myself stop. My words came out quickly as if my brain didn't know what it wanted to say first so it was trying to get it all out at once. The more I talked the angrier I became. I was hurt and I wanted to retaliate. I wanted to make him angry enough to come out and say how he felt instead of dropping hints. I didn't want to feel as weak as I had last night in my dream.

"I know this isn't your thing," he started, his words picking up pace as he began to feel my anger. "It's fine. It's done, it's fixed. We saved the day. Aren, you need to get a grip." A hint of sarcasm had crept into his voice when he started talking but it had backed out when he got to his last words. I drew a deep breath, forcibly relaxing my shoulders. All of my cuts and the bruises forming around them were aching from the tension in my body.

"Sorry. It's been a long week." My voice was clipped as I offered my weak apology.

"I know," was all he said. "I'll see you later." He didn't wait for me as he headed toward the door. I followed him anyway, trying to play my apology out to the end. He let himself out and I paused to wave at the door before closing it. He waved back as he got into the little truck he frequently borrowed from his dad. I could almost feel the lack of commitment in his movement though. I shut the door, not bothering to watch him exit the driveway.

I went back to my laptop and jabbed rather viciously at the keyboard to complete my slideshow for the second time. It was while I was saving the final project I remembered I had no way to get the slideshow to the school without taking my entire laptop- I had left my only flash drive at school. I growled at the bulky laptop then shut it down, slapping the screen closed so hard it issued a loud click in protest. I left it on the table as I got up to change my bandage and find something I could take for the pain.

CHAPTER FOURTEEN

It was noon when I finally decided to admit defeat and trudge over to the school with my laptop. Between the slideshow and Sawyer I wasn't feeling fit to appear in public so I figured I'd better get it over with before my simmer became a boil. I swerved into the visitor's parking space and braked hard. Throwing the car in park, I pulled the keys from the ignition and hopped out with my laptop under my good arm.

The secretary directed me to Mrs. Donovan when I asked if she knew who had my flash drive. I peeked in the small window in Mrs. Donovan's door to make sure she wasn't in the middle of class before opening it.

"Hi, Mrs. Donovan. I came by to get my flash drive so I could give you the new slideshow," I announced. She immediately rummaged around on her desk to produce the drive.

"Here you are," she said, handing it to me. "I'm so sorry you had to go back and redo the entire thing. I should have gotten those pictures to you earlier."

I was watching my laptop boot up while Mrs. Donovan spoke. She didn't sound like she was sorry about it. But then again I don't think I had recovered from the sting of my less than stellar morning with Sawyer. She looked like there was more she wanted to say when she noticed the bandage on my arm. I volunteered no answer to her raised eyebrow. I put the flash drive in the USB port as soon as my computer finished booting up. Before long, I was handing it back to her.

"It's okay. Everything should be there now," I said to her. I waved and was back out the door, feeling like I had already wasted my day. I walked quickly to my car, not wanting to be stopped again.

I had just shut my car door when my phone buzzed. It was a text from Lexa. A question mark. I threw the phone in the passenger seat. I headed toward home instead of the park, squealing my tires as I took the right turn onto Main Street. I didn't want to go to the Senior Skip Day party and if I talked to Lexa I'd let her convince me otherwise. I was hoping if I were alone I wouldn't have to watch the rest of my dream come true.

No, I didn't want to be alone, I amended as Noah's face came to the forefront of my mind. I just had a need for selective company. I was getting close to the C&T now and at the last minute I jerked the car into a parking space on the curb. I knew it was a long shot that he would be here but I figured I'd try anyway.

There was a surprisingly large crowd at the C&T. It took me a moment to realize it was lunchtime. People from the nearby bank and courthouse had wandered over to grab something from the C&T's selection of sandwiches and salads. My head swung from side to side trying to see every face in the café, looking for Noah. I had already made my way to the bar and I still hadn't seen him. I ordered a peppermint tea to go and kept looking around. I knew he must have other things to do than hang around at the C&T waiting for me but I had to work very hard to keep my face from falling in disappointment.

I was still looking around when the barista, a new girl with short hair and freckles that made her look like she was twelve, came over with my tea. After paying I reluctantly walked out. Stepping to the side of the door under the faded green awning, I blew on my tea and hoped if I gave it a few more seconds Noah would show up.

As I stared down at my paper cup like I expected to find the answer to world hunger at the bottom of it I felt eyes on me. I bit back a smile but kept my eyes on my tea. I tried to get a grip while telling myself it probably wasn't Noah. I could feel someone standing close to me. I looked up, a grin spreading across my face despite the intense effort I was using to remain calm.

When my eyes focused on the person in front of me my face froze. I bit down hard on my lip, effectively erasing my grin. It wasn't Noah.

"Hi, Aren," Holden said, standing so close I didn't have enough room to breathe. I had to admit he looked perfectly normal at first glance. He was wearing jeans and sneakers with a navy blue jacket over his plain gray t-shirt. As my eyes traveled from his feet to his face I tried to regain control of my faculties.

My body had reacted in several ways at once to his sudden appearance. I felt like I had been thrown back into my dream as distrust warred with a sudden, intense attraction that had sprung up literally overnight. The unfamiliar emotion made my misgivings blossom and I took a step back from him warily.

"Is everything alright?" he asked, his face awash with concern. I tried to wipe the surprise off of my face. Randomly, I recalled the advice on those animal shows that said you should never show fear to a predator. His hand reached toward me almost instinctually but when I drew back from him he dropped it.

"Lexa's not with me," I blurted out. His brow furrowed for a moment then relaxed.

"Oh," was all he said, as if he wasn't quite sure how he was supposed to react. His eyes slipped away from my face and I took that moment to study him. I had never really paid much attention to him, at least not in my waking hours. I was starting to see how many details my dreams had right. I suddenly felt the need to reach out to him, to touch him so I knew he was real. I took another half step back, putting more space between us. Without seeming conscious of it, Holden took a step toward me denying any distance.

"I was actually hoping to get a chance to talk to you," he said haltingly. He sounded like it was difficult to find the words he needed but his life depended on it all the same. I was dying to leave but I also felt I would die if I didn't hear what was so important.

"But she- well, I thought that-" I stuttered to a halt since I wasn't really sure what I was saying. When I had seen Lexa talking to him last night I knew she was interested. But I never got the feeling that it was mutual. I wasn't sure why that made me feel the tiniest thrill in the pit of my stomach. It was quickly followed by a wave of revulsion at the idea that I was competing with my best friend for a sociopath's affection. I swallowed, forcing the feeling back down.

"It's alright. I'm sorry about Lexa, she's nice but I, I knew she was your friend," he licked his lips. His quivering voice was becoming lower and lower as he spoke and I found myself leaning closer to catch his words. "I had wanted to talk to you that day in the park but you seemed- I don't know. I just couldn't think of any other way to get close to you."

The words sent ice tumbling down my spine. I took a deep breath, held it. He watched me, waiting to see how I would respond. I finally remembered to exhale when my chest began to burn. The fiery sensation in my lungs eased a little but breathing did nothing for the chilling numbness that my disorienting sense of déjà vu brought with it.

"I know you've heard those words before. Please, Aren, let me tell you the truth. Don't you want to know?" His voice sounded strangled as if he could barely keep his emotions in check. His eyebrows came together again, this time in concern. His lips parted, but he quickly pressed them together again. His eyes darted back and forth, scanning my face frantically. My body felt heavy and for a moment I couldn't tell if I was standing or sitting, as if I were weightless. My head felt like it was full of cotton balls. It was as if I had re-entered my dream.

"I don't know what you're trying to do but you've got to stop. You have to stop saying these things to me. I'm losing my mind." My words came out fast and choppy. I wanted to get everything out before the dream took over again. Tears pricked my eyes but I was determined to remain in control. "I don't know you. I never have. Please, I'm not sure where you came from or what's happening but please, please leave me alone. This is too much-"

"Aren, I would if I could. But you know I've come for you- he knows I've come for you. He found you, Aren, and I don't know how to make you see past what he's told you. What he's put in your head- even before you saw him. You don't know your own strength yet and he's trying to manipulate you. He's in your head, Aren. He put all this in there before you even met him. I don't have a choice." His words made no sense. My eyes dropped to the sidewalk as I tried to make the cotton between my ears process what he had said. I noticed that in my futile attempt to put some distance between us I had stepped back toward the building beyond the windows of the C&T. Holden was close to me, inches away from my body. We each had a shoulder pressed up against the brick, two people seeming to have a normal conversation in plain sight of anyone who drove by. I knew life was still going on around us but I felt as if the people passing by were nothing but static, something insubstantial- nothing like the two of us.

"Why?" was all I could think to say. I was still listening to his words play over and over in my head but they made no sense.

"Noah- he-"

He stopped when I suddenly made a strangled noise. The "he" Holden was talking about- he meant Noah?

"I'm sorry it happened like this, this time. I'm sorry he found you first. Please. Can't you see what this is? I know you feel it. You're putting it together on your own, let me help you. I know you don't trust me, I know what he's told you, what he's made you think- made you dream. But I also know you've been having the dreams, the dreams about us. I know because I've seen them. Please. Please."

He was speaking so fast I only heard half of what he said. The words were echoing in my head, playing simultaneously with the words that were spoken in the dream. I shut my eyes, breathing heavy. My chest constricted and my arms felt numb. Suddenly, violently, I turned away from him. I started toward my car with quick, jerky steps, as if I were trying to walk on legs that were still asleep. He moved with me, keeping right behind me. My numbed fingers were trying to remember how to open my car door when he came up behind me.

"Please, Aren. I. Am. Sorry. He beat me to you this time and now he's using you. I can't wait for you to figure this out on your own. I need you to remember now. Please." His words were pleading but his voice had a demanding undertone that frightened me. I whipped around to face him, watching the anguish on his face as he tried so hard to convey something I was absolutely unable to comprehend, as if he were speaking Portuguese. I couldn't help the anger that welled up inside of me, the frustration at not being able to understand. He stepped closer to me, taking my stillness as an invitation to come forward.

"Stop it- just stop!" I shrieked at him as a renegade tear rolled down my cheek. I put my hands up in front of me, dropping both my car keys and cup onto the pavement. He froze and in that moment I shoved him away from me, hard. Pain shot up my left arm as I flexed the muscles underneath the cuts. Holden stumbled back, his eyes wide in surprise.

Everything seemed to slow and I registered several things at once. Holden was trying to get his feet under him to halt his backward motion but it wasn't working. There was also much more traffic, both cars and people, than I had initially registered. Suddenly our world and theirs had collided. And Holden was falling. If this was my dream all over again, I knew with sickening surety what was about to happen.

CHAPTER FIFTEEN

Without thinking, my right arm shot forward, reaching for him. I threw myself forward with everything I had and grabbed onto his wrist. An electric shock shot through my arm as if I had latched on to a bare electrical wire. I held on through the piercing pain and twisted my body, trying to throw us both toward the curb. My feet had little purchase on the ground as I tried to push off. Horns were blaring as Holden and I both lost control of ourselves and landed hard on the asphalt behind my car. I landed beside him with his arm pinned under me, my head inches from the edge of the curb. He landed flat on his back, a loud whoosh telling me the wind had been knocked out of him. He was attempting to breathe, his mouth open but no air going in or out. I struggled to my feet, not letting go of his wrist despite the pain, and dragged him onto the sidewalk. His legs were weakly attempting to push himself along while I pulled.

"Holden- Holden, I'm sorry. Holden? I'm so sorry-" I continued to ramble as I hauled him over the curb. He still lay on his back, half of his body on the sidewalk now. I let go of him, unable to stand the shock of his touch any longer. I finally heard him draw in a ragged breath, let it back out. Soon his lungs remembered how to process air and he sat up, shoulders heaving. I think I continued to ramble. At least, I must have been rambling because

Holden lifted his hand to ask for silence. I clamped my lips together. They threatened to come apart again so I pinched them between my thumb and index finger. My limbs were still tingling with adrenaline and the aftershock of his touch. I was still seeing the scene from my dream where Holden had actually been struck by a vehicle.

"Aren, I know," he finally said in a tone that made me want to begin my apologies from the start. I dug my fingernails into my lips, concentrating on the pain. He let out a harsh bark of what could have possibly been considered laughter. "I should have seen that coming. I forgot."

"What-"

"I was there last night. I saw your dream. Didn't you feel me there?" he asked.

"How-" I sank onto the sidewalk beside him.

"I can do what you do, Aren. Well, mostly. Once you learn to control your own dreams you can find your way into the dreams of other people. But you're probably much better at it than I am, once you remember how. You always have been."

"Always have been?"

"I don't know why but we come back. Haven't you already started having the flashbacks? Every time, every single time, I'm always trying to find you. I always seem to remember first. That's why I should expect things like this, even if I didn't see your dream." Holden motioned toward the traffic and the patch of pavement we had become friendly with.

I watched him. I didn't have anything to say. I wasn't even sure I could speak if I tried. I couldn't figure out what I was supposed to do with what he was saying to me. The part of me that felt like I was dreaming wanted to embrace everything he told me. I wanted to go with the crazy, get good and comfortable with the outrageousness of everything he said. But the part of me that wasn't sure if I was actually asleep kept asking how I could possibly process this- where would this fit? My brain didn't have enough room to hold everything it had been exposed to in the past few days. I wondered if this was how Alice felt when she fell down the rabbit hole. She had been so accepting of it all- at least more accepting than I could possibly be right now. Kudos, Alice.

Holden's breathing had returned to normal and he was trying to stand. I stood swiftly, thinking I could help him up but I swayed on my feet as gravity expressed its reluctance to allow me free movement. Holden reached for me, grasping my elbow and watching me to see if I was going to kiss the sidewalk again. I inhaled sharply at the sting of his touch. When I looked up from my traitorous feet I saw Holden studying me intently. I straightened but he didn't release my arm. He held it gently but firmly, the sting having subsided to little needle pricks. Every part of me was aware of the contact and I froze with the unexpected notion that I didn't want to do anything that would make him draw away. Holden looked into my eyes and I was once again drawn into the warmth of his. He stared as if he could read my mind just by looking at me.

The moment didn't last long, however. I felt Holden's hand slide above my elbow and grip me, hard. I opened my mouth to protest but our private bubble burst again as a horn blared. Holden half dragged, half flung me around and away from him, shoving me toward the building. I lost my footing and slammed against the wall. It slowed my decent but I landed hard on my left arm anyway. I couldn't bite back the cry of pain as I felt my already broken skin split open again.

It was then that I processed what else I had heard. A horn followed by squealing brakes. People yelling. A dull scraping that ended with the sound of metal being rearranged by an impact with a firmer substance. I was lying on the ground and could see nothing but white. I blinked, wondering if I had hit my head. I got my legs under me and scrambled backwards, ignoring the burn in my arm as I pulled myself away. My head swung back and forth, trying to find Holden, to find anyone.

A large white SUV had jumped the curb, clipping my rear bumper and slamming into the brick storefront. I heard people calling out but I couldn't understand their words. An older woman came up behind me and leaned over to offer me her hand.

"Are you alright?" she asked, her face radiating concern. I took a few shaky breaths but I couldn't find my voice. My head nodded up and down a few times erratically. I reached out and she helped me to my feet. She put a motherly hand on my shoulder, still watching me.

"Holden-" I squeaked, finding the effort to talk harder than I thought it should be.

There was a blur of movement then. A man in his forties wearing jeans and a polo came over to me followed by a few onlookers. People had streamed out of the C&T as well as the bank across the street. Cars had stopped to either offer assistance or to check out the scene so they could say they had been there or both.

"Hey, are you hurt? Are you okay?" the man in the polo asked. He was clutching his left shoulder as he stooped, trying to look up into my face. I gave him the same shaky nod I had offered the woman.

"Holden," I repeated. I breathed in deeply, willing myself to speak, "he was with me. Someone was with me."

For a moment I expected the man and woman to exchange a look that said I must have hit my head too hard because no one had been with me. I started to take back what I had said, to change my story and insist that no one had been with me. My vision started to blur as I turned my focus inward to sort out whether or not I had actually been standing here with someone.

"The boy over there?" He pointed to his SUV. "He's fine, he's fine. I am so, so sorry. I don't know what happened, the wheel just turned and I couldn't hit the brakes fast enough- are you okay? Are you sure?" He kept asking me. I had to wonder if he were really concerned or if he just wanted to make sure he wasn't getting sued. Sadly, you never knew with people these days.

I finally registered his words about Holden and took a shaky step forward. The woman kept her hand on my shoulder. The man in the polo stepped back quickly, as if he were afraid I was going to lunge at him. Several people in the crowd were asking if I was okay. Some of the faces registered as familiar but I couldn't recall any names to save me.

"Holden?" I called out. I stopped in my tracks, halfway around the SUV. The ground tilted under me for a second. My fear, my distrust, my anxiety all hit me at once. My legs wobbled beneath me and the woman's guiding hand became a steadying grip. I looked at her, grateful.

I stood there, overcome by emotion. My breathing became labored. I had saved Holden from falling into the street and being hit only to have a car jump the curb at us. Did that mean although I could see things in my dreams I didn't have the power to change them in the real world?

I looked up and caught a glimpse of a red streaked blonde head surrounded by a group of people. Another shot of adrenaline burst through me and I steadied my shaky legs by pure will.

"I'm okay," I said to the woman. She didn't look completely convinced, but she removed her hand from my shoulder for the first time.

"You should go to the doctor," she instructed me.

"I will, I think I'll go. I'll go now," I answered. My immediate compliance to her suggestion seemed to have caught her off guard. She backed away but then realized encouraging me to drive after such a shock might not have been her best idea.

I ignored her, busying myself with digging in my pockets for keys. My fingers were stiff and it took several swipes with my hand to realize they weren't there. I stared down at my pockets as if I were willing the keys to appear. My breathing was starting to pick up when I remembered I had dropped them. I looked up at my car. I took in the scrape across the right side of the bumper. Paint was missing and the plastic had deep grooves in it. I wasn't looking forward to explaining that to my parents. I tried to tell myself it wasn't my fault but I couldn't help feeling responsible. I took a step toward my car, every part of me bent on getting out of there.

"Are you sure you should drive?" the woman asked me. "I can take you."

"No, I'm fine. Just shaken a little. It's not worth the trouble, I promise," I flashed her a smile, praying it was a convincing one. I hoped she hadn't picked up on the quiver in my voice.

I moved around to the driver's side of my car, searching for the keys. They were halfway under the car and I had to drop down to a knee to be able to pick them up. I hauled myself off the ground, keys in hand. I looked around, taking in the cars stopped on the street and the crowd that had gathered. The front of the guy's SUV was smashed against the bricks with steam pouring out of the engine. I figured he was going to have to wait to be towed out. I slipped into the driver's seat. Everything in me was screaming to get out of there. I put the key in the ignition, took a breath, and turned it. I was putting the car in drive as soon as the engine started.

I glanced behind me then peeled out of the space. I needed to get home, I needed to be alone. That was the only way I would be safe. Holden was trouble and I couldn't believe I hadn't trusted my first instinct to run. I stared at the road intently, denying myself the option of glancing in the rearview mirror.

CHAPTER SIXTEEN

No one was at the house when I skidded into the driveway. At the last minute I decided to turn my car around to face the street. I knew it wouldn't keep my parents from noticing the damage to my bumper but I was hoping it wouldn't be so obvious.

It took me three tries to find my house key on the key ring and fit it into the lock without dropping it. I burst into the house and slammed the door behind me, sliding the dead bolt home. I headed straight for my room, trying to dig my phone out of my bag as I walked. I stared at the screen. I had no new messages. I scrolled through my contact list to find Noah's name. He was the only one who would understand what had just happened and I desperately needed to tell someone. I was already to the P's when I realized I hadn't seen him. I went back up the list, slower this time. Again, I didn't see it. It took me a moment to realize I had only given him my number, he had never given me his. I stared at my contact list, willing his name to appear. My chest started to ache as if I were being denied oxygen. I sat the phone down on the nightstand.

I kicked my shoes off and flung myself onto the bed. My left arm was throbbing. I had an ache at the base of my skull and my heart was still beating too fast. My phone rang and I reached for it automatically. I hit the answer button and said hello without looking at the caller ID.

"Aren? Where are you?" a female voice inquired. I blinked, sat up. I had been expecting Noah to magically hear my wish for his call. I had to work though my intense disappointment before I could recognize the caller. Obviously I didn't do it fast enough because she spoke again. "Aren, I thought you said you were coming out here? Sawyer said he saw you this morning and you were a- you were in a foul mood."

"Lexa, I'm sorry. I forgot. I got so wrapped up in-" I faltered and she jumped in.

"Aren, you're my best friend and we've know each other forever but I don't know what's with you lately- you haven't really been yourself. I know that stupid project was stressing you out but it's not like you had to do it. You could've said no. I mean, what's going on with you? You've been so wrapped up in your own stuff I haven't even seen you. But if you're going to act like this then maybe it's best that we aren't going to be seeing much of each other soon since you had to go to your fancy college and leave the rest of us here. I didn't think you cared so much about getting praise from everyone else but it looks like that's all you care about." Lexa paused for a breath.

"Lexa, please, let me-" I was cut off again.

"No, Aren. I just figured out that I don't know you at all and I don't want to talk right now." My phone beeped as Lexa hung up dramatically. I stared at it, blinking as tears came to my eyes. Lexa's words had stung. I told myself that sometimes she gets worked up like that and flies off the deep end before thinking. Lexa has always been impulsive.

But maybe she was right. I had spent a lot of time on projects I said I didn't want to do but that I hadn't turned down. I knew I had been rude to Sawyer this morning. I hadn't even thought about Senior Skip Day or Lexa. The excuse of almost being ran over by a car seemed to fall flat, considering I wouldn't have been there for my near death experience in the first place if I'd been where I had promised I'd be.

I lay back on the bed again, letting the phone fall out of my hand. My heartbeat was starting to return to normal since my body had exhausted its supply of adrenaline. The back of my head throbbed so hard I thought I might throw up. I shut my aching eyes, trying to sort out what had actually happened today and what I had dreamed. The harder I tried to separate the two the more they kept getting jumbled up.

My phone rang and I reached hesitantly for it. I was careful to check the caller ID this time before I answered but the unknown number flashing on my phone told me nothing. My throat went dry. I sat up to try to catch my breath. My sudden movement reminded me that I had been lying down for a reason. I cradled the back of my head with one hand while I answered the call with the other.

"Hello," I said, sounding breathless. My caller would probably think I had been running a 5K, unless they knew me.

"Hi," Noah's voice responded. My heart swelled at the tone of concern I heard in his voice. I bit my lip, trying to get myself under control. "Are you alright?"

"I- well- it sounds ridiculous but I ran into Holden," I paused. Noah's sharp intake of breath was loud enough to be heard over the phone.

"What did he say?" Noah asked.

"Not much," I temporized. "He says he knows what I can do. Did you know he can do things like I can? At least, that's what he said."

There was a pause.

"I know of him. I wouldn't say we were friends but I had some ideas about him. He's nothing like you though." Noah's words instantly banished any pain I may have been feeling from my friends' criticisms. All other thoughts of Holden were driven from my mind as Noah spoke again. "Where are you? Do you want to maybe meet me somewhere and we can talk?"

My heart gave a little jump at the thought of seeing him. I knew I shouldn't be so excited when everything was getting so confusing. Trying to rein in my smile I said, "I'm at home now but I can meet you somewhere."

"How about the park?"

I opened my mouth to voice my agreement when I remembered Senior Skip Day. It was possible some people were still there, maybe even Lexa and Sawyer, and I wasn't ready to face them.

"Um, is there somewhere else? Maybe the C&T?" I countered.

"Ok, C&T it is. I'll be there soon," he said as he hung up.

I gathered my bag and flip-flops before making a quick stop in the bathroom for something for the headache that had returned the moment I had hung up the phone. Keys in hand, I headed out the door for the second time today.

CHAPTER SEVENTEEN

This time I parked in a lot off Main Street, which would hopefully mean I was less likely to get ran over. I backed my car into the space so a concerned citizen wouldn't notice my bumper and tell my parents before I had a chance to. I locked the doors and headed toward the café.

I was surprised to see that the SUV had already been towed away and someone had swept up the debris from the crash. Looking closely I could see some marks in the brick wall but otherwise couldn't tell I had almost been mown down here earlier today.

I saw one man at the counter in the C&T when I walked in. Other than that the place was empty barring employees. I waved to Maggie who was bustling around behind the counter and walked toward the back of the café. I had just sat down at a table for two when Noah walked in. He scanned the room quickly then made a beeline toward me. I smiled as he approached and he returned the grin.

"Do you want anything?" he jerked his head in the direction of the bar.

"I guess we should have something, huh?" I asked. I didn't want to upset Maggie by taking up space in her cafe.

"Give me a minute," he said and he headed for the bar. Since he was the only person waiting to be served he was back in no time, a mug in each hand. He sat one down in front of me. "Peppermint tea," he explained. I smiled at his thoughtfulness and wondered briefly how he knew. I swirled the liquid around to cool it.

I kept my eyes on my drink while I tried to gather my thoughts. I didn't want to be one of those girls who blew everything out of proportion just to get attention. Yes, I wanted Noah's attention but I didn't want to look like a total nut job to get it. The fact he said he understood what was going on with me was practically unbelievable in itself. I was still waiting for the moment when he told me everything I was saying was too much for him and he ran away screaming.

"Aren?" Noah said softly. I could feel him watching me. I looked up and met his gaze. "What happened?" he prodded.

"I had stopped here earlier today-" I paused, remembering my only reason for stopping was to see if I could find him. Was that only a few hours ago? "-and I ran into Holden. He told me that he knew about my dreams. And he said he knew about you." I wasn't really sure how much detail to go into because I wasn't sure how much was actually real. I bit my lip as I tried to sort reality from my dream before I continued. I could still feel the throb at the base of my neck and I concentrated on the pain to make the conflicting images in my mind go away.

"What did he tell you about me?" Noah asked. Regardless of the sharp edge to his tone I was grateful for a direction in my thinking. Nothing I remembered being said about Noah seemed very flattering, however, and it made me embarrassed to repeat it.

"He said he'd known you for a long time and that you had dreams like mine," I spoke haltingly, trying to edit what I could recall.

"That's all he said?" Noah asked.

"That's all I really remember. He just came at me with all this stuff. I was a little stunned, and then there was the truck," I said offhand.

"Truck?" Noah looked puzzled.

"Yeah, there was an SUV that lost control and almost creamed Holden and me. We got out of the way but it hit the building." I gestured vaguely toward the door. "And my car," I added sourly. I still wasn't sure what I was going to do about that. I guess technically it was the responsibility of the SUV driver to fix it. I still felt like I had caused the accident by trying to save Holden.

"What?" Noah looked at me in disbelief. "That actually happened?"

"It was awful. Like something right out of my dream. Well, not exactly. In my dream, the SUV hit Holden. It was so scary. Is it always this hard to keep everything straight? I can't tell if I'm awake or asleep half the time." The pitch of my voice was starting to rise so I clamped my mouth shut against the simmering hysteria. I took a deep breath and held it in my cheeks. Noah reached across the table to put his hand lightly on my injured one, being careful of the cuts and scrapes. A shiver of delight swept through me but disappeared as quickly as it had come.

"What did you mean by 'that actually happened'?" I asked him once I realized what he had said. His smile faltered a little as he hesitated a moment before answering me.

"I mean I had seen something similar happen to you in my own dreams. I was worried." His smile regained its confidence.

"Aren, this is real. Right now, us, together, we're real, I promise. I know it's hard to hold on to reality sometimes but it gets easier," he said in a soft tone. He renewed his lopsided smile and I couldn't help but smile myself. I moved my other hand slowly to my mug and raised it to my lips. My throat had gone dry but I didn't want to make any movement that might cause Noah to withdraw his hand. It took several attempts to swallow the mouthful of tea past the lump in my throat. The hand that brought the mug back to the table was shaky.

"I see two versions of everything in my head. One from my dream and one that actually happened. And I feel everything I felt in both scenarios- some of them aren't that much different. How do you tell which ones are real?" I was practically whispering. Noah leaned in toward me to catch the last part of what I said.

I pressed my lips together in a tight line, waiting for any answer he could give. I was suddenly very certain if it weren't for him I might already be locked away in a padded room somewhere. I couldn't believe how lucky I was that he had come into my life at exactly the right time, something I couldn't remember ever happening to me before. Maybe he was so perfect because he was a fabrication of my imagination. I bit down on my lip harder. I didn't want to give voice to this thought in case saying it out loud would make him disappear. I glanced over his shoulder to see if anyone was looking our way with expressions that may indicate I was talking to myself instead of sitting at a table with another person.

"Unfortunately," he started, "it takes time to sort it all out. I thought I was losing my mind when it happened to me. I didn't have anyone to talk to. I wouldn't wish that on anyone. I promise I will do anything I can for you so you never feel the way I felt," he gave my hand a squeeze to emphasize what he said. "Just start at the beginning and tell me everything. We can sort out what's real and what isn't as we go."

"It started with my dream last night. I tried to be aware of it, to control it. But I couldn't do it for long." My mouth tugged down at the corners when I remembered how awful the dream had been. It definitely didn't take any shape I would have chosen for myself. "I saw my friends- Sawyer and Lexa. But they said horrible things to me. And then I saw you. I tried to get to you but Holden was in the way. He was saying crazy things about being able to help me. He just kept coming at me, so I shoved him. That's when I woke up."

Noah was still for a moment, watching me. "What did he say?" he asked.

"He said I should know the truth, that he wanted to help me. That he knew what was going on inside my head. Today he said the same things to me. That he could do what I can do. He said you could, too. Is it really the same for you?" I murmured.

"Not exactly," he finally said, his eyes searching for the right words on the ceiling. "I don't think I'm as strong as you are. I can control my dreams but you'll learn soon enough. And I can sometimes see things that are going to happen but I haven't been able to actually make things happen, like I suspect you can do. Sometimes I can see other people's dreams if I think about them hard enough." At this, he grinned sheepishly at me. My face colored.

"Can I do that?" I wondered aloud. I wasn't really expecting an answer since I asked the first thing I could think of to take his attention off my burning face. He gave me one anyway.

"Probably. It took me a while to figure it out but I'd say you'll pick up faster since you have me to talk you through it," he grinned.

"Maybe I can figure out what's going on with Sawyer and Lexa. They won't talk to me- except to tell me how much they don't want to talk to me." I winced as I remembered my brief but painful conversation with Lexa.

"You may be able to do more than that," Noah mused. "You may be able to apologize to them through your dreams. You can do things I've never seen before." He looked at me through his lashes and his thumb drew small circles on the back of my hand, making it tingle. Hope blossomed in my chest, not only at the idea of being able to make everything right with my friends but possibly cementing things between Noah and myself through my dreams. His attention was intoxicating and I desperately wanted nothing less than for it to continue forever.

"How is it that I've never heard of anything like this before except in bad science fiction movies?" I joked. Noah seemed to take my query seriously.

"Maybe you're just lucky. I thought I was the only one when I was going through it. But you have me," he smiled his signature lopsided grin at me. I almost swooned at the implication that he was mine. "I don't think it's coincidence that I found myself here, where you are.

When I started having dreams about you I thought I'd made you up so I'd have someone like me."

I was shocked that he said exactly what I had been thinking. I wished I knew how to tell him he wasn't alone, to return the comfort he had given me- but I didn't know how.

"So- you weren't at the Christmas parade?" I asked. Sheepishly he bowed his head, shaking it side to side.

Trying to think of something else to say, my eyes started roaming the café. That was when I noticed the clock. It was a little after four. I tried to remember where the day had gone but I couldn't find the lost hours. I realized Mom would be home soon, that she might already be home. If I didn't want to have to do any more explaining than necessary about where I had been and what had happened to my car, I needed to head that way. Plus the festivities at the park would be over now and my friends may be headed here. I didn't feel I could face them, at least not yet. My longing to stay with Noah was suddenly outweighed by an intense urge to be at home in the sanctuary of my bedroom. I briefly thought about how nice it would be if I could combine the two wants. Realizing I was thinking about Noah in my bedroom, I felt my face becoming hot again.

Regretting the words before they were out of my mouth I said, "I think I need to go. I don't want to have to explain anything to-" Noah cut me off.

"No, I understand. As much as I would like for you to stay..." he trailed off. I suddenly felt the urge to pinch myself. There was no way he could possibly be telling me what I wanted to hear out of sincerity.

"I do want to stay," I gushed, desperately hoping he wanted to hear it as much as I wanted to say it. He smiled at this and squeezed my hand gently.

"Come on, I'll walk you out," he offered. He let go of my hand and the cool air that replaced the warmth of his touch was more upsetting than I expected. Dropping my head so he didn't see my disappointment, I gathered up my half empty mug but Noah reached out to take it from me. He deposited it along with his own in the plastic tub beside the trashcan. He came back to me in a few swift strides and took my uninjured hand in his. He was so close to me I could smell his cologne, clean and fresh and very Noah-like. He led me out of the café to the sidewalk, grasping me tightly. I returned the pressure of his hand, not wanting him to let go.

He pulled me to his side and we walked in silence to my car. I was glad he wasn't trying to continue our conversation as we walked. I wasn't sure I could talk while he was holding my hand. His touch felt solid and secure and I hadn't realized how much I needed that until I had it. I was already mourning the moment when he would let go.

He walked me to my car door. He pulled me around by my hand to look at him. His eyes roamed my face for a moment before he brought his free hand up to run his finger along my jaw. My mouth opened slightly as I took in a huge gulp of air. My stomach tensed as he smiled at me. I wet my lips in anticipation of the kiss I desperately wanted, wondering what he would do if I threw myself at him.

"I promise you'll be fine," he said. "I won't let anything happen to you if I can help it." All I could do was smile at him. My heart dropped a little as he stepped back from me, dropping my hand. "I'll see you soon, okay?" I nodded, attempting to regain control of my emotions. I reluctantly reached into my pocket for my keys.

Just in case he changed his mind about the kiss I took my time unlocking my door and sliding in. He stood outside the door, waiting to close it for me. After he shut the door I started the car as he turned to walk away.

Now that my time with Noah was up all I wanted to do was get home. The anger, confusion, adrenaline, fear, and giddiness of my day equaled an emotional tailspin that had left me exhausted. Without Noah to buoy my spirits all I wanted to do was lie down, though I wasn't sure I would ever be able to quiet my mind enough to sleep.

CHAPTER EIGHTEEN

When I pulled into the driveway a few minutes later Mom's car was already there. After some debate I decided to turn the car around to face the road, the damaged back end facing the neighbor's hedge instead of my dad's line of sight when he came home. I turned off the ignition and sat for a moment. I tried to tell myself that as far as the car thing went it wasn't my fault that I got hit by some crazy person. It wasn't like I was anywhere I shouldn't be. Still, I couldn't shake the feeling that I had done something terribly wrong. Something that made the guy driving the SUV the victim instead of me. Of course, if my parents hadn't already heard about it from someone else in town it would be a miracle. I sighed, gathered my things, and got out of the car slowly.

The doorknob didn't resist when I twisted it. Thankful that I didn't have to try to unlock the door with my fast fading coordination I stepped into the house. I paused, listening for Mom. I was rewarded with banging sounds from the kitchen.

"Hi," I said as cheerfully as I could manage when I ambled toward the island.

"Hi," Mom echoed as she rooted around in a cabinet. She finally came up with a baking sheet, which she placed on the stove. That accomplished, she turned to me, dusting her hands together as if she had just climbed

Everest.

"Where've you been?" Her question sounded conversational. I silently berated myself for feeling like I should be in trouble. I hadn't done anything wrong I told myself- at least not in the real world.

"The C&T. The school asked me to add some more stuff to the slideshow." I knew one didn't have anything to do with the other but she didn't know that.

"Oh, I'm sorry, honey. Did you get it finished?" Mom asked, turning back to her baking sheet.

"Yeah. At least I'd better be. I don't have time to do anything else to it," I said, bitterness creeping into my voice. That slideshow had come to represent most of what was wrong with my life these days- the project I was volunteered for that I didn't know how to do that put me at everyone else's mercy that was never done.

I wondered if now was the time to bring up the accident as I watched Mom move around the kitchen. My stomach felt a little queasy and I played with the keys in my hand. I knew I needed to be the one to tell her but I couldn't think of how to say it.

"I'm going to go lie down for a bit," I finally blurted out. Without saying anything further I walked through the kitchen and down the hall to my room.

I shed my bag and shoes then curled onto my good side. My body was tired but my mind had a few things it demanded to straighten out before I could sleep again. I would hate to see what would happen if I went to sleep with so much on my mind.

The last question I wanted to ask myself but the first one that popped into my mind was why me? As cliché as it sounded, I couldn't help but consider it. I had been perfectly happy, perfectly ordinary a week ago. As much as anyone would want to think of themselves as uniquely individual, I was- or had been- fairly unremarkable. Given the choice, I preferred it. Now even the sunlight filtering through my curtains looked strange and new. The feeling inspired panic due to an inability to determine if the newness was good or bad.

The recap of my day sounded like the thirty second

"on our last episode" bit before a science fiction TV show. The most difficult to process was Holden. I felt a physical aversion to him that demanded I stay away at all costs. But his words were like a siren's song. I couldn't help listening and, if I were to be honest with myself, I knew I wanted to hear more. But Holden's intensity frightened me. I wished I knew what drove him to such lengths. I wondered if it could be something as simple as the truth.

Holden had asked if I had started to recall other lives. As far as I could remember I had had only one glimpse of what may have been another life, the girl in the field. If what Holden said was true then it was only one of several versions of me that had existed before now.

I wondered how I could prove or disprove this theory. It was frustrating to think everyone else knew something about me that I couldn't see for myself. I rolled onto my back to see if I could find the answers on the ceiling. It only took a second of searching to see that nothing had been written there since the last time I looked.

Perhaps, though, I did have another way.

I had only been daydreaming when I threw that guy from school across a hallway but from what I had been told it seemed to have been effective. I flinched reflexively. I had never been a violent person and the thought of what I'd done was frightening. I gave myself a mental shake, bringing me back to my half-baked plan. It was true I was given to daydreaming so it shouldn't be too hard. I just wasn't sure if it counted if you were trying to daydream.

I took a deep breath and nestled back into the mattress, tucking one of my pillows under my head. I closed my eyes, continuing to breathe deeply. I thought about Noah and Holden outside of any familiar surroundings. Were there other places that we had been together? My mind began to drift, focusing first on one face then the other. I felt my mind reaching out as if trying to find where these pieces belonged.

❧ ❧❧ ❧

There was a heavy fog, the kind so thick you could feel it soaking through to the skin. The fog diffused the light in such a way that I couldn't tell where it was coming from. Differentiating morning from evening was impossible. As for the landscape, I could only see the vague shapes of the trees that marked the edge of a forest. I watched the fog roll and dance along the strip of grass between the trees and the stronghold from where I watched. Everything was deep green shrouded in a cloak of gray. Inside, everything was gray as well. The walls and floors were gray stone. My hands rested in the lap of my gray woolen dress. The chair I sat on was made of wood so old and worn that it looked gray.

I was in a low ceilinged room that was sectioned off from a larger room by a hanging of plain gray cloth. A part of me said there was somewhere else I was supposed to be. Before my body could get up from the chair my awareness moved to the edge of the gray cloth and peered around it.

A large hall with a vaulted ceiling waited behind the section of cloth I was peeking around. Down the left side of the room I could see other partitions set up by more cloth being draped between the ceiling supports. I glanced back at where I had been a moment ago and realized my body was still trying to convince itself to stand. No, not my body exactly but the one I had looked through to see outside. The rough hands and hard set of the shoulders were not mine but something in the eyes, just like last time, told me this person was part of me. She must have been just a few years older than the present me but her face bore lines that hinted at a life much harder than mine had ever been.

People were moving around in the hall. Everything seemed to happen around a large, heavy table that stretched from one end of the room to the other. Long benches ran the length of the table and each end was punctuated by sturdy looking chairs. The furniture had a dull shine that came from being treated with oil and all the edges had been worn smooth from much use. More benches lined the wall opposite me. Large hearths were present at each end of the room. My line of vision shifted slightly and I could see into the far left corner to a set of stairs that explained where all the people were coming from.

I glanced around the hall again and noticed it was filling with people rather quickly. I saw men and women, young and old, coming up the stairs, each carrying something. Some placed their burdens on the table then stepped back to talk to whoever was nearest while some rushed back down the stairs. Between the two fires a cheery glow was cast over the entire room making everything appear a warm gold instead of the dull gray I had witnessed from my little partition. Remembering I had left the girl behind, I turned to look for her.

She had made her way out of the alcove and was helping a boy with a stack of carved plates. She took them with deft hands and wove in and out of the people standing around to place the plates at regular intervals on the table.

The noise in the room had been on the rise as people came up the stairs to linger in the large hall, but now the sound ballooned and burst as a large crowd comprised of men in heavy cloaks tramped in together. Children ran to them, searching for fathers or brothers. The women gravitated toward this group as well and waited their turns to welcome their kinsmen home. There were few around the table that didn't move toward the men. I was sad to see I was one of them. I continued placing plates until my arms were empty then stood on the other side of the long table watching clusters of people move lazily away from the stairs toward seats. I smiled and waved occasionally to a passerby, obviously knowing most everyone but not so well as to have rushed to them with their other family members.

Everyone had moved away from the stairs in time for a smaller, yet somehow louder, group of young men to come traipsing into the room. The group moved together, laughing and talking, toward the head of the table nearest the stairs. A large man with a thick beard emerged to stand before the heavy chair at the head of the table. He raised his hands and said something I didn't understand. Everyone in the room called out something equally indecipherable in answer. As the newcomers seated themselves I- the other me- started walking toward them. She stood to the side of the man who had spoken. Seeing her, he stood and kissed her soundly on the cheek. She smiled warmly before embracing him.

He looks like my uncle Rob, I registered. I shook my head. Surely everyone I knew couldn't have been born time and time again.

The man motioned her toward a seat on his right. She put up a token resistance before agreeing. Instead of taking the seat directly to his right however, she moved down a space or two on the first bench until she was somewhere in the middle of it.

I followed her gaze around the circle of men, hoping to catch a glimpse of another face I knew. I didn't see anyone who reminded me of Holden or Noah. She looked down the length of the table as well but didn't seem to find who she was looking for either. The man at the head of the table began to address the crowd. I couldn't really hear his words but they seemed to be quite dramatic from the way he was waving his arms around. There were cheers from around the table then the gathering started passing bowls of various foodstuffs around. The room became quieter as everyone settled down to the task of eating.

A small girl darted from the stairs to the table where the other me sat. The woman turned to embrace the girl with the long reddish blonde braid running down her back. The girl was saying something almost too fast to understand by the look of concentration on the woman's face. The girl gave up speaking and began to tug on her arm. The woman glanced to the head of the table where her kinsman gave the slightest nod to indicate permission.

The woman stood and the girl took her hand, leading her toward the stairs. I was after them in a moment, practically on top of them as they walked down the stairs.

The staircase was a wide affair with shallow steps made of fitted stone. The little girl had to stretch her legs to take them one at a time. Light shown from sconces hanging on the walls making shadows bounce and jump as they moved. The staircase had a landing about midway down where the stairs turned back on themselves and continued down. As we neared the bottom we could hear men's voices. The little girl let go of the woman's hand and dashed down the last few steps. She ran full tilt toward a blonde man, throwing herself into his arms. His laugh was a loud, deep boom as he spun her around, hugging her fiercely. The blonde man set the little girl down then looked up at the woman. His face, so like Holden's but not quite, broke into a smile as he moved toward her.

My heart found its way into my throat as I watched the woman that was so like me and Holden move toward each other like magnets. They seemed to be restraining themselves from jumping into each other's arms like he and the little girl had done. Finally, he wrapped his arms around the woman firmly, swinging her from side to side slightly. He planted a chaste kiss in her hair before pulling back to look at her. His hazel eyes glowed golden in the firelight.

Other voices that had been growing louder as they approached now quieted when the woman and this version of Holden came into view. The couple, feeling eyes on them, drew apart. The woman turned to approach the two newcomers that stood behind Holden, though with more restraint than she had shown when she had greeted him. An older man with gray in his beard and too many wrinkles to count stood holding the hand of the little girl who was still beaming indiscriminately at the gathering. He resembled the man who currently sat at the head of the table upstairs considerably. I thought a brief frown flickered across the face of the old man but it was gone so fast I couldn't swear I had actually seen it at all.

The woman curtsied to him and he smiled while reaching his free hand toward her. She came forward so he could give her a fatherly peck on the cheek. Behind him was the last of the party, a man with dark wavy hair and brown eyes with flecks of green that shone mischievously. This time I heard the lungful of air I- she-sucked in at Noah's eyes.

Noah stepped forward, his arms raised in her direction and she moved stiffly toward him. She gave him a perfunctory embrace then backed away as soon as she possibly could. This Noah didn't seem to notice her reserved manner given his smug half smile. He glanced in the direction of Holden, following the woman's gaze. Noah reached out and took her hand to place in the crook of his arm, preventing her from going back to Holden. This time I caught the look of satisfaction on her father's face, proud that she had finally seen reason.

Just then the little girl, who was swinging the old man's hand to and fro, looked toward the stairs where my awareness watched these events unfold. Her eyes widened slightly and it felt like she was looking right at me- the present day me that was intruding on the entire scene. I gaped at her, unsure of what was happening. I didn't have long to think about it though because a loud bang caused me to jump as if I had been shot.

CHAPTER NINETEEN

The bang sounded again and I was wrenched completely from my daydream. Confused as to where I was I began looking around. I paid dearly for the swift movement with a sudden flash of pain through my skull.

"Aren? Open up, please," I heard my father's muffled voice from the other side of the door.

"It's open," I said in a voice so low I wasn't sure if he heard me. I threw my legs over the side of the bed and put my elbows on my knees. I put my head in my hands only to remove it suddenly when pain shot through my damaged appendage.

Dad opened the bedroom door. He was still wearing his scrubs. He let the door swing half closed behind him and came to sit beside me on the bed. Noticing the pain on my face when I had put pressure on my arm he reached for it. I held it across my body while he looked at the myriad cuts. There were tiny drops of blood that had oozed from some of them, probably when I clawed to safety from the SUV. He peered under the bandage and I kicked myself for not cleaning my arm up. He took his time, not speaking while he looked me over. I wasn't sure what he actually wanted but being in no hurry to find out I kept silent.

"I heard there was quite a commotion downtown today," he finally said, as if commenting on mild weather.

I moaned inwardly at his attempted casualness. "Is that what happened to your car?"

Damn, he'd noticed. "Yeah, the back fender got clipped," I said, trying to be equally casual. "Luckily that was all that happened," I said, implying that the car not being totaled was cause for celebration.

"Yeah, I heard you almost got ran over," he said. He raised an eyebrow at me but the quizzical look became serious when he paired it with a frown I didn't understand. I was halfway almost involved in an accident that didn't have any human casualties. I would have called it a win. "Toby came to the office to get checked out after it happened. He said he was sorry if he gave you and your friend a scare. His mechanic thinks something malfunctioned with his steering."

"We were fine. I'm okay," I stammered.

"I'm not sure why you were there in the first place. Didn't you have to be at school today?" he asked.

"No. It was Senior Skip Day. They had a picnic down at the park for anyone who wanted to come but it wasn't mandatory. I mean, I was morally obligated not to go to school today," I said with a grin. His frown grew more severe but he made no immediate comment. At least he'd heard of Senior Skip Day so he couldn't think I was making that up.

"Who were you with today? Did they get hurt?" he asked, continuing to pry.

"Um, Holden? He's fine, I guess."

"I haven't heard his name before." Dad stared, looking for any blink or twitch that would give me away. I wasn't sure why I was getting the third degree.

"He's a freshman at the college. He's actually a friend of Lexa's. He's kinda like a peer mentor type person, you know, he answers her questions about the college, classes, stuff." I could hear myself start to ramp up toward full on blathering as my words came out faster and faster. I clamped my mouth shut to keep myself from explaining my way into trouble.

"Never heard of him before," Dad remarked again. I didn't answer. I rubbed gently at my temples and prayed he would get to the point soon. I couldn't remember him ever coming in here about something so trivial. Was he mad I didn't say anything about almost being involved in an accident? That seemed a little much to me.

"Aren," Dad said, his voice clipped. He let out a breath so forcefully his shoulders sagged for a moment. He caught himself and straightened before continuing. "I'm a little worried that maybe you've been under too much stress. I mean, with you hurting your arm earlier this week and then, well, I'm sure it's not your fault that you almost got hit, but the timing- well- sometimes when people are under a lot of stress they do things for attention, a cry for help-" Dad trailed off when he looked up at me. I know my face displayed every ounce of the shock I felt.

"Really?" was all that actually came out of my mouth.

"Aren," Dad backpedaled, "I'm just worried. That's all. If there's something on your mind-"

"No," I cut him off. "There's nothing on my mind. Nothing but regular school stuff and graduation and college. I might be stressed but I mean- so I had an accident-" I waved my left arm in the air- "so I happened to be standing on the sidewalk when someone lost control of their vehicle. And, yeah, I happen to have a new friend I forgot to give you blood work on but-" I sputtered to a stop. I still couldn't believe what he was insinuating. When he didn't try to slow me down I knew I had been right. I felt betrayed. My parents had always trusted me but now it seemed they were inventing reasons to revoke that trust.

Dad was quiet for a moment. "Ok," he murmured. "Like I said I'm- we're- just worried, that's all."

Great. Now he was invoking the royal "we." I guess this had been the hot topic of conversation around here when I wasn't in the room. I stood up. "My head really hurts," I said as I brushed past him. I didn't want to give Dad the satisfaction of being able to play caregiver. I went to the bathroom and rummaged around for my medicine. It wasn't exactly where I'd left it and I wondered if Mom or Dad had been counting my pills. He followed me, stopping just outside the door. I ignored him. As bad as my head was hurting I wasn't going to be able to filter what I said. I swallowed a few pills with a handful of water from the sink then turned purposely toward the door. Dad stepped back to allow room for my exit.

"I'm going back to bed," I said over my shoulder. Dad didn't respond and I shut my door as soon as I crossed the threshold.

I quarantined myself in my room for the rest of the evening on principle. It had been close to six when I had my bizarre conversation with my father. I hadn't been hungry so I felt no need to go out to see what was for dinner. Besides, I'm sure Dad had been eager to give Mom the scoop on my current mental health status.

I did lie down but only so I was comfortable while I contemplated my dream. I was elated by the fact I'd been able to make the dream happen. What I wasn't sure of was its reliability. Had that actually been me and Holden and Noah? Or was I making things up and pretending I saw a former life? I couldn't deny that the woman had looked a lot like me. I had heard somewhere that when you dream your mind can't invent new faces so it uses people you know or even strangers whose faces you may have registered on a subconscious level. Maybe I was dreaming about Holden and Noah because I had seen them around town before?

I didn't see how that would explain why I had gone to Holden. At best Holden made me feel uncomfortable. My instinctual reaction was Holden equaled bad news and I didn't take that lightly. Still, as forthcoming, even eager, as Noah has been to talk to me about my dreams, he had never made crazy claims about previous lives. Of course, I guess I was going to have to adjust my views on what was crazy unless I was ready to check myself into the psych ward. That would really make my parents happy.

I stretched and shoved my pillow behind my head. I was more tired now than before my nap. In fact, I seemed to be tired all the time. I wondered if this was something that happens with the dreams.

I thought about what Noah and Holden said the dreams could do. Being almost run over by a truck this morning was giving some weight to the idea that I could influence events. I couldn't deny that saying it in so many words did make me sound less sane than I would have liked. But since I was already on the ocean of crazy, I decided to ride the boat a little while longer. I wondered if I was the one who had caused my friends to turn against me without provocation. Maybe I read what happened in my dreams into what they said during my waking hours. I recalled Lexa's phone conversation. She hadn't been anything but clear in her anger but I wasn't sure I'd deserved it.

On impulse I reached for my phone. I found Lexa's name in my favorites and dialed, waiting to hear the phone ring. After what seemed like years the phone rang once. Then it rang again. Lexa's voicemail message kicked in after that. I pulled the phone away from my ear and hit the "end" button. She declined my call. The thought made my chest ache.

I put my phone back on the nightstand. I couldn't make things right if she wouldn't talk to me. I contemplated Noah's dream premise, wondering if there might be another way to apologize. If I had started this fight in my dreams maybe I could end it there, too.

I hauled myself back out of bed and changed into the first t-shirt and pair of cotton shorts I put my hands on. Breaking my own self-imposed quarantine, I made my way to the bathroom to brush my teeth. I could hear my parents in the living room talking heatedly about something. I wondered briefly if they were talking about me. I had rarely, if ever, heard my parents have any kind of argument and for a moment I felt a deep stab of guilt. Trying to ignore them, I brushed my teeth as quickly as possible. Their conversation stopped all together when I turned on the water to rinse off my toothbrush. They were definitely talking about me.

Wishing I could ignore the hurt that rose inside me, I dashed back to my bedroom and shut the door before one of them came looking for me. Belatedly I realized I should have taken a look at my stitches but I wasn't going back. The last thing I wanted was to give them an opportunity to help me so they could ease their guilty conscience.

Pulling the blanket over me I felt the last of my strength drain away. I was dreaming before I realized I was asleep.

CHAPTER TWENTY

I was standing in one of the soccer fields at the park. The sun was shining down gently, warming my face. Though it was extremely quiet, the silence felt comforting instead of unnerving. I turned around slowly, taking in my surroundings. I didn't see another soul in any direction. I rotated again, faster this time, trying to decide what I should do. I stopped spinning when I felt the tug of something around my legs. I looked down and saw the long brown homespun dress that was clinched at the waist with an apron. My dream-self shrugged as if this inconsistency were to be expected.

The dress did not in any way impede my movement as I started across the soccer field toward the playground. I felt like I was moving at a dizzying speed but the swings didn't seem to get any closer. I swept my head from side to side, looking for...someone. I knew there was someone I needed to see, needed to talk to. Who was it?

An image, superimposed on the landscape in front of me, came to mind. I saw Lexa and Sawyer appear in my field of vision before the sun blinded me momentarily. I struggled to focus on where they were standing, just beyond the swings. I wasn't sure if they'd been there all this time or if I'd conjured them out of nowhere. I told myself the only thing that mattered was that I reach them. I began to pick up speed, my skirt swishing around my ankles.

When I came closer I saw they weren't alone nor were they still near the swings. They had moved in the blink of an eye to the picnic tables. Lexa and Sawyer sat opposite one another. Allison occupied the space beside Lexa. Ethan had appeared on the previously empty swings. Hana was beyond him as if unsure if she wanted to swing. She tried to catch my eye as I moved toward the picnic table but I looked away to concentrate on the transition from the soft grass to the shifting mulch.

I reached the picnic table but no one took notice of me. I stood a few feet from the edge of the table not knowing what to do. Allison, Sawyer, and Lexa were in deep conversation but I couldn't hear any of it. I didn't see their mouths moving but I could see them nodding their heads and gesturing. I waited a few more moments but no one ever looked in my direction.

The longer I stood there the more uncomfortable I became. I leaned forward to put my hands on the table for support. Instantly their conversation stopped. In a blink Allison was gone. I opened my mouth but nothing came out. My words seemed to be literally stuck in my throat. I moved my jaw up and down a few times in an attempt to make them come out. Sawyer and Lexa both stared at me expressionlessly.

I bowed my head, willing myself to talk. As if an obstruction had been suddenly removed from my throat I took in a huge lungful of air in preparation to speak.

"Lexa, Sawyer-" I cut myself short as I realized the picnic table was empty. I looked up. I could see them beyond the large wooden fortress on the playground. They both stood facing me, not speaking.

"Please!" I called loudly to them. They stood as still as statues. I started forward, not taking my eyes off of them. The mulch seemed more treacherous than usual, the deep uneven piles slipping and sliding under my feet like loose sand. I refused to take my eyes from my goal to check my footing, however. It made for slow going but I was determined to reach them before they disappeared again.

"Lexa! Sawyer!" I called out when I was a little closer, begging them not to move again.

"I'm sorry!" I called desperately, my words echoing across the park. They blinked as if they hadn't realized I was still here.

"Please!" I could detect a hint of hysteria in my voice that I hadn't realized was simmering inside me. I continued to move forward. I was halfway between the abandoned table and the fort now. I reached a hand out toward them. My arm felt heavy and the motion seemed to take energy away from my forward momentum. Still, I didn't retract it. "I'm sorry for what I did, what I said. Please! I'm sorry!"

The wind was picking up and I was screaming to be heard. My hair whipped around my face but I kept my eyes on my friends. They hadn't moved but I wasn't sure if they'd heard me. I leaned forward, now fighting against the wind as well as the mulch to keep my footing. My dress whipped and whirled around me making progress even more difficult. I noticed the bright sunlight had dimmed. The harsh shadows had disappeared as clouds swept between the sun and us. I felt a new sense of urgency.

"Lexa! Sawyer! I'm sorry! You have to forgive me!" I was screaming, feeling both remorse and anger bursting out of me. The wind, the disappearing sun, my inability to reach them had frustrated me beyond the point of sanity but I wasn't leaving until I knew they understood how sorry I felt.

I was still attempting to move forward but I couldn't tell if I was gaining any ground. They hadn't moved from the play fort, a set of monkey bars forming a gateway between them and me. I still felt impossibly far from them when I reached both of my arms out and lunged across the space between us. My hands closed on wrists and I followed the line of their arms up to their faces. They seemed stunned by my arrival, as if they hadn't seen me coming. I threw one arm around each of their necks and hugged them fiercely. Slowly, hesitantly, they put their arms around me, returning my embrace. My anxiety was replaced by a feeling of warmth. I didn't try to speak again; I only hugged my best friends.

I felt a sudden shift, as if they had both stood up straighter. The movement caused me to step into them and I could feel the rough homespun being pressed against my body as it met with theirs. I pulled back, my hands still on their shoulders, to see that Sawyer and Lexa had been replaced.

Noah and Holden looked at me as if it had been them standing there all along. I looked around, but I couldn't spot Lexa or Sawyer. I turned back to Noah and Holden, my hands resting on their shoulders and each of them resting a hand on my waist.

I studied them in the fading light. The clouds that had muted the sun were now darkening the sky. My gaze swept from one face to another, trying to force myself to remember something- anything- about our lives together. I pulled back to get a better look at them and their hands slipped from my waist.

This seemed to startle them out of their reverie. They both reached for me then seemed to notice each other. I backed up another step.

"Aren," Holden said, not taking his eyes off of Noah. "Please let me explain. I don't know why but every time, every life, you seem to remember everything so much later than we do. I know we sound crazy. But it's dangerous for you to meddle before you remember the rules." He turned from Noah to look at me. Noah's sudden laugh started both of us.

"You're the one that sounds crazy," Noah corrected him. "Aren and I have had many conversations about this and while they might have been bizarre they weren't completely unhinged. That's your department." He turned his face toward me. "He's always been this way."

"Are you saying he's right?" I asked Noah. The wind was starting to pick up again and my voice sounded small. I cleared my throat. All the fight had been drained from me when I had reached Lexa and Sawyer. I wasn't sure I had anything left to endure whatever these two had to throw my way.

Noah looked from me to Holden and back again.

"He has some of it right. We've known each other for a very long time, Aren." He gave me a meaningful look through his dark lashes.

"Yes," Holden said quickly. He hesitated, as if he didn't know how to proceed but the desperation on his face said he had no other option. Holden took half a step toward me, putting a restraining hand on Noah's shoulder as he did so. "You're remembering your gifts so much faster than you're remembering how to control them."

"She knows all about them," Noah cut him off. He pushed Holden's hand away. "We've covered the subject and none of our discussions were as insane as what you've been trying to say."

"Did you tell her about how dangerous it is to try to interact with other people's minds? About how sometimes when you set things in motion it's hard to undo them?" Holden barked at him, his fists clenching.

"Other people?" I echoed.

"Yes, other people. Did he tell you it can be dangerous to mess with other people's minds? Your friends that were here earlier? You weren't just talking to them in your mind, you were reaching out to theirs. The human mind is a delicate thing- if you aren't careful you could destroy theirs- or cause their minds to wall themselves off- possibly permanently. Some of us can only talk to each other," Holden shot Noah a glance before continuing, "but some of us have a wider range. I think the reason you're the last one to remember has something to do with you being so much stronger. You've always been strongest."

"And the things- things that I do or I dream? The SUV?" I asked. Emotions washed over me so quickly that I could barely keep my feet against their onslaught. A wave of guilt at having possibly injured Lexa and Sawyer was replaced with nausea that crippled my entire body. A sudden adrenaline rush from the memory of the SUV made my knees buckle.

"Yes." This time it was Noah who answered me. "You have the ability to set things in motion, to make things happen- or at least influence them. The limits are a little fuzzy though. In some lives you've been able to make things happen while you are awake. You're one of a kind, Aren." He said this almost reverently.

"How many times have we done this?" I put my hand to my head. Around me, the world had grown so dark I could no longer make out the shapes of the playground equipment. In fact, I couldn't be positive we were still on the playground at all. Faint lights like distant balls of lightning blossomed around us but were gone so quickly I couldn't tell what they were. I felt my throat catch and I bent my head down, trying to breathe. The reflections of the flashes of light lit up the ground beneath me although I couldn't have said exactly what I was standing on. The ground was smoother now than the mulch would have allowed for. The lights seemed to slow, not blinking in and out quite so fast. I risked a glance toward the sky and saw something moving in what looked like a mirror made of light. I fixed my gaze on one, staring into it.

I saw myself in a carriage dressed all in black. I barely had time to recognize my face before I was gone. I turned to another light on my right. This time it was Holden, his head wrapped in cloth against the desert sun. I saw Noah standing in the rain, a bowler hat on his head. I could almost feel the lights on me and now I turned instinctively, trying to see as much as I could in the flickers of memory. I started to notice with each tableau there was a tightening behind my eyes. As the pain grew worse I had to shut them against the moving portraits around me. I felt as if my head would explode. There was too much to remember to fit it all in at once. My knees, already shaking, finally gave way and I sank to the ground.

"Who are you?" I moaned.

"I'm not sure we know anymore," Holden answered hesitantly. "We've come back so often I couldn't tell you where it started. I can't remember all our lives, at least not yet. I do know that every time we-"

"What matters is that we've found each other," Noah shouted over top of Holden's words. "I can help you,

Aren. It's hard when all this is happening and you have no one to turn to. You have that luxury- one I didn't."

I kept my head bent so as not to look at either of them. The intensity of the light around me was so strong that the reflections bouncing off the ground were starting to hurt my eyes.

"No, Aren!" Holden's voice sounded strained. I saw his feet move closer to me. He jerked back suddenly as if he had been forcibly stopped. "If you want help we'll both be here for you. Sometimes one view of the past can be subjective. You can't shut me out. For better or worse- we belong together."

"Yes, we do," Noah said, including himself in the "we." I wasn't sure that was what Holden had meant as I recalled how I had greeted them home in the stone hall. That scene, however, had felt completely incongruous with my life now. It was Noah who had come to mean so much to me in the short span of time we had had together. I felt a tug toward both of the men before me. I also felt a desire to distance myself as much as possible from what they were trying to tell me. My head still pounded with the reality they were trying to paint. It was as if my brain had reached its capacity for memories, real or imaginary.

The flashes around me had started to pick up like we were standing in the middle of a dance floor bathed in strobe lights. I tried to keep my eyes on the ground but even it seemed to shift with the pictures around me. I'd given up all hope of finding my feet again. It was probably a good thing I did because seconds later the earth began to shake. The quaking increased in intensity and I was knocked from my knees onto my stomach. I lay there, arms over my head, not knowing where Holden or Noah was. My stomach felt like I was taking a long drop on a roller coaster I couldn't recall boarding.

❧ ❧❧ ❧

The soft morning sunlight illuminating my room amounted to cruel and unusual punishment when I awoke with a pounding in my head. I rolled over to press my face into my pillow so I could moan melodramatically but ended up banging my left arm and hissing in pain. I returned to my back, careful of my arm this time, and made faces at the ceiling instead. This was not how my morning was supposed to go. It made me shudder to think I had an entire day to get through with this luck.

I looked over at my clock to discover it was a little after seven in the morning. The assembly, which would debut my slideshow, started around nine. I had plenty of time to get ready then sit around and hyperventilate. Not just because of the slideshow, I reminded myself, but because of Sawyer and Lexa as well. My stomach braided itself into an admirable pretzel thinking about it. I wasn't sure what to say to them, or what they would say to me. Thinking back to my dreams, I wasn't really sure what I might have done. Visions of Lexa and Sawyer sharing a hospital suite while lying in comas flashed in my mind.

The dream. The memory of it brought back feelings so strong I winced as if I were expecting a physical blow. Hope, confusion and fear all tried to occupy the same space at once.

Trying to push that aside I lay still and listened, attempting to discern if my parents were still in the house. I didn't hear anything but that didn't mean they weren't lurking in the kitchen or living room. I rolled out of bed and padded to the door, breathing heavy from the workout my emotions had supplied.

I found no one in the kitchen and I didn't hear anything from the living room. I peeked out the window to see that my car was the only vehicle in the driveway, its mangled bumper shining in all its glory in the morning light. I turned up my nose and huffed, sounding pathetic instead of haughty.

I headed back to the kitchen. Although my stomach was still trying to earn its Girl Scout knot-tying badge I figured I needed to eat something. I found a package of Pop-tarts in the pantry and popped two in the toaster. The coffee pot had just enough coffee left in it for one cup so I grabbed the nearest mug and poured the dark liquid into it. I sipped cautiously while I stared out the dining room window past the gauzy curtains. Crisp, clean morning light streamed through the window. The curtains made the light dance across the furniture and the floor. It was such a warm glow that I felt myself calm, my breath grow even. I was trying to remember something, a morning like this in an entirely different place, a different time. It was as if the dancing light had hypnotized me.

I was so lost in staring at the patterns on the floor that I jumped when my Pop-tarts were ejected forcefully from the toaster. I shook my head and plunked the tarts onto a napkin then carried my balanced breakfast to the dining room table.

I kept my eyes on my food instead of the light on the floor as I ate. The last thing I needed was to start drifting off into dreams any time my body was still for five seconds. It seemed I was spending more time asleep than awake lately. At least, I think I was. I tried to sort out what the real Noah and Holden had said to me yesterday versus their dream selves but after a few minutes I decided it was an exercise in futility. I wished Noah were here to help me make sense of this.

The thought caused my emotions to start boiling all over again. I wondered where Noah was right now. And what he was doing last night while I was here, trying to earn my way into the loony bin. I was afraid to text him in case he didn't want to see me. I knew I would die at the slightest hint of rejection even if it were something legit like he had class or a doctor's appointment. I didn't want him to know how much I wanted to see him. The feeling I got when I was around him was indescribable. I was completely unprepared to deal with it. I silently muttered an apology to all the girls I'd made fun of when I saw them mooning over some guy.

I thought about the way he had taken my hand yesterday. The memory made me blush. I wanted to see him so badly, to be near him to see if he would touch me again. I had never held a guy's hand before. I didn't think I would ever get enough of the feeling.

Suddenly Holden's face pushed its way into my thoughts. It was the Holden I had met in the stone hall, his arms out to me. I felt a longing to be with him as well. This was followed by a pang of embarrassment that turned into guilt and finally revulsion. How was it I suddenly had two guys in my dreams? One who so much as admitted he was trying to be friends with Lexa, my best friend, just to try to get to me?

I looked down at the shredded Pop-tart on my napkin. My hands had not been idle while I'd been sifting through my thoughts. I popped one of the larger pieces in my mouth and focused on chewing the sweet pastry. My mug was still half full but the coffee had cooled considerably. I nudged the mug away from me. After a few more bites I decided I had to get ready to face my friends. If I still had friends.

Taking a shower was quite a challenge since I quickly discovered how badly soap stung the gash on my arm . I did my best to wash my hair with one hand and keep my left arm out of any stray bubbles. Trying to towel off was even more fun.

I didn't spend a lot of time examining the cut on my arm while I was trying to replace the bandage. I had been told after the first day or two the bandage wasn't medically necessary, but I didn't want to look at it. By the time I had tugged on jeans and a plain blue T it was a little after eight- still early.

I took my time finding where I had thrown my bag and shoes. When I grabbed my phone off of the nightstand I checked automatically for any missed calls or texts. A pang of sadness shot through me when I saw no one had left me either. With nothing more to do in my room, I wandering into the living room and threw myself on the couch. I started to reach for the remote then drew back. I wasn't in the mood to watch TV.

For the first time this morning I allowed myself to think about what I was going to do when I got to school. Believing I could fix all my problems with dreams was equally as laughable as it was insane. I was hoping Sawyer would let me apologize. Lexa would be another story though. Lexa was quick to get angry and very slow in forgetting. It went beyond being stubborn. I could think of plenty of times I petitioned her on someone else's behalf. Remembering that made being on this side of it even worse.

I glanced at the clock on the wall. Just past eight thirty. I considered sitting for a few more minutes but I was on my feet and headed for the door before I had fully dismissed the idea. Maybe if I could get there early I could catch Lexa before she got to the auditorium.

My stomach did another aerial flip when it saw the back of my car. Somehow I kept forgetting it had actually happened. The poor mangled bumper gleamed in the morning sunlight. I set my jaw, determined to ignore it, at least for now.

One problem at a time, I told myself.

CHAPTER TWENTY-ONE

The parking lot of the school was filling up quickly. I dismissed any delusions of parking close to the building and settled for a spot on the far side of the upper lot. I made sure my phone was on silent before throwing it and my keys in my book bag.

I threaded my way slowly through the cars. There were no spaces drawn in the lot and sometimes people were creative with how they parked. I swung my head side to side trying to spot Lexa or Sawyer's vehicles but I didn't see either.

There were clusters of students, parents, and teachers milling about outside the school. It hadn't occurred to me to invite Mom and Dad but I'm sure several other parents had already told them all about it. After last night I was perfectly fine spending as much time away from them as possible. A tiny twinge of sadness told me that my bravado may not be completely genuine.

One problem at a time.

I spotted an empty bench at the bottom of the stairs leading from the upper lot and made a beeline for it. I scanned the faces of people milling about but I saw no sign of Lexa's bronze highlights or Sawyer's bespectacled face. So I sat back to wait, trying not to look as awkward as I felt.

Although it seemed like I was sitting on the bench for

hours, it was probably only a few minutes before I saw Lexa coming down the stairs from the upper lot. She was walking with Allison, who was talking animatedly. I sat still, unsure if I should flag her down or not. My eyes must have been boring holes into her, however, because she started looking around as if I had called out to her. When Allison noticed me she smiled and waved as if nothing were wrong. Maybe she didn't know. I was fine with that. Lexa followed Allison's line of sight. When she saw me she hesitated for a moment before starting over, sitting down on the bench without saying a word.

I was afraid to speak so I just looked at her. She offered a half smile.

"I've been a little stressed lately," she stated bluntly.

"We all have," I rushed to agree. Afraid she might take it to mean I was belittling what sounded like the beginning of an apology I said, "Lex, I'm sorry-"

I was prepared to continue but she cut me off.

"I know. I went off yesterday, I'm not even really sure about what, but then this morning I realized that it may not have been the best thing I could've done," she shrugged as if to say it wasn't something worth talking about any more. Emboldened by her relaxed attitude I couldn't help but chuckle a little.

"You're just mad you had to endure Senior Skip Day without me," I said to her. She groaned and rolled her eyes.

"Ugh, it was awful," she admitted. I could tell by the shift in her tone that our discussion about yesterday was closed and would never be brought up again.

One down, one to go.

I began to feel nervous all over again at the thought of having to face Sawyer. While I considered Lexa's blow up to be in character for her even if it wasn't exactly warranted, Sawyer was a different matter. I had been a jerk to him. After my conversation with Lexa however I was feeling the tiniest bit hopeful. It was obvious I hadn't put her in a coma. My attempt at an apology last night might have even softened this conversation- if that were possible. I had nothing to worry about.

I told Lexa about my near death experience at the C&T. At the last minute I decided to leave out the Holden part. I felt extremely guilty talking to him behind her back and I didn't want to make her mad at me again. This time I would deserve it.

I had just completed the story, ending with my escape, when Sawyer came down the stairs from the upper lot. He saw Lexa and me on the bench and started toward us. My stomach rolled at his unreadable expression.

"Hey," I called eagerly. "Sawyer, thanks for all your help yesterday. I'm sorry I was- insane."

Sawyer nudged the edge of my flip-flop with the toe of his shoe then looked up at me. "I know," he said cryptically as a smile spread across his face. His smile calmed my churning stomach. I returned his grin then narrowed my eyes at him, bolstered by what looked to be my second successful apology.

"You know I appreciate your help or that I'm insane?" I asked.

"Yep," he replied, his smile widening. I kicked out half-heartedly. He dodged me easily.

"Okay, kids, let's take this party inside," Lexa announced. She stood and linked her arm with mine as we started toward the door, joining the masses headed into the auditorium.

Once inside, we made our way toward the front half of the huge room. The auditorium was loosely divided into four sections and seniors were front and center. The three of us found seats as far back as permissible and sat down on the itchy fabric-covered chairs that were entirely too small for anyone's comfort.

Teachers were scurrying around on stage, placing papers on the podium or pushing buttons on the projector. Even the teachers looked like they had a little extra skip in their step this time of year.

The auditorium seemed to echo and magnify everyone's voices. The roar was almost painful. The three of us sat in silence since no one had anything important enough to say to make screaming over the noise worth it. Finally Mr. Jones approached the podium and called for everyone's attention. It took several minutes before this was actually achieved though. Mr. Jones smiled down at us from the stage while he patiently waited for the roar to subside.

"I want to welcome everyone to the celebration of our sixty-eighth commencement here at Jefferson High. It's good to see all of the students, parents, and friends this morning. As another school year comes to an end we want to take a moment to celebrate our seniors in particular- to look back on their time here with us and to wish them well as they continue their journey."

Mr. Jones settled into a cadence not unlike that of a televangelist and I tried to get comfortable in my seat. I glanced to my left where Lexa sat with Sawyer just beyond her. Lexa was doodling in a notebook while Sawyer was using his hand to prop up his head. I hadn't thought to time my slideshow but I was praying it was short. I didn't want to go down in senior class history as the girl responsible for keeping us trapped here longer than necessary.

Mr. Jones wound down, thanking everyone again for attending, and introduced Mr. Garrard, the principal. Mr. Garrard was an unusual principal. He was a sweet fatherly figure who roamed the halls, smiling, occasionally poking his head into classrooms to make faces at us. He didn't seem to have a care in the world. He knew all of us by name as well as most of our parents. His friendly demeanor, however, wasn't an indicator that he was unable to deal with troublemakers. I'd seen him break up some intense fights.

Mr. Garrard made a short speech about how proud he was of us and how we were special compared to the other classes he had seen graduate. To illustrate his point he recalled a few quick stories about this or that memorable moment during the year and gave his congratulations to several students who had earned scholarships to various colleges.

I had finally slumped down into a semi-comfortable position but I still couldn't focus on what was being said. The harder I tried the more my mind wanted to do anything but pay attention. I felt like there was a lot of unprocessed information I needed to weed through. Something Lexa had said about how she felt different this morning. Did she mean the regular kind of I slept on it and now I feel differently or was it something else? While I had achieved my goal of patching things up with my friends I didn't have definitive proof that I'd done it using anything other than a good old-fashioned apology. But it had been the easiest apology of my life. If it had been the dream I could get used to this.

Holden's warning about the dangers of messing with someone else's mind echoed in my head. I didn't see how this had been dangerous at all. Of course, I was still skeptical that my dream had done this.

My mind drifted to the moment when Lexa and Sawyer had become Noah and Holden. I recalled the feeling that the three of us had known each other for a long time, much longer than my definition of a "long time" had previously encapsulated. They seemed so familiar to me. I could still see the scenes from other times and places- other lives, if I believed Holden and Noah.

I hadn't been paying attention to anything on the stage until all the lights dimmed save the bright projector screen. I let out a moan as I rolled my eyes and slid farther down in my seat. Lexa shot me a smile and I stuck my tongue out at her. Music from a pop compilation CD was broadcast over the PA system. Someone hit play on my slideshow. I could feel my cheeks getting hot. I shut my eyes, hoping to tune the whole thing out.

Predictably, my mind wandered back to Noah and Holden as it did every time it was given a moment of freedom. I didn't have any new thoughts on the subject though. I was hoping going over and over things would help me come to a conclusion but instead I just kept seeing the same frustrating images in my mind.

I took a deep breath against the aggravation I felt coming on and tried to relax. Music continued to play, punctuated here and there with laughter as someone recognized a photo of themselves or friends. Sometimes I wondered what they were laughing at but my eyelids were so heavy I couldn't open them. I let myself drift off, hoping I could get in a nap small enough to forgo any dreams.

༄ ༄༅ ༅

I was lying on the ground watching puffy white clouds race across a bright blue sky. As I watched, the blue faded quickly through the colors of the rainbow into black night. Stars came out in droves as the last of the clouds made their way across the sky. Shooting stars flashed and ribbons of color danced close to the horizon on my left. Then the sky dimmed until all the stars were gone. A faint light appeared above my head, washing everything gray. The cycle began again. I wasn't really sure what it meant but for the first time in ages I felt like I was alone inside my head.

Unfortunately, the feeling didn't last very long. I felt a change, a subtle shift that annoyed me more than it unnerved me. I wanted to close my eyes against the intruder but it seemed wrong to also shut out the wondrous march of day to night to day again that the sky was embarking on. I felt a weight growing on my body, pressing it more firmly into whatever I was lying on. It was as if I only had so much room in my world and the interloper was causing everything to compact to make room for him.

"Aren? If you can hear me, please, I need to talk to you. If you can hear me, meet me in the park. Aren?" The voice sounded familiar but I couldn't place it. There was something timeless about it that made it hard for me to discern if it belonged to someone young or old. A great hope welled up inside me that this could be the person who could finally explain everything to me. But my hope fell as quickly as it soared. It could all be more unverifiable stories, if not outright lies.

There was a sudden release of pressure. I felt weightless, expecting to float into the ever-changing sky. Instead I plummeted downward.

༄ ༄༅ ༅

"Aren!" Lexa hissed.

My head had slipped off the hand that had been propping it up. I woke, blinking, trying to remember where I was and found myself looking up at Lexa. She was standing, as were the rest of the seniors. She reached down and yanked me up. I had to shift a few times to get my feet under me. Swaying, I grabbed the chair in front of me for support.

The lights had come back on in the auditorium and Mr. Garrard was behind the podium again. I had dozed through the entire slideshow. Of course, it wasn't like I didn't know what was on it. Mr. Garrard was saying a few canned inspirational words before sending us out the door for the "last" time. Of course, we all had to be back here this afternoon for graduation rehearsal but that didn't seem to count.

"Good morning, Sleeping Beauty," Lexa quipped out of the side of her mouth, biting back a laugh. My eyes felt gritty and my mouth felt full of sand. I tried to swallow to get rid of the bad taste but my throat was too dry.

The audience began to clap and cheer. I got an elbow in the ribs from Lexa, who motioned me to start toward the doors with our classmates. I walked stiffly, as if my legs were half asleep. We exited into the foyer and continued until we were outside in the warm May sunshine. Students paused just outside the doors while they waited for friends and family who would exit after the senior class. I had to push my way through the bottlenecked students as I headed toward the parking lot. If I left now I could avoid the impending traffic jam. I had to get to the park as soon as possible.

There was a tug on my arm and I turned to see Lexa and Sawyer. I had forgotten they'd been behind me.

"Hey, where ya going?" Lexa asked.

"I have some errands," I blurted. "I was just going to take care of those before rehearsal. Why?"

My "why" had come out a little severe but Lexa either didn't notice over the din of the crowd or she chose to ignore it seeing as how we had just patched up our last misunderstanding.

"Some of us were going to grab something to eat

before rehearsal. You want to come?" she asked. Traitorous as always, my stomach hadn't been hungry until she'd mentioned food. Now it growled hollowly.

"Where? Maybe I can catch up with you later." Lexa frowned at this response. I tried to look apologetic. "I'm afraid I'll forget if I don't go now. I really need to take care of some things."

"I'm not sure where we're going. I'll text you," she said. I heard Ethan calling Lexa's name just then. I took the opportunity to bolt for the parking lot.

CHAPTER TWENTY-TWO

As I headed away from the school the foot traffic became less congested. I found my car right where I'd left it, which doesn't always happen in this parking lot, and climbed in. There were a few other students leaving but not many. Luckily, I didn't have a problem negotiating around the parked cars and out of the lot. I turned toward the park when I got to Main Street but I kept going past the first entrance in case someone was watching me. I didn't want to try to answer questions about what kind of errands I could possibly have to do at the park. I turned at the second entrance. It was only then I asked myself where I was supposed to be going. All I knew was to go to the park.

Actually, all I knew was I had dreamed I was supposed to go to the park. I still wasn't sure how much of this was real and how much of it was me losing my mind. I desperately hoped this would answer some of those questions. If someone, anyone, were waiting for me then I would know at least some of it were true.

My stomach lurched as a realized I didn't know who was waiting for me. Part of me had assumed it would be Noah but what if it were someone entirely new? I hadn't considered the possibility that there may be even more people involved in this. Before my mind let me go too far down the conspiracy theory road an imaginary pendulum swung back in the other direction, taking my thoughts with it. What if I really had dreamed all this up? What if I sit in the park all day and no one comes? What if I'm running around chasing spectres my brain has invented?

I tried to concentrate on where I was going but it wasn't easy trying to keep my self-doubting thoughts away. I was driving slowly through the park, my head twisting from side to side as I looked for a familiar face. There weren't many people in the park today. A few were walking the track and several moms had their toddlers on the playground. No one looked like they were waiting for me.

I parked on the far side of the soccer fields. I shut off the car and sat there, looking around but seeing no one. I got out, determined to walk every inch of the park if needed to settle the questions surrounding my sanity.

I had just locked the door and stepped onto the sidewalk when I caught sight of a lone figure near the lake making his way toward me. My vision blurred, making it seem like I was watching two or three figures occupying the same space, all of them headed in my direction. I blinked, trying to separate the projections from who was actually there. When my vision finally cleared I saw a single person whose name I couldn't remember.

I started walking, both of us moving slowly and stately. It was as if time had no meaning. I had begun to think that maybe it truly didn't. Now that I was staring at him from across the wide swath of grass separating the sidewalk from the lake visions flashed violently through my mind, showing me other times we had spent together. All the seemingly insignificant moments we shared that added up to a connection that couldn't be defined with any word I currently possessed in my vocabulary. The parade of images became a blur, fading quickly like dreams were supposed to.

We stopped when we were within inches of each other. We didn't touch. Neither of us spoke. I'm not sure the words we needed existed. We just stared. I could tell he was also experiencing something like the onslaught I had just been exposed to. I watched minute twitches of emotion cross his face. Every line seemed so familiar yet so new to me.

"Tell me you heard me," he said.

"I heard you."

"Do you believe I'm not crazy? I'm not lying to you? Why else would you have come here today?"

It was a very good question. I had no plans to be here. I only came because of the dream. Even then I wasn't sure who had spoken to me. I watched him, not answering immediately.

"Please-" he said, his voice thick. He reached out to me hesitantly, moving slowly as if he were waiting for me to bolt. It seemed to take him hours to reach across the few inches between us. When I didn't turn and run, he lightly brushed my hand with his fingertips. When I didn't disappear, he took my hand lightly in his, pulling me toward him. My hand felt numb and a tingly sensation raced up my arm. I was so close to him I had to lean my head back to look at him.

"I want to tell you everything, but I don't want to scare you," he swallowed hard to force the words back down his throat. His eyes darted back and forth as he searched my face, which was too close to be able to take in all at once.

"I can't believe this," I said breathlessly. His face fell quickly, disappointment splashed across it, but he recovered as best he could.

"I know the feeling," he said. His hand tightened around mine. My legs quivered.

"Why -" I stopped, not knowing what I was trying to ask.

He shook his head. "I don't know. Or if I do, I can't remember. I can't tell you how many times this has happened. I only started remembering things a few months ago. Something must have registered subconsciously, though. I had already come here to the college."

"Where are you from?" I asked him curiously. I hadn't given any thought to the notion that sometimes we may come back on opposite ends of the world. He laughed a little.

"Oregon," he answered quietly. I grinned, wondering what would have ever possessed him to think coming to college in our sleepy mid-western town was a good move. With a catch in my breath I wondered if it could actually be me.

I searched his face for a moment more then pulled back from him. His arm trailed after me as his hand tried to keep hold of mine. Eventually he had to choose between letting me go and tripping after me. He slowly let my hand slide from his. I took a few steps toward the lake and sank down into the grass. I tried to make it look like that had been my intention from the start but the truth was my legs could no longer support me. All the blood in my body seemed to have rushed to my head in a group effort to help me sort out what was going on. He hesitated before coming to sit beside me so close that our knees touched.

"Aren?" he asked, trying to look into my down turned face.

"It's like it's all there in my head but I can't accept it," I began. "I don't have any precedent that says I can and not be insane." I didn't realize until I said this that it was true. All this time I had been working toward believing what my dreams had been telling me but the truth was I simply didn't know how to accept it. I looked up at Holden. If anyone understood what I was saying, it had to be him.

And Noah.

Since the first time I met Noah this was the longest I had gone without him sneaking into my thoughts. Now the shiver of delight I got when I thought of him had turned into something else that I had no name for.

"I don't know where to start," Holden confessed. "I barely have a handle on it myself but when I realized I wasn't the only one I wanted to make sure you didn't have to go through it alone. And when I saw you," he looked away from me, hesitating, "I didn't want you to be alone- ever."

Though he spoke quietly I could clearly hear the conviction behind his vow. Thinking back to our first few encounters I saw that he had planned to stick around regardless of how I felt about it.

As I studied his face, I imagined I could see features belonging to a dozen other lifetimes. All of them had been dear to me or, at least, dear to the person I was. I wasn't sure if I was the same person every time or not. I may never know the answer to that question even if I had done this too many times to remember. My mind felt like it hit a brick wall as something reminded me that the ideas I had begun to entertain were completely foolish. Possibly dangerous, even.

This whole time Holden sat beside me, not moving, while watching me. I wouldn't be surprised if my thoughts were being displayed on my forehead as if a scrolling marquee had been installed there. My eyes wandered from him to the lake and back again.

"You've accepted this?" I asked.

"Yes," he said simply. "I thought I was going crazy. The dreams, the memories, the- accidents." His eyes darted to the cuts and scrapes on my arm. "Somehow the worse things got the more it made sense. One day it all clicked into place. No matter how crazy a person is I don't think it means they can reach out to another person's mind."

His reminder about the way our minds worked opened up an entirely separate problem for me. If the idea that I had lived multiple lives didn't make me crazy, the things that my mind could do would drive me mad if I didn't learn to control it. I didn't know how I could learn to control something I was still struggling to believe.

"What if I can't believe this?" I asked him.

"That's happened before," he whispered after some time. "I don't think it went well. Even if you don't remember, I'm sure you can imagine what happens when you're afraid of your own mind."

I looked down at the large bandage I wore against doctor's orders because I couldn't look at the stitches without being sick. The cuts started to throb dully under my attention. I shifted my focus back to him but I couldn't make the pain go away.

"What about Noah?" This was the last question he wanted to hear. He took a deep breath.

"I don't remember as much about him as I remember about you. Essentially we are the same in each life. He always finds us. But it seems no matter how he begins his life it always ends the same. No matter what he says, he wants power more than anything- and he doesn't care who he hurts while he's after it."

I felt as if a spell had been lifted and my logical fear of the person in front of me returned. It had been Noah- not Holden- who had come from nowhere to rescue me from my own mind.

"How can you be so sure?" I demanded. "He's been nothing but kind to me. He's helped me."

Holden was expecting any reaction but this. He drew back as if my anger had forcibly driven him away. His mouth opened but he didn't say anything. I continued to glare at him, trying to figure out why he would say something like that about the one person who had kept me from going out of my mind. Noah hadn't come after me like a deranged lunatic, unlike Holden's approach.

"He- I can remember. I can remember our other lives. Once he was my brother. Noah went to your uncle, our clan leader, and persuaded him to make your father marry you to himself instead of me. You were the only child between your uncle and your father. And he wanted that power. That and the power you have in here." He pointed to his temple.

I recalled the image of me greeting both men in a stone hall along with the man who must have been my father. The scene replayed over and over in my mind but I had no proof that any of it was true.

"I don't remember," I said flatly. What I recalled had to be dreams, not past lives.

"You will, you have to. But until then, please, stay away from him. I know he'll try anything to get his hands on you before you know who you are." His words were almost a whisper, but they caused me to bristle again.

"The only one who has tried to influence me is you. Noah- or whoever- has tried to help me keep my sanity through this. He's not all doom and gloom like you." I stood up, anxious to be away from him. "And another thing- I know who I am. I may or may not believe these dreams are real but they don't change anything."

Holden remained seated in the grass, looking up at me. My voice had started to rise as I spoke and I looked around to make sure there were no park patrons within earshot. I turned back to Holden who still watched me as if he expected everything he said to click into place in the next second. I felt sick with emotional overload. I wasn't sure how I'd gotten to my feet and remained there. I had to think hard about how to put one foot in front of the other. I really, really wanted to get away. I stumbled haltingly toward the parking lot, digging in my pocket for my keys.

I was concentrating so hard on walking that I didn't hear Holden behind me. My feet had hit the pavement when I heard Holden say my name, so close to me I almost jumped out of my skin. I turned, overbalanced. Holden had to grab my arm roughly to keep me from falling. I was at once grateful for the rescue and angry at his interference. If I wanted to fall on my face that was my own affair.

"Fine," he said to me, causing me to look at him quizzically. "Don't believe what I tell you about him. You have no reason to," he said bitterly. "But if you won't believe me then don't believe him either. Not until you've remembered everything."

His grip on my arm was so tight I was quickly losing feeling in my hand. The pain distracted me from being able to comprehend his words immediately. When understanding dawned, despair seemed to sweep over me like a fast rolling fog. He was asking me to cut myself off from the two people who professed to know the real me while I waited to remember something I didn't even believe was in me. I stared at him, my mouth agape. He looked like he was going to continue to speak but he hesitated when he saw my face. I used his moment of doubt to wrench my arm out of his grasp.

It was only a few more steps to my car. I was sliding behind the wheel when Holden started toward me again. I slammed down the lock, afraid of what he would do if he reached me. I didn't look behind me to see where he was as I peeled out of the parking space and slammed the gear shifter into drive.

CHAPTER TWENTY-THREE

It was so quiet in the car I could hear my stomach growling, which did nothing to help my mood. I was further agitated when I looked at the clock and realized I didn't only miss lunch but I was also in imminent danger of being late to graduation rehearsal. Since I was giving a speech before the ceremony I was pretty sure my absence would be noticed. I swore under my breath as I halted at the stop sign. I counted to three then moved out into traffic to make my way as quickly as I could to the school.

I opted to skip going up and down each makeshift aisle in the student lot looking for somewhere to park and settled on the first place I saw. I was only a few minutes late. Surely I couldn't be the only one. I locked my door and slammed it shut. I was on the far side of the lot from the stairs but I refused to run. I compromised by trying to stretch my legs to cover as much ground as I could with every step. All that accomplished was making my shins hurt.

My legs still felt a little wobbly but I made it across the parking lot and down the stairs without incident. I didn't see anyone lingering outside, which made me nervous. I began to worry that they had changed the time or the place without telling me. I threw open the heavy metal and glass entry door and stepped inside, glancing around to see if anyone was waiting to point and laugh at my tardy entrance. There were several other students milling about but no one seemed to notice me. I could hear more people inside the auditorium. I assumed from the din that rehearsal hadn't started on time. I scanned the foyer again, this time looking for friendly faces. Seeing no one, I moved into the auditorium.

Mrs. Donovan was near the stage, talking to the junior attendants. Seniors milled about in various clusters, some sprawled in chairs, others sitting on the edge of the stage. My heart was pounding in my head and my stomach echoed like a hollow cavern. I swept my head from side to side trying to find Lexa but on the third sweep I had to stop walking while I searched. Gripping the back of the nearest chair I scanned the room slowly. I finally found Lexa standing near the front of the auditorium talking to Allison and Hana. With my destination fixed firmly in my sights I made my way down to the girls.

"Hi," I said, giving a small wave.

"Where've you been?" Lexa asked me. "You never returned any of my texts."

"Yeah," I said, scrambling for an answer. I decided to go with the truth. "I left my phone in the car."

She seemed to be unable to find fault with that so she simply nodded.

"Are you ready for this?" Hana asked me. I started to open my mouth to give some kind of witty response but the look on her face made me unsure of what she was talking about.

"I'm ready for it to be over," Allison quipped. I nodded in agreement.

"I'm not really sure how walking across a stage is so difficult that it requires practice," I added. Suddenly I felt a goofy grin sliding into place. This was the first time in what felt like forever that I'd had a meaningless conversation. I turned as Lexa let out a short laugh, whether at what I'd said or the look on my face I wasn't sure. I couldn't really find it in me to care.

Movement from the junior attendants caught my eye as they broke away from their huddle around Mrs. Donovan and rushed up the aisles.

"Everyone," she called in a voice that echoed off of the back wall, "please come forward when your name is called. We are going to review seating. Then we will practice your entrance and go over the schedule for tomorrow's graduation."

Conversation died down for the most part as we waited for Mrs. Donovan to start calling names from her clipboard. I could see her lips move as she read the first few names to herself before looking up.

"Aren, you're right here," she said to me, pointing to the first seat in the first row. I suddenly felt extremely self-conscious. With a glance at Lexa I moved slowly to my seat, praying my wobbly legs would hold me up. I sat down and Mrs. Donovan continued through her list.

Hana's name was next and I gave her a half smile as she took the seat beside me. We sat silently and listened as Mrs. Donovan called out more names.

I seized this opportunity to start in with the pep talks. Tomorrow I was going to have to stand in front of a packed auditorium and give a speech that felt like it had been written by a stranger a hundred years ago. As much as I would like to tell myself there was no pressure in reading a few words in front of people I had known my whole life my stomach was telling me a different story. My lack of lunch was giving the butterflies plenty of room to flutter around. I hoped I wasn't expected to read the speech as I hadn't brought it. This made the butterflies kick their flight into warp speed.

"Aren, you're green," Hana said softly to me.

"I didn't bring that stupid speech- I hope I'm not supposed to read it," I said. Saying this out loud made it sound stupid so I stopped talking.

"I doubt it," she whispered. "Mrs. Donovan knows we aren't really excited to be here so I'd say she'll let us go as soon as possible." She glanced at Mrs. Donovan. "It doesn't look like this is her first choice for how to spend her day either."

I looked up as she continued to call out names. She did seem about as excited as we were. When everyone was seated, which didn't take long when the graduating class was less than a hundred people, she had us all stand. We walked back out of the auditorium in a neat, single file line into the foyer and across the entryway into the gym/cafeteria where we were to report tomorrow for roll call.

Our line barely reached down one side of the cafeteria. We lounged against the wall while Mrs. Donovan went around the line answering questions, though I'm not sure what kind of questions anyone could have yet. The anxiety I felt about my speech had passed. Now I was anxious to get out of here. Holden and Noah had once again crept into my thoughts and I wanted to be alone to sort them out.

After a few more moments Mrs. Donovan called for me to start our march back through the foyer and into the auditorium. I wasn't overjoyed at the prospect of leading our procession and started praying now that I wouldn't fall on my face tomorrow. Luckily I made it down the long sloping aisle of the auditorium without any major snags. I made a mental note to wear shoes with a low heel for the ceremony.

"Now, after everyone is seated, I will say a few words," Mrs. Donovan informed us, looking down from the stage. "Then Aren will give her speech."

"Aren," she turned her attention to me. "You will come up on that side of the stage-" she pointed toward my right- "give your speech then exit on the other side to go back to your seat. Mr. Garrard will say a few words. After that we will start the reading of the names-"

Mrs. Donovan continued walking us through how graduation would proceed, finishing by asking if there were any questions. Her tone indicated she was in no mood to entertain any but a few people didn't take the hint. I sat there while several people asked questions, none of which I heard. I was leaning on my armrest, my head cradled in my hand. A large yawn escaped me.

I was so lost in my own thoughts I didn't hear Mrs. Donovan excuse us. It was Hana tapping me gently on the shoulder that brought me back to reality.

"Hey, wake up. Time to get out of here," Hana said

cheerily. I blinked and stood to stretch.

"I'm out of it today," I felt compelled to explain.

Hana observed the throng of people trying to get out of the auditorium via the doors in the back then walked past the crowded aisles to the side door at the edge of the stage. I followed her as she led the way outside.

"Well, I think I'm going home to take a nap," she told me.

"Yeah-" I started to second her motion until I remembered what happened when I slept. Hana looked at me for a moment as if she were waiting for me to continue. I was saved when we heard Lexa calling my name.

"Hey!" I shouted back at her. Students were streaming out of the front doors now and Lexa was elbowing her way through, her head bobbing in and out of view.

"How did you guys get out so fast?" she asked when she caught up to us. Hana jerked a thumb in the direction of the side door. Lexa raised her eyebrows and mouthed "oh."

"I'm off guys, see you later." Hana waved as she joined the other seniors who were making their way to the parking lot.

"See ya," Lexa called after her. Then she turned to me. "What've you got planned for the rest of the day? Any more errands?"

My brow furrowed at her tone that implied she might not have believed I was out running errands this morning. After a beat I decided I was just being paranoid. "I don't have anything."

"Good, come on. I need you," Lexa grabbed my good wrist and started dragging me toward the upper parking lot.

"For what?" I asked.

"You-" she said pointedly- "have been neglecting your duty to help me find something to wear tomorrow. Now it's down to the eleventh hour and I need help. This is not something I can do alone."

I snorted. She could very well do this on her own, she just didn't want to.

Lexa had released my wrist once she felt sure I wasn't going to head for the hills. We reached her car quickly, which was parked much closer than mine. Thinking about my car reminded me of where I had gone this morning, which caused my face to warm with something akin to shame. Lexa had thought Holden was interested in her. As far as I knew she hadn't spoke to him in days although I had seen him twice. I had almost been killed because of him. Or perhaps it had been the other way around, I still wasn't sure. And now he was trying to convince me we were old souls destined to find each other again and again. The fervor of his words made a chill run down my spine.

"It's open," she called to me from inside the car.

I yanked open the door and threw myself inside, bashing my forehead on the opening in my scramble. I pulled the door closed behind me and put my head in my hands, trying to massage away the pain. Lexa didn't even try to stifle her laugh as she started her car and joined the mass exodus from the student parking lot.

"So, what's been up? I feel like I haven't seen you at all this week." Another stab of guilt swept through me. I had to get that under control.

"Yeah, it's been a weird week." I felt the need to explain myself but I bit my tongue. I was afraid if I started talking I would spill everything and there was no way I could tell Lexa. The hollow in my stomach turned sour as a profound feeling of loneliness took residence there.

"So," Lexa continued when she accepted that I wasn't going to elaborate, "did you ever convince your parents to let you go with us for senior week?"

I was a little startled by the reminder that there was something beyond graduation. My week had seemed to be moving toward Saturday's festivities as an end to a book, not a chapter.

"No luck," I sighed.

I had begged my parents to let me go to the beach with my friends but they held tight to the argument that they didn't have the money to send me. Once I realized how much I would have to fork out for the trip versus how much money I had from my sporadic babysitting stints –and the fact that my parents were counting each cent of graduation money so they could make sure it all went toward college– I had let the matter die slowly with the tiniest bit of relief. Lexa didn't have to know that though.

"That sucks," she sympathized. "Hana told me yesterday she can't go either. And I'm not sure I'm going to be able to put up with Allison talking about Ethan for a week."

"Really?" I asked, genuinely surprised. I hadn't paid much attention to Allison considering all that was going on. Now that I thought about it I was surprised she'd been hanging around so much lately.

"Oh yeah. Driving me crazy. She's talked to me more in the last few weeks than she has our entire lives. Ever since Ethan broke up with what's-her-name."

"Stacy," I supplied automatically.

"Yeah, her," Lexa nodded.

We had finally crawled our way out of the parking lot and were headed toward the interstate. This meant we had some serious shopping to do. Jefferson didn't have much in the way of variety when it came to shopping. That meant if we needed something more than groceries or notebooks we had to take the thirty-minute drive to the next town over. They boasted a real mall that housed about forty stores. To us it was like Fifth Avenue. This was the reason you could find every high schooler in a fifty-mile radius hanging out there on any given weekend. As we hit the four-lane highway I looked out the window. The sun had dipped behind a growing cover of clouds that looked fairly murky. The dark sky rolling in reflected the way I felt. My mood had only blackened as the day went on. I wondered briefly if I had the power to change the weather as well. Feeling ridiculous for even allowing myself that thought I stuck my tongue out at my reflection in the glass.

"Where are we going first?" I asked her. I was almost afraid of the answer. Lexa was famous for going to every store in the mall only to return to the very first article of clothing she saw in the very first store- about four hours later. "I do have to be home before midnight," I half-joked.

"I figured we'd just kinda walk around and see what we see," she said vaguely, ignoring my comment about having to be home before midnight.

Good thing the mall closes at nine.

"So," she drawled, "let's hear the story on this Noah guy you've been talking to every time I turn around. Spill."

My body tensed. My mind started rushing through everything that had happened since I met Noah. There didn't seem to be much I could tell her. I sighed, trying to figure out where to start. She took this as a sigh of longing and grinned.

"Um, I don't know what to say," I said honestly. "You were there when I met him at the C&T. Then he just sort of kept showing up."

"Has he asked you out?" Lexa probed.

"No. I mean, he's asked me to meet him at the C&T but that's it."

"Do you like him?"

My lips parted to respond in the affirmative but then I paused. I hadn't seen Noah since Thursday afternoon. I tried to tell myself that it had only been twenty-four hours but it seemed like years. I knew it was all because of Holden and the things he had said. But the little seeds of doubt he had planted seemed to be taking root whether I wanted them to or not.

"Come on," Lexa cajoled when I didn't answer, "you must like him. I've never seen you with that stupid grin on your face before."

"Yeah, I like him," I admitted, though I could hear my heart wasn't in it. At this point I wanted nothing to do with him or Holden if this confusion was what it caused. But a part of me felt like my world would be much emptier without Noah. Possibly without both of them.

"I see," Lexa was trying to be calmly conversational but I could hear the excitement in her voice. "He goes to the college, right?"

"Yeah. Freshman," I stated rather smugly. It didn't matter who you were, every high school girl wanted to be able to boast a college boyfriend.

"I've never seen him before. He's hot."

Her comment called to mind his beautiful green-flecked brown eyes that I could stare into all day. And his wavy hair that looked so silky I wanted to run my fingers through it. I could feel the flush creeping into my face. I thought once again about how long it had been since I'd seen him. This time Holden's words lost some of their potency when facing how much I wanted to see Noah. The need to see him overpowered even my growling stomach. I began to fantasize about the prospect of the date Lexa hinted at. I shivered as I remembered the soft touch of his hand on my face in the parking lot of the C&T.

"Lexa, I really like him." A dam burst somewhere inside, filling me with euphoria at both the remembered and imagined moments spent with Noah. "I'm not sure what to do. The other night I wanted to fling myself at him. He's so smart, too. I mean, he's amazing-"

Lexa laughed. "I knew it! Look at you- all crazy over some guy. I always wondered if I'd ever get to meet the man who met your lofty criteria."

"Ha, ha," I said dryly. Lexa had teased me for years about my high standards when it came to boys. I had come to think she meant to distract me from thoughts about what was wrong with me if no one wanted to date me. Occasionally someone would ask me out but I had never been interested, usually because it was the guys at school who asked everyone out. I never mentioned them to Lexa because she would have wanted to overanalyze why I didn't go out with whoever it was. The truth was I just hadn't seen the point in dating.

"So, what's he like? Where's he from?" she asked when I made no other response to her jab about my high standards.

"Um, I'm not sure where he's from. We haven't talked about it. Mostly it's about our classes or projects we have going on. We talk about our day, you know, normal stuff." When I said it like that it sounded like we had the most boring conversations. But other than talking about dreams I couldn't really think of anything else Noah and I had spoken about. Lexa seemed unimpressed as well.

"When are you going to see him again?" she asked.

This time the sigh of longing that escaped me was genuine.

"I don't know when I'll see him again," I admitted.

"He hasn't called or text or anything?" she asked.

"No, I haven't heard from him. But it's only been since yesterday."

"Why don't you call him? Or at least text him? You know, just to tell him 'hi' or something." Lexa suggested.

"I couldn't," I protested. "What if I look clingy or desperate? I don't want him to think I'm stalking him."

"You've given him a whole day without talking to you, I don't think that puts you in the stalker category. But the weekend is coming up. Maybe he'll ask you out. He's crazy about you," Lexa said with a grin.

Lexa always thought everyone was crazy about someone. This time though I wanted her observations to be true.

"Ok, enough," I told her, ready to get out from under the microscope for a second. "What's going on with you?"

"Oh, nothing," she said in a way that meant there was definitely something.

"Ok," I said, not taking the bait. I looked out the window as if I was completely uninterested in whatever she wanted me to pry from her. She gave it a moment before she spoke again.

"Hey, do you remember that guy from the other day? Holden?"

I was glad I was facing away from her. I don't think I could control my expression as my eyes widened and I sucked in a breath. This was not where I wanted our conversation to go.

"Maybe. That guy at the C&T?" I asked coolly.

"I don't see how you could forget. Noah went after

him pretty hard. What was with that, by the way? Did he tell you?" I saw Lexa's reflection look my way but I kept my gaze on the scenery that was flying by.

"No, he never said," I answered truthfully. Holden had given me an idea of what it had been about but Noah hadn't explained it to me himself. "So what about him?"

"I don't know," she started. "I just think he seems nice. And, I mean, if he goes to the college and I'm going to be starting there in the fall, maybe I'll be seeing a lot more of him."

"You like him?" Disbelief colored my words. I realized my reaction was due in part to some jealous notion that Holden belonged to my world now.

"Yes," she said defensively, "why?"

"Sorry," I backpedaled. "I was just surprised."

I was having trouble thinking about Lexa and Holden together. No matter what he said, or what I dreamed, I told myself I didn't want anything to do with him. But I didn't want my best friend to have anything to do with him either. I suddenly recalled what he had told me about why he started talking to Lexa in the first place. Some cruel part of me wanted to tell her, to let her have a taste of what it feels like to not be wanted. Maybe it would make her stop thinking about him. But I knew I couldn't do that to her.

Wanting to smooth things over I asked her for more details, even though I didn't want to hear them. "What did you guys talk about?"

"Oh, you know. School and stuff," Lexa answered taciturnly. I shot her a look but I didn't say anything. Usually you couldn't get Lexa to shut up about her latest love interest.

Soon Lexa was turning off at the exit that led to the mall. We sat in companionable silence until she pulled into the parking lot and started to circle the massive building. I knew I was in trouble when she parked at the far end. The far end meant we were going to start at one side of the mall and work our way down the entire length. On the way back would be when purchases were made, if any were made at all after hours of trudging from store to store. I prayed it would only be one circuit of the mall-when she began making multiple laps we were in real trouble.

I got out of the car when Lexa shut the engine off.

"Ready?" she asked me enthusiastically.

"If I have to be," I responded as I fell in step with her.

CHAPTER TWENTY-FOUR

I only made it through one store before I was begging for a side trip to get something to eat. I settled for buying a pretzel at the stand outside the enormous department store we had just trekked through. Lexa, impatient to find her next great buy, went ahead of me into another clothing store while I took a seat on the bench facing its entrance. The soft, warm pretzel tasted like ambrosia. My stomach, empty for so long, started to make noises at the unexpected intake of food.

I tried to eat as slowly as possible. I told myself it was because I didn't want to scarf it down and make myself sick but it was really because I wasn't in the mood to be shopping. I felt like I owed it to Lexa though considering how difficult I'd been this week.

I had finished my pretzel and was fishing around in the bag for a napkin when a shadow fell over me. Thinking Lexa had finished her second store I put on my yes-I'm-enjoying-myself smile and looked up. I froze for a moment in confusion before my smile became genuine.

Noah stood grinning down at me, his hands in his pockets. He was so close I had to look up at an uncomfortable angle to see his face. Thinking back to the conversation on the way here I realized my memory of his brown eyes didn't do him justice. He was wearing a dark green t-shirt with some kind of stylized blue bird on it over dark jeans with his signature smile.

"Hi," I said.

"Hi, yourself," he responded. He took half a step back in case I had designs on getting up but I had no intention of standing. After a beat Noah sat down beside me on the bench.

"What are you doing here?" I demanded.

"Hey, it's a public place, I'm allowed," he joked. My face flushed as I realized my tone was less than cordial. "I just needed to get out for a little while, you know?"

"I guess so. I wouldn't have thought the mall would have been your first choice," I said, hoping this explained my disbelief at his being here. I wondered if it was possible that I had subconsciously reached out to him to let him know where I would be. It wouldn't be the craziest thing I'd heard this week.

"It's a change of scenery," he shrugged. I nodded, not wanting to open my mouth and say something else completely ridiculous. "What are you up to?"

"Shopping with Lexa," I responded automatically. "She's in there. I skipped lunch today," I explained as I held up the empty pretzel bag.

"So I guess everything worked itself out between the two of you?" he asked. I smiled, recalling his advice that I try to use my dreams to help smooth things over with Lexa and Sawyer.

"Yes. Everything's good," I told him.

"What about you? Do you believe me?"

The look in his eyes was a silent plea. He seemed so alone and vulnerable, looking for someone else to understand him. I felt strained, my resolve to give up trying to make sense of it all thrown back in my face at the first opportunity. It was as if the entire mess refused to give me room to breathe so I could figure things out.

"I do," I heard myself say, shocking both Noah and myself. "I'm not really sure I know what it means though."

I watched his eyes widen slightly. He flashed me his crooked smile and I lit up inside. I knew people said this feeling faded after a while but I couldn't imagine ever becoming immune to his smile.

"Aren, you're amazing," he said. The light inside me became a beacon. The rational part of my brain asked me how someone could have this effect on me but the emotional side was so busy basking in Noah's glow that she didn't answer.

"You're a natural," he continued. "Aren, do you realize how incredible you are? You could do anything with your gifts. Anything you want could be yours."

I blushed at the complements. I wanted so badly for him to be happy with me.

"Noah, I..." I tried to respond to his flurry of flattering remarks but I couldn't think of anything to say. It was taking everything I had not to throw myself at him right there in the middle of the mall.

"Aren, I want-" he hesitated- "I can't stop thinking about you. Could we spend more time together?"

As he spoke quietly, his eyes drifted away from my face to the floor. I watched him while attempting to process his words. I must have been dreaming. Noah looked back at me when I didn't say anything, searching my face for a sign of acceptance or rejection. He looked so innocent, so vulnerable, that my heart ached.

"Noah," I breathed slowly, "I think I would like that."

His face lit up like a kid's at Christmas. He started to open his mouth then closed it. He tried again.

"I can't wait to show you everything I know. It means so much to meet someone who I can really talk to, who knows what's going on. It's like a dream come true. There won't be anything we can't do. Aren, I-"

"Aren-"

Noah and I both turned when we heard Lexa calling my name. Her tone said she couldn't believe anything was taking me so long but she hesitated when she saw what had been keeping me. I could already see the questions burning in her eyes. Lexa also didn't know when to leave things alone, however, so she continued her approach.

"Hi," Lexa said brightly as she came closer.

"Hi," Noah acknowledged. He and I stood at the same

time. He turned to me, "I'm sorry I kept you. But I'll see you soon?"

I saw the same flash of vulnerability in his eyes.

"Yes," I told him huskily. He grinned before he turned and walked away.

"What the...?" Lexa turned a quizzical expression my way. I was still tongue-tied. I took a moment to toss my empty pretzel bag into a nearby trashcan while I gathered my thoughts. Lexa waited patiently. Or, as patiently as Lexa knew how to wait. When I didn't say anything a few seconds after turning back to her she figured I needed prompting. "Did you know he was going to be here?"

"No," I responded. "He just appeared out of nowhere."

"And?"

"And what? What do you think, Lexa?" I was trying to turn my impatience into teasing. "We talked."

Clearly Lexa didn't expect me to stop without giving her details. She stared at me, waiting. I couldn't help wanting to torture her a little by holding back.

"Talked about what?" she finally asked.

What could I say we talked about?

"Nothing much," I mumbled in an attempt to mollify her. "He just said he would like to maybe spend some more time together."

She clasped her hands together and gave a melodramatic squeal of delight. I had underestimated how much I would need to tell Lexa to satisfy her, however. She glanced over her shoulder, probably to make sure Noah wasn't standing behind her, before she commenced her interrogation that would make the Spanish Inquisition look like old ladies gossiping at afternoon tea.

"Is that exactly what he said? I need to know exactly how he worded it," she pressed. "Did he make plans or suggest anything? Did he say anything before that?"

I felt the blush creep back into my face as I thought about what he had said.

"I knew it! What did he say?"

"He just said, well, he told me he couldn't stop thinking about me. And that I was amazing." Even repeating what he said felt unreal. I couldn't believe he could feel that way about me. My nose wrinkled involuntarily as a flicker of self-doubt invaded my thoughts. Without him standing in front of me it seemed I might have made it all up.

Lexa, however, was over the moon at this revelation. She grinned widely then frowned when she noticed my face.

"Stop it. Right now. Do you hear me?" she spoke harshly with all the authority of a mother hen. "He likes you, Aren!"

I rolled my eyes at Lexa's uncanny ability to read my face.

"Don't we have some shopping to do?" I asked, suddenly very tired of the spotlight. Immediately, Lexa hooked my arm in hers and started towing me down the mall.

"Of course we do. I can always talk *and* shop," she grinned as she dragged me to the next store.

CHAPTER TWENTY-FIVE

Lexa dropped me off at my car sometime around eight thirty. She had found a dress and heels for graduation as well as a pants and boots ensemble in case she woke up in a completely different mood tomorrow than she was in today. She waited to make sure I got in my car with no trouble before waving and driving away.

As expected, Mom and Dad were already home when I got there. I realized belatedly I should have probably called them to let them know I was going to be late. I sighed. *Too late now.*

I let myself in the house like nothing was amiss and strolled into the living room. Mom was on the couch reading a book while Dad flipped through channels way too fast to actually see any of them.

"Hey," I said.

"Hi," Mom started in a tone that said she was trying to hide her annoyance under a layer of casual disinterest. "How was your day?"

"We had graduation practice and stuff," I told them. "Then I helped Lexa with some errands."

Errands sounded much more respectable than shopping for unnecessary clothes.

"Oh," Mom said. "Well, I didn't know you were going to be late so dinner's in the kitchen. We already ate."

"Thanks," I said, trying to sound as cheerful as I could.

Mom turned back to her book so I took this as a dismissal.

I went into the kitchen, throwing my bag on the counter, to see what was for dinner. I found mashed potatoes, mac'n'cheese, and chicken in the fridge. I heaped food on a plate and put it in the microwave. I watched the seconds tick down then pulled the plate out before the microwave dinged. I could hear muted conversation coming from the living room and decided to take my plate to my room. I threw my bag over my shoulder, put my fork in my mouth, and carried the hot plate gingerly in both hands while willing my left arm not to give out.

I sat the plate on my desk before putting my bag down and shutting the door. I dug into my dinner, telling myself I didn't care about whatever it was Mom and Dad were whispering to each other. Instead, I thought about what I was going to do with the rest of my evening. I didn't have to get up early tomorrow but upon remembering that tomorrow was graduation I began to get a little nervous

I inhaled my dinner, finally full for the first time all day, and quietly walked with my plate back into the kitchen. Mom and Dad were still talking, though they weren't whispering anymore, probably because they thought I was still in my room.

"-probably normal. She's had a lot on her plate and that can be stressful," I heard my mom say, though there was a lingering doubt in her voice.

"This isn't the first time she's been under stress," Dad answered lamely. It seemed like they were wrapping up a discussion that had lost steam a while ago. I couldn't tell if it was due to the subject having been exhausted or if it was because they had been having the same conversation over and over. I rolled my eyes, cursing the microscope an only child is placed under.

After a pause, Dad continued. "I'm just pointing out that this happened rather suddenly, this shift. She seems so preoccupied lately. And there's her figurines, then her car-"

"Just a bad week," Mom interrupted. The words sounded tired-like they have been used too many times already.

"If this bad week goes on much longer..." he let his words hang ominously in the air. Mom didn't give him any kind of answer.

I was a little dazed. It was as if they were talking about another person, not me- their daughter. I padded back down the hallway toward my room a few paces then came down the hall again, this time making more noise. I went into the kitchen and placed my plate in the sink, rattling the other dishes as I did so.

"Aren, is that you?" Dad called as I started to head back to my bedroom. Biting back the question of who else could it possibly be I made my way into the living room, stopping in the entryway. Dad gestured to me. "I wanted to take a look at your arm."

I walked over and dutifully held out my arm. He looked up at me questioningly as he began to remove the bandage. When I didn't offer an explanation he felt the need to ask. "Why do you still have the bandage? It doesn't need to be covered up."

"I don't like to look at it," I answered as he pulled off the last of the medical tape.

"I guess that makes sense." His comment made it sound like it added up to more than me not liking to stare at stitches all day.

Dad gently moved my arm this way and that to look at the stitches as well as the small scratches around it. When he was done with his inspection he let go of my arm. I tried to massage the unbroken skin on my forearm, endeavoring to relieve some of the soreness from the unaccustomed movement. I hadn't realized how much I had been avoiding using my arm.

"It looks like it's healing up well," he said as he sat back in his chair, almost like he couldn't believe it. "You probably need to wash it, carefully, and then put some of that antibiotic on it. If you can stand it don't bandage it tonight."

I nodded and took the opportunity to make an exit. I

headed toward the bathroom and dutifully washed my arm as carefully as I could. I felt exposed without my bandage but I was determined to do my best to follow Dad's instructions.

After caring for my arm, which made it feel even sorer, I changed into shorts and a t-shirt even though I didn't feel the tiniest bit sleepy. Sleep and all that came with it had become almost worse than being awake. I wasn't sure if I would ever be able to sleep again.

Confined to the safe haven of my room thanks to the conversation I had overheard, I reached for the book on my nightstand. After re-reading the same paragraph three times I figured reading wasn't going to work. I put the book back on the nightstand, frustrated.

I couldn't think of anything I wanted to do so I just sat there. I looked around, taking inventory of my stuff. I would be packing up everything pretty soon to head east for college. It still seemed surreal to me. Every summer for as long as I could remember had ended with starting back to school here with the same people. I had nothing to compare what it would be like to move away and it made me nervous. I had never been very good with stepping into the unknown.

This made me want to laugh as I realized my entire week had been spent thrashing around in previously unknown territory. I tried to think back to the beginning of the week but it seemed so far away it might as well have been years ago. All of a sudden I felt so tired I could barely lift my arms to tug down the comforter on my bed.

As I was burrowing underneath it there was a soft knock on my door. I paused, unsure I had actually heard anything. The knock sounded again and this time Mom said my name.

"Yes?" I called tentatively. Mom opened the door and stepped in. Evidently she had drawn the short straw as to who was going to come talk to me.

"Going to bed early?" I wasn't quite sure if it was a question or a statement but I decided to comment anyway.

"It's been a long week. I'm hoping if I go to bed now

I'll get a little sleep before I remember I have to give a speech tomorrow."

"I can understand that." Mom said it in a way that made me unsure if she really did understand, but I let it go. She came over and sat on the edge of my bed. "I just wanted to check on you. I haven't seen you much this week and I know a lot's going on right now."

"I'm fine," I said immediately. Mom's eyebrows drew together slightly and I realized that wasn't going to be enough to satisfy her. "It's been a hectic week with all the end of the year stuff. I'll be a lot better once I get tomorrow over with."

Mom watched me for a moment then decided she had the best answer she was going to get.

"Ok. Well, get some sleep," she said with a little smile. She planted a butterfly kiss on my forehead and turned off the light before closing the door behind her.

I lay in the near darkness with my eyes wide open. As strange as the day had been I anticipated it would not compare to what would happen after I closed my eyes. I wasn't sure what direction my dreams would take and I didn't know if I was up to the task of trying to keep them under control. I thought back over my day. The morning with Lexa and Sawyer who appeared to have forgiven me. Holden asking me to meet him in the park. Then running into Noah at the mall.

Remembering Noah made me smile to myself, but there was a new wariness in the back of my mind. As much as I wanted to deny it I also felt a certain pull toward Holden. I wasn't sure how to describe what I felt for each of them but I knew it was both more complicated and intense than I would have liked.

I also wasn't sure if my mind was up to the task of separating the fact from the fiction. Both of them had told me things in my dreams as well as my waking hours that would easily convince someone to lock all of us up in the nearest mental ward. A week ago I would have said they needed to be carted away if I had heard their story second hand. But some grain of truth seemed hidden in their words, no matter how fantastical it sounded. There was something that tied the three of us together for much longer than any one person's memory could recall.

I wasn't sure when I'd accepted that I was what they said I was. Part of my mind asked why I wasn't breaking down in hysterics but I didn't have a good answer. Instead of searching for one I let myself sink farther and farther into the calmness that had come so unexpectedly.

ye ye ye

My hands were cold against my face, which had already been warmed by the open fire. I could hear the wind howling at the mouth of the cave and knew from the sharp tang in the air a blizzard was on its way, if it wasn't already here. The smell differed from the musty smell of fungus that grew in the dark and the small puddles of stagnant water that would never dry without the sun. I could smell the pungent odor of furs that hadn't had quite enough time to cure before we'd moved on from where their previous owners had been hunted down. The scent was both repugnant and comforting. I drew the large animal hide closer around me to ward off the chill that battled for a place near my skin.

I couldn't see much around me for the brightness of the fire. The large blaze burned steadily and my eyes stung from the smoke that was trapped in the cave with us. I squinted, trying to see around the fire to count how many of us were jammed together. People were bundled in furs like me, huddling in groups to stay warm. The area outside of the fire's light was so dark I couldn't make out individual shapes, but I knew more people were there. This news wasn't alarming in the least, however. I knew these people, I trusted them. They were family.

I was suddenly aware that I was an intruder in the consciousness of another person. Through her I could smell the sharp scent of the bitter cold that seeped into our hiding place from outside. I looked behind me and discovered the storm outside was obscured by the narrow exit that twisted its way out of the room we had sheltered in.

Having nothing else to do, I turned back to stare at the fire. I could simultaneously see the entire room from a distance and see through the eyes of the person I had once been. The double vision was dizzying and I prayed she wouldn't move very much. My prayers were too late as shouting came from the mouth of the cave, causing her to stand quickly, simultaneously dropping her furs. The instant cold was shocking and she bent to pick up the hides and wrap them around her again.

Men carrying crude torches walking single file came into view around the bend in the entrance. Their clothing and hair was covered in snow and ice. Some of them had half filled sacks slung over their shoulders, the sight of which was met by cheers from the gathered crowd. I could smell the blood seeping through the bags. The hunters had returned with food, however meager.

One of the men broke from the line to walk straight for the girl that was me. Without saying a word he put his hands on her shoulders and drew her to him, kissing her roughly on the mouth. The kiss made my head swim and my stomach seemed to drop to the floor. I had never been kissed before and I wondered if it actually felt like this. The intensity made me feel self-conscious but from what I could see from across the room no one thought this behavior was anything but ordinary.

I tried to see his face through her eyes, which was covered in shadows from her body and the wrappings around his head. Slowly, reluctantly, they pulled away from each other. She reached up and touched his face. It was then I saw the green flecks in his brown eyes that sparkled in the firelight under the shaggy brown hair so dark it was almost black.

Instantly everything went dark. The wind was knocked out of me as I landed hard on my back. I threw my hands out, grasping at the ground. I twisted my head from side to side but I couldn't see anything. I blinked, hard, thinking my eyes were still closed. I heard nothing, not even my own heartbeat. I didn't feel the warmth of the fire anymore, or the cold. There was no breeze, no scent in the air that gave me a clue as to where I was. I wanted to scream, just to hear something, but the scream was stuck in my throat.

Just when I thought I was about to go crazy from sensory deprivation a bright light blazed to life, stinging my eyes. The only thing that overpowered the pain was the realization that I still possessed the gift of sight.

"Aren?"

The voice, so quiet as to almost go unnoticed all together, was behind me. I struggled to turn my head but I simply couldn't move.

"Aren."

This time my name wasn't a question but a statement. A dark figure came from my left side to stand between the light and me. His face was in darkness but the light shown through his dark hair.

I wanted to stand or speak but I couldn't even make myself twitch. I wondered how I was still alive since I couldn't feel air going in and out of my lungs.

He reached down to me and effortlessly pulled me up. The painful shock of his touch broke some kind of spell. I took a deep breath and felt the air rush in. It was as if I were coming to life.

"Aren," he said my name again, softly, like a prayer. "I have missed you. Every time- not knowing if I would find you again- scared to say anything when I did-"

His words hit me so hard I felt like I had been punched. The wave of compassion for him hurt so much I thought I would fall to the ground again.

"I would do anything for you," Noah said gravely.

I knew he meant every word. My chest swelled as my emotions ran so wild I didn't see how they could be contained in my body. My breath, only newly restored to me, ceased. I had never felt so much for anyone before. I thought about pinching myself but I already knew this was a dream. The realization was like a needle puncturing my overfilled balloon of happiness.

"Just because it's a dream doesn't mean it isn't real. You should know this by now," he said, seeing the conclusions I had just come to play across my face.

Slowly he reached up and placed his hand under my chin, turning me to look him full in the face. He moved closer, it didn't take much, until our bodies were touching. The heat from his body felt warmer than the campfire.

"All I want," he whispered so close to my face that I could feel his warm breath, "is for you to stay with me. You don't understand how powerful you are yet. We can do anything together."

Power.

Something about that word frightened me. I still didn't have a firm grasp of what it was I could do and yet everyone wanted to keep telling me how powerful I was. I didn't want to be powerful. I didn't want to be anything. Tiny doubts began to tug at me. What if the only thing that had brought him to me was my power?

I turned my face away. I felt his arms move to encircle me, pulling me into him. It felt so natural that I went limp in his arms and let him hold me.

The rush of freezing air around my body told me he was gone. I opened my eyes and brushed my hair out of them. I was alone and cold. The bright light had moved overhead, leeching the color out of everything. I couldn't see Noah anymore nor anything else I recognized.

"Noah?" I called out, desperation seeping into my voice. I paused, but I heard no reply. I started to move forward. My body felt like it weighed a ton. Picking up my foot and putting it back down exhausted me. I looked around, trying to figure out where I was going. Everything looked the same. I couldn't tell if I was on a plain that continued on and on forever or if I was trapped in a bubble. I lifted my foot to take another step but the effort seemed too great. I put my foot back down, not gaining an inch.

I heard a scratching noise and turned my head. I thought I could see something moving not far from me. Slowly, I tried to turn my body to face the movement. As I watched, long dark wisps began twisting in the air in front of my face becoming darker and darker as they undulated. Suddenly, one of the lines became a tear. It was as if the space in front of me was ripping open. Beyond the slit I could see movement in the darkness. I wanted to back away from the hole in nothingness but couldn't move. As I stood there hesitating someone bounded through, feet first, and landed in a heap in front of me. I wasn't prepared for the pang of disappointment at the sight of blonde hair instead of brown.

"Holden?" I asked the tangle of limbs in front of me. I heard a sucking sound and looked up in time to see the rip he had tumbled through disappear. I looked back down. Holden had rolled to his back and was sitting up. I leaned down and he grabbed my arm.

"Are you alright?" he asked.

"Yes," I said, puzzled at his question. "Are you?"

"I didn't think I would ever reach you," he said, ignoring my question. He got to his feet while refusing to relinquish my arm.

"What are you talking about?" I asked. Still gripping me tightly, he looked me over as if he were searching for missing limbs, or extra ones.

"He was trying to keep me out." He looked back toward the now nonexistent hole he had come through.

"Who?"

Holden looked back at me. "Noah," he finally said, as if the answer should have been obvious.

At the mention of his name I felt little tremors under my feet. Holden moved closer, his hands on my shoulders.

"What's going on?" I demanded.

"I'm sorry- he doesn't want me near you. Please- I don't have long. He has more control here than you realize." The intensity of the tremors began to increase. Holden shook my shoulders and brought his face close to mine. "Please listen. He will do anything, say anything, to have you. But it's not because he cares about you."

I pulled back from him as far as his grip would allow. I wanted to strike out at him but the only thing keeping me on my feet was his hands on my shoulders. He winced when he saw my reaction.

"I'm sorry- I'm sorry I didn't get to you first. But that means I can't wait for you to come to these conclusions yourself. Be careful. He doesn't want to be with you- he wants your power."

The tiny doubts that had been dancing around earlier pressed in on me again.

"What would you know about what he wants? What I want?" I shrieked angrily. This time, he was the one who pulled his face away from mine though he didn't let me go.

The ground beneath our feet was bucking wildly now. I reached out instinctively to Holden so I wouldn't fall. Sounds of the ground rumbling and heavy things falling filled the air.

Small cracks began to open below us. We tried to move out of the way but it was as if we were glued to the spot. More and more ground fell away and soon we were falling. We tried to hold on to each other out of fear but I could feel my grip slipping. When I finally let go he disappeared.

I didn't have long to wonder what happened to him because a few seconds later I landed with a thud on something hard. I squeezed my eyes closed, not wanting to see where I was now. I began to hear the buzz of quiet conversation around me. I peeked out from between my lashes and saw almost everyone I knew standing in some kind of pit below me. They were milling around, talking to each other, all clad in black. Then I realized they weren't below me so much as I was above them. I opened my eyes wider and realized I was on the stage of the auditorium at graduation.

I leapt to my feet, trying to look in all directions at once to see if anyone had noticed me lying on the floor behind the podium. No one even glanced in my direction. Suddenly, as if there had been some sort of signal I didn't hear, everyone stopped talking, took a seat and looked expectantly toward me. I looked blankly back at them as I clung to the podium for dear life.

I glanced down. It was my speech. I was supposed to give my speech today. I began to panic- I hadn't looked over it once since I'd written it. I could make out the title and my name on the paper but as I stared at the words, praying they would make some sort of sense, they disappeared all together. I was looking at a blank sheet of paper. I glanced at the impatient crowd then back down again. The words did not reappear.

"If you don't have anything to say, maybe you should get down." Someone called out, their words echoing in the silent auditorium. I scanned the crowd, trying to see who had spoken. The voice had sounded so familiar...

Lexa stood amongst the seated throng who were so still I wondered if they had been frozen. Relief swept through me at the sight of her. She smiled at me and I smiled back.

"Just sit down so we can get this over with," she called to me, laughing. I let out a long breath. There was nothing more in the world I wanted to do than get this over with. I started to walk away from behind the podium but Lexa called out to me again.

"There is nothing you can say now that will make this any different."

I turned toward her, catching the hard edge underneath her joking manner. I wanted to ask what she was talking about but apparently she needed no prompting.

"You can't stay here and we know that now."

I wasn't sure what she was talking about. And I wasn't going to get the chance to ask before she called out to me one last time.

"Good-bye."

I was plunged into total darkness. Spots flashed before my eyes as they tried to adjust. I squeezed them shut. I heard the crackle of a fire and the voices around me. I could smell the damp smell of the cave and the tang of the animal hides. I could feel arms around me. I felt someone's lips pressing themselves to mine and I opened my eyes.

This time, however, I was looking into hazel eyes under a tangle of blonde hair.

CHAPTER TWENTY-SIX

I woke Saturday morning gasping for air. My first thought was I had something I urgently needed to do. When I couldn't figure out what it was I leaned back into my pillows. The gray morning light seeping into my room did nothing for my mood. I lay there, not wanting to get up until the dream was gone. What I had seen left me feeling lonely and confused. The underlying panic made me want to scream.

After a few moments I decided staying in bed wasn't going to help me get rid of the dream. I stood and stretched. The gray light outside gave me no clue as to the time so I reached for my phone. It was eight. Graduation wasn't until one, which meant I had an entire morning to kill. Great.

I stared at my phone, noticing it had something else to tell me besides the time. I had one text message. I didn't blink as I looked at it, afraid I was still dreaming. It was only two words but they were enough to shave off a tiny bit of the doom and gloom that I felt.

Good luck.

It was from Noah.

I put my phone back on the nightstand. I took a deep breath, staring at the ceiling. He was being nice, that was all. I can't read into it. Deciding I had to treat it like a text from anyone else until further notice I forced myself to put it out of my mind.

I wandered out into the kitchen to see if anyone else was out and about. Mom was sitting at the table, reading the paper and drinking a cup of coffee. Dad must have had to go in to the clinic this morning. I headed for the coffeemaker to see if there was any left for me. I poured myself a cup and went to sit at the table, steeling myself for any awkward conversation but determined to act as normal as Mom would want me to be.

"Morning," Mom greeted me when I sat down. She pushed the paper away and picked up her coffee cup.

"Morning," I answered after my first tentative sip.

"How do you feel? Are you ready for today?" she asked. I shrugged off her questions.

"I guess so." I took another sip. When I didn't elaborate Mom tried a different tactic.

"What are your plans for the day?"

Plans? All I had been thinking about was graduation. I hadn't realized graduation was only a part of my day. What was I going to do with an entire day?

"I don't know. I'm guessing Lexa will call with some emergency- her hair maybe," I said. Mom laughed. Her laugh took me by surprise and I jumped a little.

"That sounds about right," Mom commented as she stood. She took her coffee mug to the sink and rinsed it out. "Do you want breakfast?"

My stomach heaved at the thought of anything solid. "No, thanks," I told her, trying to infuse my voice with all the gratefulness I could muster.

"Ok," Mom called as she left the kitchen.

I sat, staring into my coffee mug, trying to figure out how to kill some time. The few hours between now and graduation seemed like they would stretch on forever. If I didn't find something to do I would go crazy. I figured I could always call Lexa so I could be on hand when the emergency hit. There was always something with her- her hair was wrong, she didn't have the right color of eye shadow, she had the wrong shoes- it was only a matter of time before she turned on the Bat Signal.

"Your phone is ringing!" Mom called from the hall,

ending my deliberation.

I got up, coffee forgotten, and ran to the bedroom. I scooped up my phone and put it to my ear without looking at the caller ID.

"Hey," Lexa said, sounding more cheerful than I had ever heard this early in the morning. "We're going down to the C&T for breakfast. You want to go?"

"Yeah, just let me get dressed," I told her.

"I'll pick you up. See you in a minute." Lexa didn't wait for a reply before she hung up.

I threw my phone on the bed and began rooting around in the piles of what I suspected were clean laundry that Mom must have deposited in my room. I pulled on jeans and a blue t-shirt then searched for my bag. I realized I hadn't asked who all was going but I guessed it didn't matter as long as I had something to keep my mind occupied. There were two things I was actively trying to avoid thinking about- the first was my graduation speech and the other was Holden and Noah, all of the above inspiring surges of nausea.

I was telling Mom my plans when Lexa appeared at the door. I followed her to the car, both of us so full of nervous energy that we were practically skipping. The sky overhead was full of clouds but it didn't dampen our mood.

"So," Lexa said as we headed toward town, "are you excited?"

"Excited to get it over with," I told her as I looked down at my hands.

"I just hope I don't trip across stage or something!" Lexa exclaimed. I shot her a look, even though she couldn't see me. There were many people clumsier than Lexa, me being one of them. While it seemed every graduation had at least one name that went down in history as the person who tripped across stage I was hoping this year would be different. And if it couldn't be different, I hoped it wouldn't be me.

Before I knew it we were parked at the C&T. Lexa hopped out, barely pausing for me to exit the car before she started toward the door. I paused, asking myself if coming here felt any different this morning, since by this afternoon I would be an adult. It didn't. I sighed and followed Lexa.

I could hear more than see Ethan when I walked in. Lexa had hurried to our usual table in the back where Ethan, Sawyer and Hana were already gathered. Everyone was talking loudly to be heard over the Saturday morning crowd.

I zigged and zagged my way through people, hugging the far wall from the counter as it was packed three deep with patrons, to make it to the table.

I smiled a little stiffly as everyone shouted their hellos and took a seat next to Ethan, who was in the middle of a story about last night that was so confusing I couldn't have followed it if I wanted to.

"Hey," Hana called to me from across the table. I looked up to see her sliding a plate with a huge, untouched cinnamon roll in my direction. The C&T was famous for their homemade cinnamon rolls that were the size of dinner plates. The problem with their popularity was you had to be here at dawn if you expected to get one. I noticed two more half eaten ones sitting around the table. I smiled and gingerly tore off a piece of the roll trying, and failing, to keep the warm, gooey icing from getting all over me.

"Do you want anything?" Lexa asked me from behind my chair.

"Just coffee, if you don't mind," I requested. She nodded and starting fighting her way to the counter. I reflexively hugged my injured arm to me, glad I didn't have to try to elbow through the crowd.

"What are you doing after graduation?" Ethan turned to me expectantly. I frowned at him.

"Do you mean, like, 'what am I going to be when I grow up' or 'what am I doing tonight'?" I asked.

"Uh, sure," Ethan answered. I rolled my eyes.

"Not sure and don't know. Respectively." I flashed my teeth at him. "What about you?"

"I think Katie is having a party at her house." Katie was the cheerleaders' co-captain and one of the most popular girls at school. "And I think several people are going bowling." Ethan shrugged as if to ask what else is there to do around here.

"Those sound like very good options. It must be tough, having only hours left in which to make this important decision," I told him.

"Yeah, I'm still on the fence," Ethan agreed. He glanced down at my arm. I had forgotten to bandage it this morning. "Wow. Nice. Bet that will leave a scar."

I frowned at him as I moved my arm away. I dropped back into my own thoughts. I felt like I was still walking around in a dream. I looked around the room, wondering how to convince myself I wasn't dreaming. The hum of activity as people rushed to and fro made my eyes go out of focus. I turned back to the table. Hana was saying something but I couldn't hear a word.

"Here you go," Lexa said as she pushed a mug in front of me. I smiled my thanks at her and she took the free seat beside me. She sipped and tore into my barely touched cinnamon roll.

I looked across the table at Sawyer. He caught my eye and smiled his goofy grin, then turned his attention back to Hana, who was talking and gesturing wildly. I realized I hadn't spoken to Sawyer much since Thursday. Guilt washed over me again when I remembered how I had acted then tried to make everything right in a dream. Now I felt afraid to say anything to Sawyer in case he suddenly remembered that he only dreamed I apologized. And even though Lexa and I had hung out yesterday I was also feeling uneasy about her. I tried to tell myself I was being paranoid but I couldn't shake the feeling of guilt that said I had copped out on making a real apology.

"Hey, guys," Allison greeted everyone though she only had eyes for Ethan. Her face fell slightly when she noticed there wasn't an open seat next to him so she settled for a seat next to Hana.

I looked around at the faces of all my friends. It didn't feel like the hundreds of other times we had sat here together. I felt like I didn't know them anymore but the truth was they didn't know me. I was still running to keep up with the changes that were happening. And I couldn't share it with any of them, not even my best friend. They would never understand that I had somehow moved beyond them. I was beginning to accept that I possessed something they couldn't comprehend. And I had barely scratched the surface. The feeling of loneliness I sometimes had in a dream, a regular dream, intensified.

I forced my attention back to my friends. They were all talking over each other as they tried to expel their nervous energy. Hana, who was listening to something Allison was saying, glanced at me. She raised her eyebrow slightly but then looked away as if she understood I didn't have an answer to give even if she voiced the question. I tugged another piece off of the roll and chewed stiffly.

I felt a feather-light touch on my shoulder a second or so before I heard someone speak.

"Aren-"

I whipped around to see Holden leaning over me, his face inches from mine, occupying the space where my ear used to be. For a moment it was like I was back in my dream. I was expecting him to pull me to him in an embrace, to feel that warm, satisfied feeling I did when I had been held in my dream.

I shook the feeling off and pulled back from him. He stood with his back to Lexa whose face I could see over his shoulder. If she had been talking, she wasn't anymore. It felt like the entire table- no, the entire room- had stopped talking and was staring at us. I felt my face begin to color.

"What?" I hissed at him, hoping everyone would go back to their own conversations if I kept my voice down.

"I need to talk to you," he said, his voice as insistent as ever.

I opened my mouth to protest but the look Lexa was giving me made me want to be anywhere but here. I knew exactly what she would say if I left with him. I watched her face cycle through surprise, confusion, and hurt to settle on anger. Holden, oblivious to what he had literally stepped in the middle of, kept talking.

"Please, Aren. Now." His insistence wasn't causing the

situation to get any better. "Ok, let's go." I pushed him away and stood quickly.

He had only moved back what seemed like a fraction of an inch and I was practically standing on top of him. I bumped him with my hips as he tried to untangle his feet from mine. Ii felt as if all the air had been drawn out of my lungs by the violent shock that passed between us when we touched. My face was burning now as everyone watched us try to extricate ourselves from each other. He finally freed himself and turned toward the door. He stretched his hand back as if to grasp mine but I pulled it out of his reach. Seeming stunned, he dropped his hand. I shoved him toward the door, trying to get away from the table as quickly as possible.

We burst out of the door as if we had been shot from a cannon. Holden immediately headed around the corner toward the parking lot. I guess we had learned our lesson about standing on the street while having a conversation.

"What's going on?" I growled at him.

"I saw what he showed you. I know what he's trying to do," Holden told me.

"You saw..." Disappointment stood between me and comprehension. I had been expecting him to take me in his arms like last night and kiss me. I was angry with myself for thinking something so stupid and angry with him for bringing me out here for this. I wondered when he and Noah had become so interchangeable in my head that I swapped them in and out of my fantasies like pictures in a frame. "You saw? You were there too? In my dream? How much time do you spend in my head? "

"I can't help it," he said.

I was becoming angrier by the second. "You can't help it?"

"You pull me in," he tried to explain.

"What do you mean by I 'pull you in'?" I spat through clenched teeth.

"Sometimes I end up in your dreams without meaning to. Like you want me there," he practically whispered. I had leaned toward him to hear what he was saying but I jerked back at his words.

"Why would I do that?" I asked harshly.

"I don't know," he mumbled. He licked his lips before continuing. "But that's not what I'm here about. I saw what he showed you last night. It wasn't true. What he said wasn't true."

The more he spoke the louder he became. He seemed to speak with such force he could barely contain himself. If he thought grabbing and shaking me would have helped get his message across I had no doubt he would have done it.

"What wasn't true?" I asked, a little less sure of myself now.

"That time, with the tribe, it wasn't him-" He looked me in the eye when he said this. I looked away as I remembered the intensity of the kiss. He went on, "He doesn't want you for you. He wants your power."

Power.

There was that word again.

I blinked. I tried to shake off my hurt at what I saw as rejection.

He wanted to talk about Noah and power. I didn't even understand what kind of power I could possibly possess that would make this entire episode necessary.

"I don't know what you're talking about," I hissed at him. Even while I was speaking my mind was replaying what Noah had said to me in my dream. About my power and how we could do anything together.

Holden pressed his lips together and shut his eyes for a moment. When he opened them he looked like he was carrying the weight of the world on his shoulders. The passion in his eyes had vanished, replaced by a deep sadness. I wanted to reach out to him but I held myself in check.

"I wish-" he started but shook his head. "Maybe it would have been different if it had been me you had met first. He's never got here first and I don't know what to do. I miss you. I more than miss you."

I started to protest, to say anything to make him stop talking, but he raised his hand and I shut my mouth.

"You'll remember. I know you will. I just hope it's

soon. Before something bad happens. I don't know what else to say." He stepped back from me and before I realized what I was doing I took a step toward him, keeping the same distance between us.

I kept telling myself I had made a decision. Holden had seemed completely unhinged from the moment I met him. Noah was the one that had been there for me, the one who understood. But now with the prospect of losing Holden I felt terrible.

"If you need me-" he began as he held out a small scrap of paper. I took it automatically, clutching it in my fist.

Without saying another word he turned and walked away.

I tilted my face toward the sky. The sun had won its struggle with the clouds, which were breaking up and heading their own way. Its warmth was a counterpoint to the soft, cool late spring breeze. A few cars moved slowly down the street as if it were any other lazy Saturday. It seemed as though I could feel the underlying buzz in the air that came with something akin to a holiday. I guess graduation could suffice as some kind of holiday in this sleepy little town.

Holden had disappeared from sight so I turned to go back in. I was going to have to face Lexa. I was sure she was in there thinking the worst. I hadn't given it time to fully register how this must have looked to her. I knew she liked Holden but I was privy to Holden's reasoning for talking to her that night in the C&T- which I could never tell her as it would in no way make anything better. My apparent friendship with Holden, which she knew would have had to develop behind her back, was a terrible betrayal. It was certainly something Lexa had never experienced from me before. Even though it wasn't what it looked like I didn't see any way to explain that to her.

I squared my shoulders as I reminded myself I had done nothing wrong even as my stomach took residence in my throat. I was coaching myself on how to breathe normally when I walked back into the C&T.

I hadn't even gotten back to the table before Lexa was on me.

"What was that about?" she demanded as she met me a few feet before I got to the table, blocking my path.

"Lexa-"

She cut me off. "I thought you didn't know each other and now you're best friends? And when were you going to tell me? You knew I liked him. And what happened to 'he's bad news, stay away'? Really, Aren?"

"Lexa, come on. It had nothing to do with me- we aren't friends. He's just crazy. He wanted to talk about Noah. I'm telling you, he *is* bad news." I tried to say this with all the conviction I could muster but my words sounded hollow, even to me.

Lexa threw her hands in the air. "I can't talk about this with you right now." She turned and grabbed her keys and cell phone off the table and stalked out of the C&T. I stared after her, afraid to turn around and face my friends. After the bells on the door quieted their protest of Lexa's rough treatment I became painfully aware of the eyes boring into my back.

When I finally found the courage to turn around it seemed everyone was making an effort to not look at me. Ethan and Sawyer were talking in hushed tones while Allison, who had taken my seat by Ethan, was leaning across the table to listen. Hana was picking at the remains of a roll and occasionally inserting a comment in the boys' conversation. I started to wonder if they had somehow missed the entire scene.

It was Allison who broke first. She turned to me and asked, "So, what was that?"

The edge to Allison's voice made me want to choke her but instead I just stared. I couldn't think of anything to say that wouldn't make it look worse than it was already.

"Uh, Hana? Could you take me home?" I practically whispered.

Hana didn't hesitate. "Yeah, sure." She got up and started to dig her keys out of her pocket. Allison still watched me hungrily, as if I were going to tell her everything at any moment. Ethan and Sawyer threw up their hands in my direction in a parody of a wave. I waved back a little too eagerly in my attempt to achieve normalcy.

I followed Hana out to her car. When she unlocked the door I climbed in wordlessly. I felt awkward but Hana had seemed the safest choice given the circumstances. Ethan was terrible at these kinds of situations and I felt things were still shaky with Sawyer. Allison was completely out of question for obvious reasons.

"Thank you," I said. She didn't look at me as she concentrated on pulling into traffic.

"No problem." I had the feeling she wanted to say more but she held herself in check.

Hana had only been to my house a few times so I had to give her directions. She seemed completely satisfied to sit in silence otherwise. Her radio was on but turned down low, just enough noise to make things slightly less uncomfortable. We had never been really close friends but I was extremely thankful for her now.

When we pulled into my drive I noticed Mom's car was gone and Dad still hadn't returned. I let out a sigh of relief at the prospect of being alone. Hana stopped the car and threw it into park so she could turn and look at me.

"You okay?" she asked.

Her sincerity made me hesitate to give the usual "I'm fine." I thought about how awful I felt at upsetting Lexa again, how hurt I was when Holden gave up on me, and how desperate I was to hear from Noah so he could make everything better.

"I don't know," I said truthfully.

"That's okay. It can take time to figure things out. If nothing else I'm sure sleeping on it would help."

Her advice seemed sound enough though I questioned why she would say sleeping on it would help when it was only mid-morning. Of course, this wasn't something that was going to straighten itself out in a minute or two.

"Thanks, Hana. I'll see you later, okay?" I climbed out of the car and attempted to shut the door. I had put too little effort into it so it barely latched. I had to fumble to open the door again so I could slam it harder. Face glowing, I backed away toward the house to watch Hana leave.

CHAPTER TWENTY-SEVEN

The house was quiet. I couldn't decide if it was worse to be left alone with my thoughts or if I'd rather face my parents. I decided it was a lose/lose situation and dragged myself to my room to stow my bag. There was a note on my door from Mom saying she had to go to town and would be back soon.

It was too early to start getting ready since I usually took all of fifteen minutes to change. I could never figure out how Lexa took hours to get ready.

I decided to kill an hour or so in front of the TV. I wasn't a big TV watcher but flipping channels was a good way to waste time. I set my phone on the coffee table and curled up on the couch. I couldn't keep from looking at the phone every few minutes though. I had expected Lexa to call with some emergency, one that would outweigh our fight, but my phone remained silent. I double-checked to make sure the ringer was on. Then I triple-checked. Finally I put it in my lap so I didn't have to keep reaching for it.

I tried to think of someone I could call. I considered Noah but I was terrified of appearing needy. Which I was- I needed him more than anything right now. I thought about the crumpled paper Holden had given me, which now resided in my pocket. I knew it had to be his number. I couldn't bring myself to look at it in case I was tempted to call him. Of course, I certainly didn't care if he thought I was needy- because I wasn't.

For an hour I flipped channels, switched positions and clutched my silent phone. I would challenge myself to see how long I could go before I looked at the clock. The longest I lasted was about five minutes.

Around eleven thirty I decided I should start getting ready. I thought if I took my time I could keep myself busy until I needed to leave the house. I turned the TV off and left the remote on the couch. In an act of defiance I left my phone as well.

I dragged myself back to my bedroom and started going through my closet. After a cursory glance at the natural disaster I didn't see anything I wanted to wear. I decided maybe I should start with getting cleaned up instead.

I stood in the hot shower for a while just letting the spray roll over me. I carefully washed my left arm, which felt like it had been used as a tennis racket. I washed my hair twice. When I couldn't justify standing there any longer I turned off the water and reached for a towel.

Much to my disappointment the clothes in my closet hadn't magically ejected the perfect something while I was gone. I went through them again, throwing a few possibilities on the bed in hopes of narrowing my choices.

Once my bed had a small mound of rumpled fabric on it I wrestled the closet door shut. Maybe I should have taken shopping with Lexa more seriously. Yesterday seemed like a dream to me. This thought distracted me so much that I jumped at a sudden knock on my door.

"Aren?" Mom called from the other side of the door.

"Yeah," I answered automatically. She turned the knob and pushed the door open.

"Hey. I just got back from the store." Mom began by stating the obvious. She glanced at the pile on the bed. "Trying to find something to wear?"

"Yeah," I said again.

Mom came over and started to half-heartedly pick through the stack on the bed, laying out the clothes in a neat stack. "I was surprised when I saw your car in the driveway. I figured you girls would be getting ready together."

I wondered briefly if this was another fishing for information expedition. I didn't trust myself to say anything that wouldn't give me away so I just shrugged. Mom kept digging through the clothes.

"I like this one." She held up a simple blue sheath dress. "Or this, maybe." With her other hand she pulled a v-necked dress with a multi-hued green pattern out of the pile.

"Ok," I said to neither one in particular. She put them back on the bed side by side. She put her fists on her hips, satisfied with her work.

"I'll let you change. I've got to put up the groceries." She was gone before I said anything.

I sat on the bed, looking at my choices. The blue dress was closer to me so I tugged it off the hanger and slipped it on. I toweled off my hair and blow-dried it. After playing with it for a moment I decided to leave it down. I had to get on my hands and knees to find shoes in the closet. I finally pulled out a dusty pair of low-heeled Mary Janes. I slapped the dust off and slipped them on, buckling them at the ankle. I briefly considered make-up but I was so unused to wearing the stuff that it made me feel funny when I did. I didn't need to feel any more self-conscious than I already was.

By the time my preparations were complete my arm was throbbing with over-use. I had bandaged it again, still ignoring doctor's orders.

I went out to the living room to find my phone. I was hoping it had decided to ring once I wasn't standing over it. No such luck. I had no missed calls or even a text. I also hadn't taken as much time as I'd hoped. It was fifteen minutes after twelve. I had a half hour before I needed to be at the school.

I made my way into the kitchen where Mom was putting up groceries and leaned against the island.

"Your father is on his way. I figured we would meet you there?" The question in her voice sounded like some kind of test. I decided to play dumb.

"Yeah, that sounds good," I told her. I liberated a banana from the bunch that sat within arm's reach and peeled it open.

"You look very nice," Mom said to me, pausing in the midst of putting cereal boxes in the pantry.

"Thanks," I replied with half a smile. I popped a piece of banana in my mouth.

"Do you have your gown and everything? Cap, tassel?" she asked.

"In the car."

"In the car?" she echoed. "Is it wrinkled?"

I shrugged. I was suddenly surprised at how unconcerned I was. I tried to make myself care about the state of my cap and gown but it wasn't working. There seemed to be so much on my mind lately that I didn't have room to be worried about the cheap polyester getup.

Mom watched me as I worked all this out. She must have decided it wasn't worth pressing the issue, which surprised me. She continued putting groceries away.

"I think I'm going to head to the school," I decided, finishing my banana.

Mom stopped to look at me again. "Ok. We'll be right behind you."

I went back to my room and hunted up my bag and keys- which took longer than I thought considering I had only put them down less than two hours ago. I threw my phone roughly into my bag, deciding the phone deserved it for not ringing when I wanted it to.

CHAPTER TWENTY-EIGHT

I took my time driving through town. Traffic was a little heavier than usual with virtually everyone headed toward the high school. I parked in the upper lot and fished my cap and gown out of the back seat. After a moment's hesitation I stuffed my bag under my seat and got out of the car with only my keys. I threw the plastic outfit over my arm, locked the door, and headed for the school.

Knots of people made my walk from the parking lot to the front door an exercise in bobbing and weaving. I waved to a few fellow graduates and parents I knew but I didn't stop to talk. I was early for roll call but I figured I could wait in the cafeteria. A few other people seemed to have the same idea, lounging in chairs that had been placed along the wall for that very purpose.

I walked all the way across the huge room to a corner and took a seat as far away from anyone as I could get. I immediately regretted not bringing my phone. I had nothing to do but sit and watch other people come in and out. The minutes ticked by as I tried my best not to look awkward. I busied myself trying to smooth the wrinkles out of my gown and untangling the strands of my tassel before putting it on my cap.

Other soon-to-be-graduates trickled steadily into the room but I hadn't seen any of my friends. Of course I wasn't even sure if I had friends anymore. I was relieved when Mrs. Donovan finally entered the cafeteria, her trusty clipboard in hand. She made a cursory glance around the room, looking from her watch to her clipboard then back at the room. I stood up, hoping her presence signaled it was time to start lining up.

I made my way over to Mrs. Donovan.

"Hi, Aren," she smiled at me.

"Hi," I said a little shakily. I slipped into my gown and held the cap in my hand.

"Everyone! Please line up for roll call," Mrs. Donovan called. The room, which had been buzzing half a moment before, went completely silent as soon as Mrs. Donovan spoke. There was a rustle of polyester as everyone tried to remember where they were supposed to stand. Mrs. Donovan made her way down the line, helping people to get into place and inquiring about the few who were missing.

Mrs. Donovan was halfway down the line when Hana came rushing in the door, sliding into her place behind me.

"Hey," she said to me, breathless, as she worked pins into her strawberry hair to keep her cap on.

"Hey," I responded, surprised someone was speaking to me.

"Ready to get this over with?" she grinned as she slipped her gown on and zipped it.

"Absolutely," I told her, trying my best to return her carefree grin.

She helped me smooth my hair under my cap as several more students filed in the door. Sawyer was sneaking in like he was late for class. He gave us a small wave and a half smile, though I wasn't sure if it was actually meant for Hana or for me. I waved anyway, continuing to pretend that nothing was even remotely out of place in our world.

Lexa wasn't far behind him with Ethan and a few other kids. They were all dashing for their spots and talking so I wasn't sure if Lexa was ignoring me or she didn't see me in her mad rush. Either way I was relieved that I didn't have to act as if I thought things should be fine between us.

"Hey, you okay?" Hana called softly to me.

"Uh, yeah," I said. I looked at her and tried to give a reassuring smile but it came out as more of a grimace. Hana made a delicate snorting sound that made me grin.

Mrs. Donovan had made her way around the cafeteria once and now came back to stand by me. The trickle of students through the door had come to a halt. Mrs. Donovan called for everyone's attention. Again, the nervous chatter died instantly.

"I will be coming around again to take roll. If you are not in your place I'll take that to mean you aren't here. If you aren't here then your name will be marked off the role and your diploma will be pulled so it can be mailed to you at a later date. If you want to hear your name called today, make sure you're where you're supposed to be."

Mrs. Donovan followed this speech up with a tight grin and immediately got to work. She said our names under her breath as she walked down the line checking her list. Slowly, the noise picked back up as we waited restlessly for her to finish.

Once Mrs. Donovan made her way around the room she and her clipboard exited the cafeteria. I assumed it was to let someone know whose diplomas should be pulled, if anyone's. I hadn't taken inventory to see who was here and who wasn't. I tried looking down the line to see if anyone was missing but my heart wasn't really in it.

Mrs. Donovan reappeared, sans clipboard, and came to stand by me. There was a dip in the noise level at the sight of her but when she made no move to speak the whispering swelled again.

"Aren, there's a copy of your speech on the podium so you don't have to carry it with you," Mrs. Donovan addressed me out of side of her mouth. My stomach dropped. I had forgotten all about my speech. I hadn't even thought about bringing a copy with me. My distress must have been written all over my face because Mrs. Donovan smiled encouragingly at me. "You'll be fine. It'll be over before you know it." With a light pat on my shoulder she moved away from me a few steps and called for everyone's attention.

"Aren?" Hana hissed at me. I looked back at her, unable to speak. She bit her bottom lip as she took in the expression on my face.

"I haven't look at that speech once since I turned it in!" I told her.

"I'm sure it will come back to you," she assured.

I turned to face the cafeteria doors. Mrs. Donovan gave some final instructions, which I didn't hear a word of. I was tugging the zipper of my gown up when she gave us the signal to start forward.

Both of my feet tried to move at the same time and I had to take a few shuffling steps to keep from falling. Luckily everyone else was concentrating on walking as well so my two-step passed undetected. I slipped into a slow, stately march that would hopefully keep me from tripping over myself again.

It seemed to take no time to cross the foyer and enter the auditorium from which "Pomp and Circumstance" was blaring. The auditorium was packed with families, friends and underclassmen. It was as if the entire town had turned out, which probably wasn't far from the truth. Most of the lights had been dimmed except for the one illuminating the aisle we were walking down. When our processional entered everyone stood to their feet calling out and clapping.

I heard a familiar whistle and looked to my left. Mom and Dad were seated about halfway between the stage and the rear doors. They waved excitedly and I smiled and gave them a little wave in return. Overcome with the excitement of it all I started looking around to see if I could find anyone else I knew, completely forgetting that I had been terrified of putting one foot in front of the other a moment earlier.

When we reached the front of the huge hall I moved down the front row to my seat. I stood in front of it as I had been instructed, waiting for everyone to find their own places. Finally, Mrs. Donovan stepped up to the podium and gave us the signal to be seated.

"We would like to welcome you to Jefferson High School's sixty-eighth commencement ceremony. The young men and women before me-"

I didn't hear anything else she said after that point. I was already fidgeting, unable to get comfortable in the Astroturf-upholstered seats. I flipped open the program that had been left on my chair. I was pleased to learn I could still read as I glanced through the list of the graduates' names.

I tried to look around for something to distract me. Being in the very front of the auditorium I couldn't really see much except for the first few rows of the section to my right. I was scanning them for familiar faces when my heart suddenly stopped. I squinted and looked again. Noah was sitting in the second row. I turned back toward the stage wondering if I was seeing things. I casually glanced back over my shoulder. It was definitely Noah in the second row watching Mrs. Donovan give her welcome speech.

A warm glow blanketed me at the sight of him. I had been trying not to think about him and what he had said about spending more time together. I thought I had dreamt it, along with his text this morning. I had put it out of my mind instead of trying to decipher what it meant. But maybe I really was his. I stopped. I felt funny saying it, even in my head, in case I cursed it.

A sharp little elbow nudged me in my side.

"Go on. You'll be fine," Hana whispered to me. My head shot up to see that Mrs. Donovan had stepped back from the podium expectantly. She was leading the audience in polite applause, which could mean only one thing. It was time for my speech.

I rose slowly, using all the powers of my concentration to make it to the podium without tripping. A perverse part of my mind wondered if the valedictorian had ever been the one to fall on their face during graduation or if I would have the honor of being the first.

I put one foot in front of the other, counting out a cadence in my head as I ascended the stairs and made my way to center stage. Mrs. Donovan flashed me a genuine smile and then surprised me by giving me a small hug. I gave her a quick squeeze in return then let go and turned to the podium. Mrs. Donovan had been thoughtful enough to put the copy of my speech on top of the other papers that sat there. The applause had died down and I glanced out at the audience, plastering a smile on my face. Most people were shrouded in darkness beyond the first row. This made me feel a little better as I told myself no one was really out there. Then, I began to read.

"Faculty and staff, family and friends, fellow graduates," I started. So far, so good.

"Last year our class sat in this same room watching as the seniors became graduates and we, the juniors, became seniors. We knew the next class to walk across this stage would be us and suddenly a year did not seem like a very long time.

"Now, twelve months later, here we are. We can look back and see that the year we thought would last decades also seemed to disappear in the blink of an eye. When we walked out of this school at the end of the term it was with the knowledge that we are not coming back in the fall. While this chapter of our lives comes to an end today another chapter begins. We gain the freedom to follow our dreams when we walk out that door." I nodded my head toward the doors at the back of the auditorium for dramatic emphasis.

"You can call it whatever you want, ambitions, aspirations, goals, but we all have dreams. Whether it's the chance to play football at Tech on scholarship-" this brought a few hoots from some of the guys who had earned said scholarships-"or a full ride to the university or college where you have always wanted to go-" a few whistles and muted claps from some of the students in the audience who had received such- "or it's finally winning the argument that a year off is best so you can decide what your next move will be-" I heard an ear-splitting whistle- "we all have a dream. Some of us have more than one. Sometimes they change. Sometimes we have two dreams that seem to be in direct opposition to one another. Sometimes it's something you feel like you could never share with another person. The important thing is that you must hold on to your dreams. Your dreams are going to be what gets you out of bed in the morning when you are miles away from your mom, who usually comes in throwing pillows at you when your alarm has been going off for too long." Laughter ran through the audience. I smiled despite myself. The knot in my stomach had loosened and I was ready for my big finish.

"Some of us are going across the country, some of us are moving across town, some of us have no clue where we will be tomorrow. Whatever your plan, at one point or another you may realize the only real thing you have is your dreams. Wherever you are going, remember to take your dreams with you." The page ran out of words so I stopped. I looked out at the audience and took a tiny step back from the podium.

Applause engulfed me, coming from both the faculty behind me and the audience before me. I felt my face flush and I smiled, looking down at my feet. I turned and began to walk toward the opposite side of the stage, glancing out at the audience every now and again, amazed that they were clapping for me. At the second stair a junior attendant reached his hand toward me to assist me in my decent. I navigated the stairs successfully but once I was on level ground I paused. I looked up sharply into the seats behind the black clad graduates as if someone had physically maneuvered my head in that direction.

Holden was staring at me from an aisle seat, smiling and clapping in my direction. I went rigid for an instant then I lurched toward my seat, determined to get out of his line of sight as quickly as possible.

I was no longer concerned with falling as I rushed to take my seat. The applause had died down and Mr. Garrard was approaching the podium. Hana patted my left hand gingerly when I resumed my seat, being careful of my injuries.

"Nice," she whispered to me.

I smiled at her, trying to show genuine gratitude. I was

a little distracted with the thought that there were three people in the world who would understand the irony of the speech I had just given in light of the past week and apparently we were all sitting here in the same room. I didn't remember saying anything to either of them about the specific time or place of graduation today. Of course, it is a small town and I'm sure it wasn't that hard to find out.

I hoped Lexa hadn't seen Holden. A little knot of nervousness, completely different from the one that had plagued me in the minutes leading up to my speech, formed in my stomach. Things were bad enough and I really didn't want this to go down in history as the day my world imploded. I turned around, trying to see where Lexa was sitting but it was no use. I turned back toward the stage.

"It is with great pride and pleasure that I announce the candidates for graduation before you have met all criteria to receive their diploma. Congratulations." Mr. Garrard concluded his little speech to delighted applause.

"Mrs. Superintendent, it would honor us if you would read the roll of our graduates who are present to receive their diploma," Mr. Garrard addressed this to someone behind him. He stepped back from the podium to take up his position beside the table stacked with the diplomas in question. A plump, pleasant-looking woman rose from a folding chair on the stage and came to the podium.

"It is an honor to be asked here to present the names of the graduates," she said with a nod and a smile to Mr. Garrard. With a flourish she produced a pair of reading glasses and fitted them to her face. Mrs. Donovan, behind her, motioned for the first row to stand. I led my row toward the stairs as the woman behind the podium cleared her throat and read the first name- mine.

CHAPTER TWENTY-NINE

I felt as if I had gone into some kind of shock when I saw Holden in the audience. I vaguely remember walking across the stage to receive my diploma, smiling as I shook Mr. Garrard's hand while he presented me with the little portfolio.

The superintendent fell into a rhythm as she read off the names of students, which wasn't helping. I was almost ready to fall asleep where I sat. I hadn't been paying attention for a long time and I was only vaguely aware that something was happening when the cadence stopped.

Mrs. Donovan had once again taken command of the podium. She motioned for us to rise, which we did as if we were marionettes on the same string. She said a few more words of congratulations then signaled for us to move our tassels from one side of our caps to the other. I jumped when the band broke out into an unidentifiable song. Caps, silly string and shouts all went flying. I was so stunned I hadn't even taken off my cap by the time everyone else's had fallen to the ground.

Hana turned and hugged me impulsively, then stepped back.

"Hey, are you going to make it?" she asked me. She smiled as she said it, as if in jest, but her voice had a note of real concern. I tried to laugh, but the sound came out wrong.

"I'm fine. I'm just kind of dazed- I guess I can't believe it's over," I tried to explain. The words didn't sound exactly right to me but it was the best I could do. A hand on my shoulder caused me to jump.

"Congratulations," Noah called to me over the crowd. His gaze shifted from me to Hana and I turned to her so I could introduce them.

Hana was staring as if he were a ghost. Her eyes narrowed like she was trying to remember something.

"Hana, do you know Noah?" I asked her. Warmth was beginning to creep back into me as Noah's presence dispelled my daze.

"Um, no, I don't," she answered, still staring at his face. Noah put his hand out to her and she shook it quickly.

"Nice to meet you," Noah said. She simply nodded. She began to scan the crowd furiously.

"I'm going to go find my parents," she told us before diving into the crowd.

I turned toward Noah who still had his hand on my shoulder. He seemed to have forgotten it was there and I reveled in the warmth emanating from his touch.

"I didn't know you were coming," I said to him as I stepped closer to avoid being bumped by passersby looking for their graduate. "I don't remember really saying anything about it to you." He shrugged.

"I wanted to surprise you," he grinned. "I can't stay long but I wanted to see you."

"Thank you," I murmured when I couldn't think of anything else. I bit my lower lip, unsure of how to proceed.

"I'll talk to you later, okay?" he searched my face and I nodded. Swiftly, he brought his face close to mine and kissed my forehead so lightly I wasn't sure it had really happened. Then his hand was gone from my shoulder and he was melting into the crowd.

"Aren!" I pivoted on my heel to see my mom and dad beaming as they pushed their way through the crowd. I was caught in a huge group hug when they reached me.

"Congratulations, honey," Mom gushed, her face full of parental pride.

"We're so proud of you," my dad added. "You did a great job with your speech."

The mention of my speech brought a flood of odd feelings rushing back to me, something akin to déjà vu but not quite. My speech about dreams. I tried to shake the feelings off as I looked into the smiling faces of my parents. I wanted to enjoy this moment since it was the first time this week they seemed happy with me. I didn't have to remind myself that their unhappiness with my odd behavior had been the result of my dreams.

"Come on," Dad said as he put his arm around my shoulders. "Let's go celebrate."

We made our way out of the auditorium slowly due to the fact that we had to navigate around tight bunches of people. I waved to a few other graduates I knew who were standing around with their families. I didn't see Lexa or Sawyer in the crowd but I did run into Ethan who gave me a bear hug that lifted me entirely off the ground. He called out both hello and goodbye to my parents before he disappeared into the crowd with a shout.

I was trying to unzip my gown as we were fighting our way out of the hot auditorium. When we stepped into the cool May breeze I took in a deep lungful of clean air, glad to be out of the packed room.

"Where would you like to go for a celebratory lunch?" Dad asked me as we stood on the sidewalk. Other families had also spilled onto the concrete and we had to weave our way to an unoccupied bit of real estate.

"Um, it doesn't matter to me. Wherever," I answered. I was scanning the clusters of people on the sidewalk looking for Lexa. I wanted to apologize, to see if there was any hope of making things okay.

"Well, let's head out before all the good places are full," Mom said. She took my good arm. "We'll all ride together." I let Mom steer me toward where they had parked.

Luckily, with most everyone still inside the school it wasn't too difficult to get out of the parking lot. I sat in the back seat, staring out the window. Mom and Dad were chattering away about places to eat with an excitement I just didn't feel.

I couldn't figure out what was bothering me. My day had suddenly taken on a surreal quality. I tugged at the skirt of my dress in frustration. My mind was fuzzy and I was having a hard time holding on to any tendril of thought. I leaned my head against the cool glass and shut my eyes.

☙ ☙☙ ☙

I was looking at a wide, hard-packed dirt street, lined with square buildings sitting shoulder to shoulder. The clapboard houses shared one long porch that started at the nearest house and continued uninterrupted to the other end of the avenue. Sturdy square posts held up the slanted roof that covered the wooden walkway. I leaned against a post and stared out toward a place beyond the last building. I was straining to see as far as I could down the road out of town that was lined with large weeping willows and sprawling trees dripping with Spanish moss.

I had stared down this road for so long I had forgotten what I was looking for. I only knew that it was important for me to keep watching and waiting.

Presently a small form crept close and slipped a slight hand into mine. I squeezed the hand without glancing away for even a second.

"Come inside?" asked a child's soft sweet voice that reminded me of honeysuckle in summertime.

I shook my head and kept staring down the road. The little hand made no move to pull itself away from mine. I gave it another quick squeeze.

After a time the little voice piped up again, "Do you know who you're looking for?"

My brows came together briefly as I considered the question. I used to know. But I had stood here for so long I had forgotten why I stood here most days. I decided to ignore the child's question.

So much time passed I forgot about the hand holding onto mine. I jumped a little when she spoke up again. "He will come, you know," she said with the blind certainty only a child can possess.

I remembered now. I was waiting for him. I had always waited for him. Whenever I found us apart I knew he would come to find me. With renewed purpose, I shifted my shoulder against the post.

"But I don't know who will be first," the sweet voice murmured.

I bit my lip. I wasn't sure I knew what she was talking about but for some reason her statement filled me with dread. Yes, I could vaguely remember that there was someone else. Another person who had appeared over and over, just like us. I wet my lips.

"What if he comes?" I breathed, my voice rusty from disuse.

The little voice did not hesitate. "He will be the same. He can't change."

I sighed. I had wished so often that it didn't have to be this way. I looked down into the cherubic face I knew so well. She smiled, causing the freckles on her cheeks to dance. I couldn't help but smile back. I tugged one of her red braids lovingly before my eyes returned to the empty road.

CHAPTER THIRTY

"Aren?" Mom was calling my name from the front seat. I opened my eyes and pulled my head away from the window. I rubbed at a crick in my neck. "I didn't know public speaking would wear you out like this." She laughed and climbed out of the car.

I blinked. Mom and Dad's decision to return to normal happy family status was making my head spin. Mom shut her door and motioned for me to hurry up.

We were in the parking lot of Scott's, the local steakhouse. This was the only place in town to celebrate any kind of occasion and the almost empty parking lot indicated that we must have been one of the first to escape graduation. Soon this place would be packed with families celebrating with their graduates. The latecomers would either have an extremely long wait or they would have to break down and drive the thirty or more minutes to the next sit down place that wasn't a Waffle House.

I rubbed at my cheek that had been plastered to the glass as we walked inside. Dad spoke with the hostess and we were escorted to a booth that looked out on the wide expanse of meadow beyond the back lot. I scooted in next to the window and my parents took the bench opposite me. I heard the clack of laminated menus being placed on the lacquered table as I stared out the window in my half dazed post-sleep state.

The server appeared to take our drink order and returned almost immediately. She was clearly expecting the large crowd that was about to descend and was already gearing up. She asked politely if we were ready to order food. I ordered the first thing I could make out on the menu, a salad, and handed it back to her. I busied myself with my straw while my parents ordered. I took a sip of water then let out a yawn so huge my eyes watered.

"Tired?" Mom asked me.

"Yeah, I guess so," I told her, wiping at my eyes.

"Looks like we got here just in time," Dad remarked. I turned to follow his gaze. It seemed everyone from the school had caravanned to the restaurant. People were waiting in a line to be seated while the poor seating hostess hopped from her counter to a table and back again.

The noise in the restaurant increased exponentially. Before our food arrived we were forced into silence when yelling across the table became inadequate.

This suited me just fine since I didn't have anything to say. I had too much on my mind and my head was starting to ache. I wondered why I hadn't seen Holden after graduation. I hadn't stayed long after the ceremony but I didn't think that would stop him. Of course, maybe he hadn't been there for me. He might have come to see Lexa, but I couldn't even pretend that might be true. He had been honest with me about the reason he had tried to befriend her. I tried to repress the smug feeling that crept up when I thought of someone choosing me over Lexa, even if he was crazy. My feelings of guilt doubled.

I mentally kicked myself. I wasn't supposed to be thinking about Holden at all. It was Noah I wanted to be with. I could still feel the tingle that swept across my skin when he touched me. I recalled the jolt I had earlier that morning when Holden had taken my hand. It had been altogether different. It was sharp and painful but exciting, mostly because it was unexpected.

No, I had made my choice. I had to tell Holden to leave me alone. If I were honest though, I had to admit I enjoyed his attention. His intensity was unlike Noah's calm and sure demeanor. But it was his intensity that scared me. Holden made me feel like I was losing my mind. If it hadn't been for Noah the dreams would have probably already drove me mad.

I took another stab at my salad. I chewed slowly, being more preoccupied with my thoughts than with eating. I had hoped that with the pressure of my speech gone I might feel like eating something but I was still too distracted to be hungry.

I kept glancing out at the meadow, since the alternative was to stare at other people eating their food. The light coming in through the windows was subdued. The sun had gone back into hiding behind clouds that had become increasingly more menacing throughout the afternoon.

"Are you done?" Mom called over to me as she watched me push croutons around on my plate.

"Yes, thank you," I said to both of them, hoping they understood I was talking about more than my salad.

"Do you have plans this evening?" Dad asked me rather casually. I briefly remembered Ethan talking about bowling. I couldn't help wondering what Lexa and our other friends were doing to celebrate.

"Uh, I don't know. I haven't really talked to anyone," I answered. He nodded at this and flagged down our server for the check.

Once we were out of the crowded restaurant Mom and Dad drove me back to my car. There was still quite a crowd lingering outside the school and the parking lot held a fair number of cars. I saw a familiar red head and asked Dad to drop me off at the front doors. Mom glanced up meaningfully at the sky that looked like it was going to open up any minute.

"Just let us know what your plans are, okay?" she asked me. I nodded, still a little confused by my parents' new plan to treat me like an adult instead of a mental patient. It made me more nervous than when they had been on suicide watch.

Dad stopped at the curb and I hopped out with my keys, leaving my cap and gown on their back seat.

I started to move through the groups of people to the last place I saw her. "Hana?" I called as I rounded a large family that was talking animatedly. I had hoped Hana's presence meant that Lexa or Sawyer were still here as well. I was determined to find Lexa so I could try to make her understand what had happened this morning.

"Hey!" I heard Hana call from somewhere on my right. I took a few steps beyond the grouping of people and saw her standing near the front entrance of the school with Holden.

I froze. I looked from Hana to Holden and back again trying to figure out what was going on. They stood in comfortable proximity like old friends.

"Um," I made an attempt at speech but an uncertain noise was all that came out.

"Aren?" Hana took a step toward me. I licked my lips and looked from her to Holden.

"We need to talk," Holden said in a low voice. He nudged Hana who turned and tugged open one of the doors to the school. Holden held the door while I followed her in, not knowing what else I should do. I heard the smallest rumble of thunder in the distance as we reentered the school I had thought I'd walked out of for the last time less than two hours ago.

CHAPTER THIRTY-ONE

To my surprise there were people still inside the school as well. No one paid any attention as three more came in and walked casually into the auditorium. The stage looked exactly as it had when I'd left. The podium stood alone and proud in the middle of the stage. The diploma table was empty of its charges and large flower arrangements with gigantic bows in our school colors stood as sentries across the stage. The auditorium floor was littered here and there with discarded programs.

I felt like I was being led to a firing squad. We didn't speak as we walked a little ways down the aisle then slid into a row. I sat in the middle of Hana and Holden. I took a deep breath to steady myself, not taking my eyes off of Hana. I planned to ignore Holden completely but I wanted to hear what she had to say. When Holden had shown up at the C&T neither of them had indicated they knew the other. Did Hana tell Holden where I was this morning? Was that how he found me?

"Hana," I said impatiently, "what's going on?"

Hana pursed her lips while she organized her thoughts. I watched her steadily; refusing to acknowledge Holden though he sat so close to me his leg was touching mine.

"I know Holden," she started slowly. She let out an exasperated breath. "I'm not sure how to explain it exactly."

"Hana, tell me," I demanded impatiently. Her eyes slid past me to Holden.

"Aren."

Holden spoke so quietly that at first I thought I'd imagined it. Hana's eyes moved back to me, waiting for me to acknowledge him. I closed my eyes, refusing to look at him even as my traitorous body turned toward his whisper.

"Aren, please," he said to me in the same quiet voice. I squeezed my eyes shut tighter. Now I knew what it felt like to be the subject of an intervention.

"Aren, Hana knows us."

The emphasis he placed on "us" made my eyes fly open. He had leaned in close to me and I had unconsciously responded by leaning toward him. Our faces were so close my eyes crossed as I tried to look at him. I jerked back. He seemed startled by this sudden movement and drew back a little himself.

I continued to stare at him. I don't think I could have been more surprised if an airplane had crash-landed in the auditorium. I had temporarily lost Hana in the equation as I tried to deal with the "us" he had dropped on me. Something inside me had clicked forcefully but I had no words to describe what had happened. The tension that was building in my head eased ever so slightly. It was like one of the last pieces of the puzzle had shifted somewhat, just enough to snap into place. The problem was I'd been working the puzzle in the dark so I had no clue as to what the picture looked like.

Holden continued to stare at me. I felt light-headed under his scrutiny.

"Us?" I asked hesitantly. I was almost afraid to say it out loud in case the roof caved in at the second mention of the word. I fought against the still indescribable feeling the term engendered to ask acidly, "What 'us'?"

Much to his credit Holden did not rise to my bait. Instead he tried to explain, "Remember my homecoming in Scotland? My sister was with us. Do you remember her?"

Once again I could see the stone hall and the steps that I'd raced down. It was as if I had a sixth sense about when the men would return though there had been one person who had beat me to them. A little girl with the palest strawberry blonde hair...

My eyes widened and my mouth dropped open as Holden nodded once in confirmation.

I felt Hana's presence then, as if she were a ten-foot tall bear that was breathing on my back. Hana knew something, possibly more than I did. Everyone seemed to know more than I did. They seemed so sure of who they were and who I was. Tears pricked my eyes and I blinked furiously. I wanted to leave but I was trapped. I did the only thing I could and turned from Holden to Hana. She had sat quietly throughout the entire exchange, watching me, her eyes wide and alert.

"You-" I started. I couldn't even think clearly enough to form the next words. My throat had gone so dry I wasn't sure I could've continued even if I had the words. I coughed to clear the cotton from my throat without success.

Concern and apology was written all over Hana's face as she met my eyes.

"I can't do what you do but I do remember the, um, other times," she tried to explain. "I don't know why but sometimes I'm there, too."

"Holden's-" I could only get out one word before my throat closed up again.

"I was his sister once," she rushed in quickly. "Not now. I wasn't even sure it was real, even though it felt like it. I thought maybe I was crazy. Until I saw him." She glanced involuntarily at Holden as if to make sure he was still there.

Anger flared inside me at the certainty in her voice. She was so sure that what she remembered was real, just like Holden and Noah. But the more I thought about what I had been told were memories the more uncertain I became. Every time I'd gotten a grasp on something it changed or rearranged itself. So many people had been traipsing through my dreams that I couldn't trust them. I felt like my own mind was betraying me, as if it answered to someone else.

Hana's eyes widened as if she could hear everything I was thinking. For all I knew, she could.

"I know this doesn't help you much," she admitted. "I don't know what to say that would help. I know you feel like you're losing it but..."

"Hana," I started but, again, I couldn't find words for what I wanted to say. I raised my voice, trying to overcome the filing cabinet lodged in my throat. "I don't know what's going on. But I really wish everyone would leave me alone."

Hana pulled back from me as if I'd slapped her.

"I just want to help," she said softly.

"Everyone keeps saying that. But if I'm going insane I think I'd like to do it on my own," I spat.

I turned back toward Holden, calculating how hard it would be to climb over him to get out of here. I looked up toward the aisle, my escape route, and gasped. Noah had just entered the auditorium.

CHAPTER THIRTY-TWO

"Aren," Noah called out when he saw me.

"Hello- Hana, is it?" Noah asked over my shoulder when he reached our row. As he was talking he extended a hand to me. I reached out almost desperately. He practically dragged me out into the aisle over Holden's lap.

"Wait!" Hana called. Holden stood to face us. Noah clasped my hand firmly in his and pulled me to his side.

"Holden, please," I begged, "all I want right now is to go home. I can't begin to think about any of this. Please just stop."

"I saw your car in the parking lot when I drove past," Noah said by way of explanation, ignoring the others. "It seems a good thing I stopped." He tugged on my hand and I moved closer to him until our shoulders were touching. He placed a hand on my waist to propel me toward the door.

"Nice to see you again," Noah called over his shoulder.

"Aren, wait." Hana was pushing past Holden who seemed to be frozen in place. Noah picked up his pace but Hana wasn't above a full out sprint to reach us.

"Aren-"

Hana placed her hand gently on my arm. Noah reacted, whipping his free arm around to knock Hana's hand away from me. He glared fiercely at her as if daring her to do it again. The shock on her face mirrored my own. I glanced around, realizing the four of us were the only people left in the auditorium, allowing our drama to play out in private.

Noah tugged at me until I was behind him, using his body as a shield. He turned to face Holden, who had found the ability to move again. Holden came forward, his face unreadable and his eyes on Noah. Hana took a few steps back out of their line of sight.

"Don't do this," Holden said quietly to Noah. Noah's hand clenched around mine painfully.

"We have nothing to say to each other," Noah responded in an equally soft tone. "We're leaving. There's nothing else to discuss."

What happened next was so fast I didn't have time to react. Holden reached out to Noah who had started to turn in anticipation of leaving. When Holden's hand touched Noah's shoulder Noah jerked like he'd been electrocuted. He pulled on my arm hard, making me stumble in my slick shoes. I lost my balance and went flying down a row, catching myself on the arm of a chair. Pain shot up my left arm as I used it to stop my forward momentum.

Noah turned to face Holden. His knees were bent as if to spring and his hands hung in fists beside him. Holden looked no less ready for a fight. Hana had backed into a row on the opposite side of the aisle watching the two with a look of alarm frozen on her face.

Noah lunged at Holden. He shoved him hard and, having the advantage of the higher ground courtesy of the graded floor in the auditorium, made Holden lose his balance. Holden stumbled back a few steps before catching himself on the back of a chair. He pushed off, flinging himself at Noah. He planted both hands on Noah's chest, shoving him back against a chair. Noah slapped him away.

"You can't have her," Noah growled. His voice was so low that it took me a moment to make out the words. It took me another moment to figure out who he was talking about. It was Holden who caught my eye when the horrible understanding hit me.

"I don't think that's up to you," Holden called to him.

"I've worked too hard this time. You weren't there for her!" Noah spat back.

I pushed myself away from the chair I had been leaning on.

"That doesn't matter! It's still up to her!" Holden replied with equal ferocity. I glanced at Hana again. She looked terrified. I wondered if she'd seen this before.

Noah was advancing toward Holden now. Holden squared his shoulders as if he had seen this coming.

"No."

CHAPTER THIRTY-THREE

It was barely a whisper, so quiet that I didn't recognize my own voice but I felt the conviction with my entire body. I started to move toward them but my stride was not as sure as Noah's. Luckily the graded floor worked for me as I didn't have to try so hard to go downhill.

I reached out and put a hand on Noah's arm. He had been anticipating a fight and reacted automatically, swinging around violently, his arm catching me full in the chest. Knocked off my feet, I flew backwards. I heard an echoing crack as my head bounced off the edge of the cheap theater-like seats in the auditorium. My vision blurred as my eyeballs ricocheted violently in my head.

"Aren!" Hana shrieked.

I could sense hazy movement as all three of them started toward me. They only made it half a step when Noah turned back to Holden.

"She's mine! Get away!" Noah shouted.

Hana was taken aback by this outburst but Holden held his ground.

"I can see how well you take care of her," Holden hissed. Even with my foggy vision I could see Holden's blurry form vibrating with anger. He tried to shove past Noah but it didn't work. The two men's faces were inches from each other now.

The intense pain radiating from the back of my skull

was spreading to my entire body. I tried to move into a more comfortable position but someone had replaced my body with a lead doll. I tried to call out, to tell them to stop, but I couldn't do that either. I wasn't sure they'd listen to me anyway. Their arguing was getting ready to reach another peak and I was waiting to see who was going to throw the first punch. Holden kept trying to catch a glimpse of me as Noah did his best to block me from Holden's view. They had also effectively blocked Hana in so she couldn't get to me either. She kept glancing from them to me with the same horrified expression.

"Ask her!" I heard Noah shout. "All I've seen is her trying to get away from you. She chose me!" There was an edge to his voice that didn't sound entirely sane. I felt panic well in me. I tried again to move but I wasn't able to. I couldn't really make out a clear picture of what was going on. My head was pounding fiercely and I felt very tired.

My ears were ringing now and I could no longer make out what was being said. I stopped trying to see or hear what was going on and instead tried to focus on blocking it all out. This had to be a bad dream and if it was that meant I could stop it. I felt like I was suffocating. I gasped for air, afraid I would never be able to fill my lungs. I felt like I was going to be sick.

Suddenly, the pain in my head stopped and I found I could breathe again. I realized I was still lying uncomfortably on the floor so I sat up. I looked toward Holden and Noah, who I could now see clearly. Noah was forcibly holding Holden back from me. It looked like they were still shouting but the sound was muffled as if a wall of thick glass had sprung up between us.

I got to my feet. I put my hand up tentatively and met the invisible barrier. There *was* something between us. In the back of my head I knew this was my doing, my way of separating myself from their fight. I felt relieved but it was quickly followed by guilt. I wanted so badly for this to end. I could feel the centuries of despair at watching this same scene play out over and over. It occurred to me that their struggle might have more to do with each other than with me. The question felt familiar but I didn't see an answer on the horizon.

I shook my head. I could see the faint reflection of myself in the smooth glass-like barrier, superimposed over the figures in front of me. I watched as Holden drew back and punched Noah's jaw. Noah's head snapped to the side but he recovered quickly to lunge at Holden. I wanted to cry out to make them stop.

I focused on my face again. This face was foreign yet familiar at the same time. I could see the me that was here, in this time, and all the other women I had been before. My mind felt stretched to its limit as all the memories came flooding back to me. A strange calm enveloped me. I was finally myself. I was whole again.

I looked to Holden and Noah. Through the years we had been everything to each other. We had been friends, enemies, even family. Each time, no matter how much I wanted to believe Noah would change, he always wanted power more than anything. I felt a profound sadness at yet another lifetime he would spend grasping for it.

And then there was Holden. I could remember all the moments in which we had found each other through time. A sudden blast of feeling, something that didn't seem wholly captured by the term "love," hit me like a physical blow. I had to put my hand against the barrier to make sure a wild swing hadn't hit me. But the swing Noah made in answer to Holden's first blow hit its mark, which was nowhere near me. I watched Holden as he stumbled momentarily, the downward slant behind him making it difficult to regain his footing. Noah advanced, matching him step for step as he stumbled backwards.

No matter how I felt about the man who was now called Holden, I realized Noah would always come between us. This time I had come very close to loving him. But no matter how much love he received I wasn't sure he could ever return it after years of seeking power before all else. Knowing this also confirmed that Holden's attention would always be split between loving me and watching out for Noah. As the memories washed over me I remembered the despair that inevitably crept into each life as I realized this would happen over and over- this feeling of coming into my memories of who I really was and how I couldn't do anything to stop it from happening again.

I closed my eyes. The barrier between us, solid as ever, made crying out to them impossible. The gut reaction that had created it couldn't be duplicated to reverse it. I couldn't stand watching them rip each other apart though.

I reached out to them, not with my hands but with my mind. I could practically see the anger and hatred they harbored for each other as if they were wearing signs on their chests. I tentatively touched their minds, the strength of their anger almost knocking me back.

I knew this body had never attempted to reach out consciously before but some part of it knew how. It seemed as ingrained in me as breathing. I pushed into their minds. I could feel myself pass over the thresholds they had each erected to keep others out but these defenses were lowered as they concentrated on attacking each other physically. When I felt fully encircled by their minds, I spoke.

"No more," I said quietly but resolutely. "If this is what remembering does to us then I wish you didn't remember at all."

The recoil from their reactions threw me mentally and physically back to the floor. I heard a deafening shatter like an infinite number of windows exploding violently. Panic overtook me again. Then everything went black.

CHAPTER THIRTY-FOUR

When I opened my eyes I felt my body spasm as if I'd been thrown in an ice-cold pond. Several people hovered over me. It took a moment to separate the faces I knew from the ones I didn't. My parents both stood to my left speaking over me to a man in a white coat with a stethoscope hanging casually around his neck. All of them turned toward me as one when I twitched.

"Hello there," the man said cheerfully. He smiled but the smile didn't reach his eyes.

"Honey, how do you feel?" Mom asked as she leaned even closer. I was starting to feel claustrophobic due to the ceiling of people. I blinked at her.

"Let's give her a little space," the doctor said. He demonstrated this by taking a step back. My parents complied by sliding down toward my feet a step or two.

"I'm okay," I reassured her.

"That's good," the doctor responded before Mom could. "Do you know where you are?"

I looked around but it didn't take much to realize where I was. I could see the ugly mint green walls and the curtains hanging from tracks on the ceiling. I heard the various beeps of machines and the crackling of a loud speaker paging someone. Panicked, I shifted my arms. No shackles. It didn't seem that I'd been brought to the asylum after all.

"The hospital," I answered.

"Yes, that's right. Can you tell me your name?" he watched me anxiously like someone would watch a baby trying to take her first steps.

"Aren," I answered, my brows coming together at what I considered a ridiculous question. I waited for him to ask me if I knew who the president was.

He must have taken my look of frustration as confusion because he began to talk slower. "Alright, Aren, do you know how you got here?"

I wasn't sure how to answer that one. I remembered what had happened but I knew I couldn't tell them that. I could hear the doc now- go directly to the mental ward, do not pass "go," do not collect two hundred dollars.

"Not exactly," I drawled. "My head hurts."

"You took a nasty fall," he declared. He said this like he was once again talking to a child. I wanted to tell him I didn't need a cool story to take back to the playground.

"We thought you were coming straight home," my mother said. "We dropped you off to get your car but then you didn't follow us home. You didn't answer your phone and when we went back to the school your car was just sitting in the parking lot and you were nowhere to be found. We were lucky they hadn't locked the school up. Why were you in the auditorium?"

Mom's rant was half explanation half condemnation.

"I forgot something," I mumbled.

"Well, anyway," the doctor started, clearly uncomfortable with my mom's outburst, "I think you'll be perfectly fine. I want you to rest up. I gave your dad something in case the pain gets to be too much. Try not to trip yourself up anymore, okay?" The doctor chuckled at his own joke then extended his hand toward Dad.

"Thanks, Pete," Dad said. The doctor just nodded before slipping through the curtain. Dad turned to me, all smiles. "Ok, Grace, let's get you home." Dad pulled down the heavy hospital blanket to help me up.

"I'm glad that's not what we named her. It would have been cruel," Mom commented.

I sat up slowly as I took stock of my injuries, first and

foremost being the throbbing in the back of my head. My vision wasn't blurry anymore but I did feel a little nauseous as Dad extended his arm to help me out of the bed. My long hospital gown made moving a little awkward and I was searching the room for my clothes before my hospital- issued socks touched the cold tile floor. I was trying not to think of who had put me in the gown.

"How long was I out?" I asked.

"Several hours. It must have been some fall," Dad answered. Mom reached under the bed and pulled out a large white plastic bag, which she handed to me.

"There's a bathroom across the hall," she pointed helpfully. "Do you need help?"

My face colored at the idea of my mom helping me dress like I was two.

"No, I'll be fine," I told her as I started out of my curtained cubicle, clutching the bag to my chest.

I took cautious steps forward, thinking of how cruel it was to put a person with a concussion in socks and telling her to walk across a slick tile floor. I knew if I fell now they'd never let me out of here.

I discovered I was at the end of a hallway comprised of curtains. In truth it was a large room that probably had about ten beds, all with the same ugly curtains suspended from tracks in the ceiling. A nurses' station was in the middle of the room and people in scrubs were moving purposefully, weaving in and out of the curtained sections. I spotted the door labeled 'bathroom' across from the nurses' station and knocked tentatively before I let myself in.

The bathroom was a large square room containing a toilet and sink with a wide shelf built into the wall. I sat my bag down on the shelf and started pulling clothes out. Grateful to be out of the hospital gown, I slid into my blue dress even though it was wrinkled from sitting in the bag for untold hours. I freed my shoes but I wasn't sure I was ready to try to walk in heels.

After I changed I stuffed the hospital gown back into the bag. I glanced at the door but wasn't ready to go back out. Sitting down on the lid of the toilet I leaned against the wall.

I didn't know what had happened to Noah or Holden or Hana. If they'd been there surely my mother would have mentioned it. I wasn't sure how to ask about them without raising any kind of suspicion but I felt sick not knowing.

After a few moments I stood up. I wasn't going to find any answers in the bathroom and the last thing I wanted was Mom trying to break down the door because I took too long. With my shoes in one hand and the bag in the other I walked back into the emergency room.

I paused outside the door. Mom and Dad were still hovering by my bed, their heads together in deep conversation. Nurses and staff were rushing here and there. The people in scrubs ignored me since I was standing upright unassisted and instead focused on going to or from whichever patient they had designs on.

The grating sound of metal on metal made me turn to my left as one of the curtains was pulled back. I saw one nurse moving the curtain, another standing by a bed. I could see wavy dark hair from where I stood. I took an involuntary step toward the bed, trying to get a better view.

One of the nurses noticed my movement and caught my eye.

"Miss?" she called to me. "Do you know him?"

CHAPTER THIRTY-FIVE

I took another step forward. A pale face, smooth in sleep, lay there. The rest of his body was covered with blankets. I looked up to see the nurse watching me intently.

"Um, no, I don't think so," I said, panicked, as I watched Noah. My eyes flickered up to hers and I could see the doubt in her face. "I mean, I've seen him before-in town. I think he went to the college?"

Now that I said it I wasn't even sure if it were true. He had told me he attended the college but that didn't mean he wasn't lying.

"What's wrong with him?" I asked.

"We aren't sure. He was brought in here like this. Doc doesn't know if he's going to wake up. We're moving him to a regular room but right now we don't know who he is. It would be helpful if we knew his name. We'd like to let his family know- surely someone's looking for him." She looked at me again as if she would find the answer on my face.

I looked down at my feet, still in the hospital socks I had been given. The nurses began to roll Noah's bed out of the emergency room. I held the sight of his expressionless face in my mind in an attempt to evoke some kind of emotion. I was so drained I could barely comprehend what they had told me. He wasn't waking up. I told myself this over and over but still had no response.

I turned back toward where I had left my parents, wanting to reach them before they came to investigate. Mom and Dad were speaking with one of the nurses as I approached. When they saw me the nurse waved a good-bye, offering a smile to me as she passed. I tried to return the gesture but my face didn't want to smile just yet. It felt like it wanted to cry.

"Ready?" Mom's question was rhetorical. I could tell by the circles under her eyes and the strained expression on her face that she wanted nothing more than to be out of the hospital- which meant I was also ready whether I liked it or not.

I put the bag containing the hospital gown on the bed.

"Let's go home," I said.

We had just walked out of the emergency room wing into a long sterile-looking hallway when Dad noticed the shoes in my hand and raised an eyebrow.

"Wait here," he said to me, turning back.

I pressed myself against the wall to keep out of the way of the heavy traffic coming and going. I could see into the next wing, which seemed just as busy as mine had been. Several people occupied the chairs that lined the hall. I had expecting screaming and nurses pushing gurneys around with paramedics sitting on top of people's chests trying to administer CPR but I guess I had come on an off day. I was completely okay with that.

Motion registered in my periphery and looked toward the nurses' station in the opposite room. I saw someone leaned over the desk with his back to me. A small spark of recognition lit up inside me. I didn't blink as I prayed for him to turn around. Finally, he turned. I could see the familiar red streaked blonde hair and hazel eyes. He had a white bag in his hand identical to the one I had been given. He started toward me, leaving his own wing of the emergency room.

My breath caught as my heart swelled to a size that didn't permit air to enter my lungs. For the first time I felt like I was seeing the real Holden. The deep connection that could only be established by losing and finding someone again and again over untold lifetimes hit me so hard it felt like gravity had released me from the earth.

I stared at him expectantly, willing him to look up and see me. Finally his eyes came up to meet mine.

They fell back to the floor almost as quickly as they had looked up. For a fraction of a second he'd seen me. Then he turned his eyes away like he didn't know me. Maybe he hadn't really seen me or I looked so bad he hadn't recognized me. I had purposely avoided all reflective surfaces so I had no idea what kind of mess I might resemble.

I took a step forward. He was still coming toward me. I went to take another step but was blindsided. I only maintained my upright position by the arms that were wrapped around me. I went rigid with shock at the sudden, violent embrace.

"Aren!" a female voice squealed in my ear.

Rich brown tresses were being disentangled from my own hair as Lexa pulled back from me. She held me out at arms' length but she still didn't let me go. I looked behind her and glimpsed Sawyer and Hana. My eyes continued to scan the hall, drawn toward Holden.

He had entered the hallway and turned toward the direction my friends had come from. At Lexa's squeal he had turned to take stock of our small group. He stared right at me and I returned his look, pleading with him to recognize me but instead he turned his attention back to negotiating the packed hallway that led toward the exit.

"Aren?" Lexa asked. She followed my gaze to Holden. Hana turned to look as well. I felt myself blush. "Do you know him?"

I tore my gaze away from Holden to stare at Lexa wide-eyed.

"You don't?" I asked her. She glanced again. He had almost made it to the end of the hall. I watched him, drinking the sight of him in, hoping at any moment he would turn to come back to me.

"No, he doesn't look familiar," she said finally.

"I don't know him," Hana said as she turned back to

us. I watched Holden reach the end of the hall and disappear around the corner. My heart felt like it was trying to leap out of my chest to follow him.

"We were so worried," Lexa said, having already completely forgotten Holden. She shifted so that she was in my direct line of sight.

"Yeah, when we couldn't reach you we called your parents," Sawyer told me.

I looked from him to Hana to Lexa. I wanted desperately to drill them about Holden whom they suddenly thought they didn't know. Lexa and I had had one of our only fights ever over him. Sawyer had seen it. Hana had been there when...

I froze. The ground seemed to fall away as I realized I was alone. I had only just remembered who I was in time to make them forget.

I was ripped back to the present by my dad's hand on my shoulder.

"Here," he said, holding out a pair of paper flip-flops like the ones you get at a nail salon. He stooped to help me take off the socks and slide the flip-flops on my feet. I tried to bend my full concentration on the task so I could escape the full realization of what I had done.

"Ready to go home?" Mom asked. Lexa put her arm through mine and Sawyer clapped me on the shoulder. Hana hovered so close to Sawyer that she was pushing him into me. As one, we all turned toward the door.

"Home," I echoed quietly. I couldn't help but see all the places I had called home in lifetimes past flash through my mind in rapid succession. Despair overtook me at the realization that after spending so much time trying to make myself remember all I wanted now was to make myself forget.

ABOUT THE AUTHOR

Sam Jenkins is an adult-sized child with an overactive imagination. She was awarded the *Gonzo Award for the Weirdest Imagination* at a young age that set the tone for much of the rest of her life. She holds a B.A. in Theatre from Berea College. Born and raised in southern West Virginia (yes, it's a state- she doesn't mean western Virginia), she currently resides in Kentucky with her Malamute/German Shepherd rescue pup Qanuk. She is not a fan of heights and her bucket list includes learning to surf and meeting penguins in New Zealand.